The White Tiger

ARAVIND ADIGA was born in Madras in 1974. He studied at Columbia and Oxford Universities. A former Indian correspondent for *Time* magazine, his articles have also appeared in publications such as the *Financial Times*, the *Independent* and the *Sunday Times*. He lives in Mumbai. *The White Tiger* is his first novel.

'Astonishingly assured and captivating...It is every bit as good as *Bonfire* [*of the Vanities*] and it does for India what that book did for New York City; and possibly what Charles Dickens did for Victorian Britain.' *Tablet*

'Richly detailed storytelling that will captivate his audience...*The White Tiger* contains passages of startling beauty – from reflections on the exquisite luxury of a chandelier in every room, to descriptions of skinny drivers huddled around fires fueled by plastic bags. Adiga never lets the precision of his language overshadow the realities at hand: No matter how potent his language one never loses sight of the men and women fighting impossible odds to survive.' *San Francisco Chronicle*

'Aravind Adiga's *The White Tiger* is one of the most powerful books I've read in decades. No hyperbole. This debut novel from an Indian journalist living in Mumbai hit me like a kick to the head... This is an amazing and angry novel about injustice and power.' *USA Today*

'Extremely bold, brilliantly written, but too determined to shock.' Nadine Gordimer

'There have been many India books this past year or two, but Aravind Adiga's debut novel, which shines a light on India's vast area of darkness, cuts through the clutter like no other.' Sudipta Datta, *Financial Express* (India)

'Fast-paced, drolly funny…Adiga shows an authentic, unforced talent for irreverence and his book – almost as if in determined opposition to the "India shining" narratives – chronicles harsher truths… *The White Tiger* can cut uncomfortably close to the bone… It makes us think about the many Indias and the many types of aspirations and frustrations they represent, but does this within the framework of an absorbing novel. It's an impressive debut.' Jai Arjun Singh, *Business Standard* (India)

'Once in a while it happens, that singular voice breaking through the polyphony of India Imagined. A voice that defies the received wisdom of the Great Indian Marketplace of Metaphors and brings to the rustle of the ever-increasing number of pages a new note of anticipation… Adiga as a storyteller drives on fourth gear… What the white tiger tells the Chinese premier in so many mesmerizing words is that he is a rare creature, not as ordinary as "Made in China". He is rare indeed – in fiction. And Aravind Adiga has only begun the story.' S. Prasannarajan, *India Today*

'In a country teeming with suppressed stories, this is sure to open a Pandora's box, unleashing ugliness, beauty, misery and brilliance. Be grateful for it.' Nirpal Singh Dhaliwal, *Tehelka*

'An intelligent and ruthless portrait of the India in the making – shining or rising, but always sinking – shot through with wit and black humour that match the author's economy with words… But the real power of this book comes from its total lack of sentimentality and the consequent realism it thus manages… In the course of the narrative, a vivid India breaks through.' Sudeep Paul, *Indian Express*

'Gritty, bitter, sardonic, nasty and terrifically appetizing.' *The Times of India*

'A brilliant debut… A marvellous narrator' *Frankfurter Allgemeine Zeitung*

'An incredible trip into the dazzling and pulsating heart of India… An unlimited reading pleasure!' *Stern*

The White Tiger

ARAVIND ADIGA

Atlantic Books
LONDON

First published in hardback in the United States in 2008 by
Free Press, a division of Simon & Schuster, Inc.

First published in hardback in Great Britain in 2008 by
Atlantic Books, an imprint of Grove Atlantic Ltd.

This paperback edition published in Great Britain
in 2009 by Atlantic Books.

1 3 5 5 7 9 10 8 6 4 2

A CIP catalogue record for this book is available from
the British Library.

ISBN: 978 1 84887 722 8

Printed in the UK by CPI Bookmarque, Croydon, CRO 4TD

Atlantic Books
An imprint of Grove Atlantic Ltd
Ormond House
26–27 Boswell Street
London WC1N 3JZ

www.atlantic-books.co.uk

For Ramin Bahrani

The First Night

For the Desk of:

His Excellency Wen Jiabao,
The Premier's Office,
Beijing,
Capital of the Freedom-Loving Nation of China

From the Desk of:

'The White Tiger'
A Thinking Man
And an entrepreneur
Living in the world's centre of technology and outsourcing
Electronics City Phase 1 (just off Hosur Main Road),
Bangalore, India.

Mr Premier,

Sir.

Neither you nor I can speak English, but there are some things that can be said only in English.

My ex-employer the late Mr Ashok's ex-wife, Pinky Madam, taught me one of these things; and at 11:32 p.m. today, which was about ten minutes ago, when the lady on All India Radio announced, 'Premier Jiabao is coming to Bangalore next week', I said that thing at once.

In fact, each time when great men like you visit our country I say it. Not that I have anything against great men. In my way, sir, I consider myself one of your kind. But whenever I see our prime minister and his distinguished sidekicks drive to the airport in black cars and get out and do *namastes* before you in front of a TV camera and tell you about how moral and saintly India is, I have to say that thing in English.

Now, you *are* visiting us this week, Your Excellency, aren't you? All India Radio is usually reliable in these matters.

That was a joke, sir.

Ha!

That's why I want to ask you directly if you really are coming to Bangalore. Because if you are, I have something important to tell you. See, the lady on the radio said, 'Mr Jiabao is on a mission: he wants to know the truth about Bangalore.'

My blood froze. If anyone knows the truth about Bangalore, it's *me*.

Next, the lady announcer said, 'Mr Jiabao wants to meet some Indian entrepreneurs and hear the story of their success from their own lips.'

She explained a little. Apparently, sir, you Chinese are far ahead of us in every respect, except that you don't have entrepreneurs. And our nation, though it has no drinking water, electricity, sewage system, public transportation, sense of hygiene, discipline, courtesy, or punctuality, *does* have entrepreneurs. Thousands and thousands of them. Especially in the field of technology. And these entrepreneurs – *we* entrepreneurs – have set up all these outsourcing companies that virtually run America now.

You hope to learn how to make a few Chinese entrepreneurs, that's why you're visiting. That made me feel good. But then it hit me that in keeping with international protocol, the prime minister and foreign minister of my country will meet you at the airport with garlands, small take-home sandalwood statues of Gandhi, and a booklet full of information about India's past, present, and future.

That's when I *had* to say that thing in English, sir. Out loud.

That was at 11:37 p.m. Five minutes ago.

I don't just swear and curse. I'm a man of action and change. I decided right there and then to start dictating a letter to you.

To begin with, let me tell you of my great admiration for the ancient nation of China.

I read about your history in a book, *Exciting Tales of the Exotic East*, that I found on the pavement, back in the days when I was trying to get some enlightenment by going through the Sunday secondhand book market in Old Delhi. This book was mostly about pirates and gold in Hong Kong, but it did have some useful background information too: it said that you Chinese are great lovers of freedom and individual liberty. The British tried to make you their servants, but you never let them do it. I admire that, Mr Premier.

I was a servant once, you see.

Only three nations have never let themselves be ruled by foreigners: China, Afghanistan, and Abyssinia. These are the only three nations I admire.

Out of respect for the love of liberty shown by the Chinese people, and also in the belief that the future of the world lies with the yellow man and the brown man now that our erstwhile master, the white-skinned man, has wasted himself through buggery, mobile phone usage, and drug abuse, I offer to tell you, free of charge, the truth about Bangalore.

By telling you my life's story.

See, when you come to Bangalore, and stop at a traffic light, some boy will run up to your car and knock on your window, while holding up a bootlegged copy of an American business book, wrapped carefully in Cellophane and with a title like:

TEN SECRETS OF BUSINESS SUCCESS!

or

BECOME AN ENTREPRENEUR IN SEVEN EASY DAYS!

Don't waste your money on those American books. They're so *yesterday*.

I am tomorrow.

In terms of formal education, I may be somewhat lacking. I never finished school, to put it bluntly. Who cares! I haven't read many books, but I've read all the ones that count. I know by heart the works of the four greatest poets of all time – Rumi, Iqbal, Mirza Ghalib, and a fourth fellow whose name I forget. I am a self-taught entrepreneur.

That's the best kind there is, trust me.

When you have heard the story of how I got to Bangalore and became one of its most successful (though probably least known) businessmen, you will know everything there is to know about how entrepreneurship is born, nurtured, and developed in this, the glorious twenty-first century of man.

The century, more specifically, of the *yellow* and the *brown* man.

You and me.

It is a little before midnight now, Mr Jiabao. A good time for me to talk.

I stay up the whole night, Your Excellency. And there's no one else in this 150-square-foot office of mine. Just me and a chandelier above me, although the chandelier has a personality of its own. It's a huge thing, full of small diamond-shaped glass pieces, just like the ones they used to show in the films of the 1970s. Though it's cool enough at night in Bangalore, I've put a midget fan – five cobwebby blades – right above the chandelier. See, when it turns, the small blades chop up the chandelier's light and fling it across the room. Just like the strobe light at the best discos in Bangalore.

This is the only 150-square-foot space in Bangalore with its own chandelier! But it's still a hole in the wall, and I sit here the whole night.

The entrepreneur's curse. He has to watch his business all the time.

Now I'm going to turn the midget fan on, so that the chandelier's light spins around the room.

I am relaxed, sir. As I hope you are.

Let us begin.

Before we do that, sir, the phrase in English that I learned from my ex-employer the late Mr Ashok's ex-wife Pinky Madam is:

What a fucking joke.

Now, I no longer watch Hindi films – on principle – but back in the days when I used to, just before the movie got started, either the number 786 would flash against the black screen – the Muslims think this is a magic number that represents their god – or else you would see the picture of a woman in a white sari with gold sovereigns dripping down to her feet, which is the goddess Lakshmi, of the Hindus.

It is an ancient and venerated custom of people in my country to start a story by praying to a Higher Power.

I guess, Your Excellency, that I too should start off by kissing some god's arse.

Which god's arse, though? There are so many choices.

See, the Muslims have one god.

The Christians have three gods.

And we Hindus have 36,000,000 gods.

Making a grand total of 36,000,004 divine arses for me to choose from.

Now, there are some, and I don't just mean Communists like you, but thinking men of all political parties, who think that not many of these gods actually exist. Some believe that *none* of them exist. There's just us and an ocean of darkness around us. I'm no philosopher or poet, how would I know the truth? It's true that all these gods seem to do awfully little work – much like our politicians – and yet keep winning re-election to their golden thrones in heaven, year after year. That's not to say that I don't respect them, Mr Premier! Don't you ever let that blasphemous idea into your yellow skull. My country is the kind where it pays to play it both ways: the Indian entrepreneur has to be straight and crooked, mocking and believing, sly and sincere, at the same time.

So: I'm closing my eyes, folding my hands in a reverent *namaste*, and praying to the gods to shine light on my dark story.

Bear with me, Mr Jiabao. This could take a while.

How quickly do you think *you* could kiss 36,000,004 arses?

*

Done.

My eyes are open again.

11:52 p.m. – and it really *is* time to start.

A statutory warning – as they say on cigarette packs – before we begin.

One day, as I was driving my ex-employers Mr Ashok and Pinky Madam in their Honda City car, Mr Ashok put a hand on my shoulder, and said, 'Pull over to the side.' Following this command, he leaned forward so close that I could smell his aftershave – it was a delicious, fruitlike smell that day – and said, politely as ever, 'Balram, I have a few questions to ask you, all right?'

'Yes, sir,' I said.

'Balram,' Mr Ashok asked, 'how many planets are there in the sky?'

I gave the answer as best as I could.

'Balram, who was the first prime minister of India?'

And then: 'Balram, what is the difference between a Hindu and a Muslim?'

And then: 'What is the name of our continent?'

Mr Ashok leaned back and asked Pinky Madam, 'Did you hear his answers?'

'Was he joking?' she asked, and my heart beat faster, as it did every time she said something.

'No. That's *really* what he thinks the correct answers are.'

She giggled when she heard this: but *his* face, which I saw reflected in my rearview mirror, was serious.

'The thing is, he probably has... what, two, three years of schooling in him? He can read and write, but he doesn't get what he's read. He's half-baked. The country is full of people like him, I'll tell you that. And we entrust our glorious parliamentary democracy' – he pointed at me – 'to characters like these. *That's* the whole tragedy of this country.'

He sighed.

'All right, Balram, start the car again.'

That night, I was lying in bed, inside my mosquito net, thinking about his words. He was right, sir – I didn't like the way he had spoken about me, but he was right.

'The Autobiography of a Half-Baked Indian.' That's what I ought to call my life's story.

Me, and thousands of others in this country like me, are half-baked, because we were never allowed to complete our schooling. Open our skulls, look in with a penlight, and you'll find an odd museum of ideas: sentences of history or mathematics remembered from school textbooks (no boy remembers his schooling like one who was taken out of school, let me assure you), sentences about politics read in a newspaper while waiting for someone to come to an office, triangles and pyramids seen on the torn pages of the old geometry textbooks which every tea shop in this country uses to wrap its snacks in, bits of All India Radio news bulletins, things that drop into your mind, like lizards from the ceiling, in the half-hour before falling asleep – all these ideas, half formed and half digested and half correct, mix up with other half-cooked ideas in your head, and I guess these half-formed ideas bugger one another, and make more half-formed ideas, and this is what you act on and live with.

The story of my upbringing is the story of how a half-baked fellow is produced.

But pay attention, Mr Premier! Fully formed fellows, after twelve years of school and three years of university, wear nice suits, join companies, and take orders from other men for the rest of their lives.

Entrepreneurs are made from half-baked clay.

*

To give you the basic facts about me – origin, height, weight, known sexual deviations, etc. – there's no beating that poster. The one the police made of me.

Calling myself Bangalore's least known success story isn't entirely true, I confess. About three years ago, when I became, briefly, a person of national importance owing to an act of entrepreneurship, a poster with my face on it found its way to every post office, railway station, and police station in this country. A lot of people saw my face and name back then. I don't have the original paper copy, but I've downloaded an image to my silver Macintosh laptop – I bought it online from a store in Singapore, and it really works like a dream – and if you'll wait a second, I'll open the laptop, pull that scanned poster up, and read from it directly…

But a word about the original poster. I found it in a train station in Hyderabad, in the period when I was travelling with no luggage – except for one very heavy red bag – and coming down from Delhi to Bangalore. I had the original right here in this office, in the drawer of this desk, for a full year. One day the cleaning boy was going through my stuff, and he almost found the poster. I'm not a sentimental man, Mr Jiabao. Entrepreneurs can't afford to be. So I threw the thing out – but before that, I got someone to teach me scanning – and you know how we Indians just take to technology like ducks to water. It took just an hour, or two hours. I am a man of action, sir. And here it is, on the screen, in front of me:

ASSISTANCE SOUGHT IN SEARCH FOR MISSING MAN

General Public is hereby informed that the man in the picture namely Balram Halwai alias MUNNA son of Vikram Halwai rickshaw-puller is wanted for questioning. Age: Between 25 and 35. Complexion: Blackish. Face: Oval. Height: Five feet four inches estimated. Build: Thin, Small.

Well, that's not *exactly* right any more, sir. The 'blackish face' bit is still true – although I'm of half a mind to try one of those skin-whitener creams they've launched these days so Indian men can look white as Westerners – but the rest, alas, is completely useless. Life in Bangalore is good – rich food, beer, nightclubs, so what can I say! 'Thin' and 'small' – ha! I am in better shape these days! 'Fat' and 'potbellied' would be more accurate now.

But let us go on, we don't have all night. I'd better explain this bit right now.

Balram Halwai alias MUNNA...

See, my first day in school, the teacher made all the boys line up and come to his desk so he could put our names down in his register. When I told him what my name was, he gaped at me:

'Munna? That's not a real name.'

He was right: it just means 'boy'.

'That's all I've got, sir,' I said.

It was true. I'd never been given a name.

'Didn't your mother name you?'

'She's very ill, sir. She lies in bed and spews blood. She's got no time to name me.'

'And your father?'

'He's a rickshaw-puller, sir. He's got no time to name me.'

'Don't you have a granny? Aunts? Uncles?'

'They've got no time either.'

The teacher turned aside and spat – a jet of red *paan* splashed the ground of the classroom. He licked his lips.

'Well, it's up to me, then, isn't it?' He passed his hand through his hair and said, 'We'll call you... *Ram*. Wait – don't we have a Ram in this class? I don't want any confusion. It'll be *Balram*. You know who Balram was, don't you?'

'No, sir.'

13

'He was the sidekick of the god Krishna. Know what my name is?'

'No, sir.'

He laughed. 'Krishna.'

I came home that day and told my father that the schoolteacher had given me a new name. He shrugged. 'If it's what he wants, then we'll call you that.'

So I was Balram from then on. Later on, of course, I picked up a third name. But we'll get to that.

Now, what kind of place is it where people forget to name their children? Referring back to the poster:

The suspect comes from the village of
Laxmangarh, in the…

Like all good Bangalore stories, mine begins far away from Bangalore. You see, I am in the Light now, but I was born and raised in Darkness.

But this is not a time of day I talk about, Mr Premier!

I am talking of a place in India, at least a third of the country, a fertile place, full of rice fields and wheat fields and ponds in the middle of those fields choked with lotuses and water lilies, and water buffaloes wading through the ponds and chewing on the lotuses and lilies. Those who live in this place call it the Darkness. Please understand, Your Excellency, that India is two countries in one: an India of Light, and an India of Darkness. The ocean brings light to my country. Every place on the map of India near the ocean is well-off. But the river brings darkness to India – the black river.

Which black river am I talking of – which river of Death, whose banks are full of rich, dark, sticky mud

14

whose grip traps everything that is planted in it, suffocating and choking and stunting it?

Why, I am talking of Mother Ganga, daughter of the Vedas, river of illumination, protector of us all, breaker of the chain of birth and rebirth. Everywhere this river flows, that area is the Darkness.

One fact about India is that you can take almost anything you hear about the country from the prime minister and turn it upside down and then you will have the truth about that thing. Now, you have heard the Ganga called the river of emancipation, and hundreds of American tourists come each year to take photographs of naked *sadhus* at Hardwar or Benaras, and our prime minister will no doubt describe it that way to you, and urge you to take a dip in it.

No! – Mr Jiabao, I urge you not to dip in the Ganga, unless you want your mouth full of faeces, straw, soggy parts of human bodies, buffalo carrion, and seven different kinds of industrial acids.

I know all about the Ganga, sir – when I was six or seven or eight years old (no one in my village knows his exact age), I went to the holiest spot on the banks of the Ganga – the city of Benaras. I remember going down the steps of a downhill road in the holy city of Benaras, at the rear of a funeral procession carrying my mother's body to the Ganga.

Kusum, my granny, was leading the procession. Sly old Kusum! She had this habit of rubbing her forearms hard when she felt happy, as if they were a piece of ginger she was grating to release grins from. Her teeth were all gone, but this only made her grin more cunning.

She had grinned her way into control of the house; every son and daughter-in-law lived in fear of her.

My father and Kishan, my brother, stood behind her, to bear the front end of the cane bed which bore the corpse; my uncles, who are Munnu, Jayram, Divyram, and Umesh, stood behind, holding up the other end. My mother's body had been wrapped from head to toe in a saffron silk cloth, which was covered in rose petals and jasmine garlands. I don't think she had ever had such a fine thing to wear in her life. (Her death was so grand that I knew, all at once, that her life must have been miserable. My family was guilty about something.) My aunts – Rabri, Shalini, Malini, Luttu, Jaydevi, and Ruchi – kept turning around and clapping their hands for me to catch up to them. I remember swinging my hands and singing, 'Shiva's name is the truth!'

We walked past temple after temple, praying to god after god, and then went in a single file between a red temple devoted to Hanuman and an open gymnasium where three body builders heaved rusted weights over their heads. I smelled the river before I saw it: a stench of decaying flesh rising from my right. I sang louder: '… the only truth!'

Then there was a gigantic noise: firewood being split. A wooden platform had been built by the edge of the *ghat*, just above the water; logs were piled up on the platform, and men with axes were smashing the logs. Chunks of wood were being built into funeral pyres on the steps of the *ghat* that went down into the water; four bodies were burning on the *ghat* steps when we got there. We waited our turn.

In the distance, an island of white sand glistened in the sunlight, and boats full of people were heading to that island. I wondered if my mother's soul had flown there, to that shining place in the river.

I have mentioned that my mother's body was wrapped in a satin cloth. This cloth was now pulled over her face; and logs of wood, as many as we could pay for, were piled on top of the body. Then the priest set my mother on fire.

'She was a good, quiet girl the day she came to our home,' Kusum said, as she put a hand on my face. 'I was not the one who wanted any fighting.'

I shook her hand off my face. I watched my mother.

As the fire ate away the satin, a pale foot jerked out, like a living thing; the toes, which were melting in the heat, began to curl up, offering resistance to what was being done to them. Kusum shoved the foot into the fire, but it would not burn. My heart began to race. My mother wasn't going to let them destroy her.

Underneath the platform with the piled-up fire logs, there was a giant oozing mound of black mud where the river washed into the shore. The mound was littered with ribbons of jasmine, rose petals, bits of satin, charred bones; a pale-skinned dog was crawling and sniffing through the petals and satin and charred bones.

I looked at the ooze, and I looked at my mother's flexed foot, and I understood.

This mud was holding her back: this big, swelling mound of black ooze. She was trying to fight the black mud; her toes were flexed and resisting; but the mud was sucking her in, sucking her in. It was so thick, and more of it was being created every moment as the river washed into the *ghat*. Soon she would become part of the black mound and the pale-skinned dog would start licking her.

And then I understood: this was the real god of Benaras – this black mud of the Ganga into which everything died, and decomposed, and was reborn from, and died into again. The same would happen to me when I died and they brought me here. Nothing would get liberated here.

I stopped breathing.

This was the first time in my life I fainted.

I haven't been back to see the Ganga since then: I'm leaving that river for the American tourists!

… comes from the village of Laxmangarh, in the district of Gaya.

This is a famous district – world-famous. Your nation's history has been shaped by my district, Mr Jiabao. Surely you've heard of Bodh Gaya – the town where the Lord Buddha sat under a tree and found his enlightenment and started Buddhism, which then spread to the whole world, including China – and where is it, but right here in my home district! Just a few miles from Laxmangarh!

I wonder if the Buddha walked through Laxmangarh – some people say he did. My own feeling is that he ran through it – as fast as he could – and got to the other side – and never looked back!

There is a small branch of the Ganga that flows just outside Laxmangarh; boats come down from the world outside, bringing supplies every Monday. There is one street in the village; a bright strip of sewage splits it into two. On either side of the ooze, a market: three more or less identical shops selling more or less identically adulterated and stale items of rice, cooking oil, kerosene, biscuits, cigarettes, and jaggery. At the end of the market is a tall, whitewashed, conelike tower, with black intertwining snakes painted on all its sides – the temple. Inside, you will find an image of a saffron-coloured creature, half man half monkey: this is Hanuman, everyone's favourite god in the Darkness. Do you know about Hanuman, sir? He was the faithful servant of the god Rama, and we worship him in our temples because he is a shining example of how to serve your masters with absolute fidelity, love, and devotion.

These are the kinds of gods they have foisted on us, Mr Jiabao. Understand, now, how hard it is for a man to win his freedom in India.

So much for the place. Now for the people. Your Excellency, I am proud to inform you that Laxmangarh is your typical Indian village paradise, adequately supplied with electricity, running water, and working telephones; and that the children of my village, raised on a nutritious diet of meat, eggs, vegetables, and lentils, will be found, when examined with tape measure and scales, to match up to the minimum height and weight standards set by the United Nations and other organizations whose treaties our prime minister has signed and whose forums he so regularly and pompously attends.

Ha!

Electricity poles – defunct.

Water tap – broken.

Children – too lean and short for their age, and with oversized heads from which vivid eyes shine, like the guilty conscience of the government of India.

Yes, a typical Indian village paradise, Mr Jiabao. One day I'll have to come to China and see if your village paradises are any better.

Down the middle of the main road, families of pigs are sniffing through sewage – the upper body of each animal is dry, with long hairs that are matted together into spines; the lower half of the body is peat-black and glistening from sewage. Vivid red and brown flashes of feather – roosters fly up and down the roofs of the houses. Past the hogs and roosters, you'll get to my house – if it still exists.

At the doorway to my house, you'll see the most important member of my family.

The water buffalo.

She was the fattest thing in our family; this was true in every house in the village. All day long, the women fed her and fed her fresh grass; feeding her was the main thing in their lives. All their hopes were concentrated in her fatness, sir. If she gave enough milk, the women could sell some of it, and there might be a little more money at the end of the day. She was a fat, glossy-skinned creature, with a vein the size of a boy's penis sticking out over her hairy snout, and long thick pearly spittle suspended from the edge of her mouth; she sat all day in her own stupendous crap. She was the dictator of our house!

Once you walk into the house, you will see – if any of

them are still living, after what I did – the women. Working in the courtyard. My aunts and cousins and Kusum, my granny. One of them preparing the meal for the buffalo; one winnowing rice; one squatting down, looking through the scalp of another woman, squeezing the ticks to death between her fingers. Every now and then they stop their work, because it is time to fight. This means throwing metal vessels at one another, or pulling each other's hair, and then making up, by putting kisses on their palms and pressing them to the others' cheeks. At night they sleep together, their legs falling one over the other, like one creature, a millipede.

Men and boys sleep in another corner of the house.

Early morning. The roosters are going mad throughout the village. A hand stirs me awake... I shake my brother Kishan's legs off my tummy, move my cousin Pappu's palm out of my hair, and extricate myself from the sleepers.

'Come, Munna.'

My father, calling for me from the door of the house.

I run behind him. We go out of the house and untie the water buffalo from her post. We are taking her for her morning bath – all the way to the pond beneath the Black Fort.

The Black Fort stands on the crest of a hill overlooking the village. People who have been to other countries have told me that this fort is as beautiful as anything seen in Europe. The Turks, or the Afghans, or the English, or whichever foreigners were then ruling India, must have built the fort centuries ago.

(For this land, India, has never been free. First the

21

Muslims, then the British bossed us around. In 1947 the British left, but only a moron would think that we became free then.)

Now the foreigners have long abandoned the Black Fort, and a tribe of monkeys occupy it. No one else goes up, except for a goatherd taking his flock to graze there.

At sunrise, the pond around the base of the fort glows. Boulders from the walls of the fort have rolled down the hill and tumbled into the pond, where they lie, moist and half submerged in the muddy water, like the snoozing hippopotamuses that I would see, many years later, at the National Zoo at New Delhi. Lotuses and lilies float all over the pond, the water sparkles like silver, and the water buffalo wades, chewing on the leaves of the lilies, and setting off ripples that spread in big V's from her snout. The sun rises over the buffalo, and over my father, and over me, and over my world.

Sometimes, would you believe, I almost miss that place.

Now, back to the poster –

The suspect was last seen wearing blue chequered polyester shirt, orange polyester trousers, maroon colour sandals...

'Maroon colour' sandals – ugh. Only a policeman could have made up a detail like that. I flatly deny it.

'Blue chequered polyester shirt, orange polyester trousers'... er, well, I'd like to deny those too, but unfortunately they're correct. Those are the kinds of clothes, sir, that would appeal to a servant's eye. And I was still a servant on the morning of the day this poster was made.

(By the evening I was free – and wearing different clothes!)

Now, there is one phrase in this poster that does annoy me – let me go back to it for a moment and fix it:

... son of Vikram Halwai, rickshaw-puller...

Mr Vikram Halwai, rickshaw-puller – thank you! My father was a poor man, but he was a man of honour and courage. I wouldn't be here, under this chandelier, if not for his guidance.

In the afternoons, I went from my school to the tea shop to see him. This tea shop was the central point of our village; the bus from Gaya stopped there at noon every day (never late by more than an hour or two) and the policemen would park their jeep here when they came to bugger someone in the village. A little before sunset, a man circled around the tea shop three times, ringing his bell loudly. A stiff cardboard-backed poster for a pornographic film was tied to the back of his cycle – what traditional Indian village is complete without its blue-movie theatre, sir? A cinema across the river showed such films every night; two-and-a-half-hour fantasias with names like *He Was a True Man*, or *We Opened Her Diary*, or *The Uncle Did It*, featuring golden-haired women from America or lonely ladies from Hong Kong – or so I'm guessing, Mr Premier, since it's not like I ever joined the other young men and went to see one of these films!

The rickshaw-pullers parked their vehicles in a line outside the tea shop, waiting for the bus to disgorge its passengers.

They were not allowed to sit on the plastic chairs put out for the customers; they had to crouch near the back, in that hunched-over, squatting posture common to servants in every part of India. My father never crouched – I remember that. He preferred to stand, no matter how long he had to wait and how uncomfortable it got for him. I would find him shirtless, usually alone, drinking tea and thinking.

Then there would be the honk of a car.

The pigs and stray dogs near the tea shop would scatter, and the smell of dust, and sand, and pig shit would blow into the shop. A white Ambassador car had stopped outside. My father put down his teacup and went out.

The door of the Ambassador opened: a man got out with a notebook. The regular customers of the tea shop could go on eating, but my father and the others gathered in a line.

The man with the notebook was not the Buffalo; he was the assistant.

There was another fellow inside the Ambassador; a stout one with a bald, brown, dimpled head, a serene expression on his face, and a shotgun on his lap.

He was the Buffalo.

The Buffalo was one of the landlords in Laxmangarh. There were three others, and each had got his name from the peculiarities of appetite that had been detected in him.

The Stork was a fat man with a fat moustache, thick and curved and pointy at the tips. He owned the river that flowed outside the village, and he took a cut of every catch of fish caught by every fisherman in the river, and a toll from every boatman who crossed the river to come to our village.

His brother was called the Wild Boar. This fellow owned all the good agricultural land around Laxmangarh. If you wanted to work on those lands, you had to bow down to his feet, and touch the dust under his slippers, and agree to swallow his day wages. When he passed by women, his car would stop; the windows would roll down to reveal his grin; two of his teeth, on either side of his nose, were long, and curved, like little tusks.

The Raven owned the worst land, which was the dry, rocky hillside around the fort, and took a cut from the goatherds who went up there to graze with their flocks. If they didn't have their money, he liked to dip his beak into their backsides, so they called him the Raven.

The Buffalo was greediest of the lot. He had eaten up the rickshaws and the roads. So if you ran a rickshaw, or used the road, you had to pay him his feed – one-third of whatever you earned, no less.

All four of the Animals lived in high-walled mansions just outside Laxmangarh – the landlords' quarters. They had their own temples inside the mansions, and their own wells and ponds, and did not need to come out into the village except to feed. Once upon a time, the children of the four Animals went around town in their own cars; Kusum remembered those days. But after the Buffalo's son had been kidnapped by the Naxals – perhaps you've heard about them, Mr Jiabao, since they're Communists, just like you, and go around shooting rich people on principle – the four Animals had sent their sons and daughters away, to Dhanbad or to Delhi.

Their children were gone, but the Animals stayed and fed on the village, and everything that grew in it, until there was nothing left for anyone else to feed on. So the rest of the village left Laxmangarh for food. Each year, all the men in the village waited in a big group outside the tea shop. When the buses came, they got on – packing the inside, hanging from the railings, climbing onto the roofs – and went to Gaya; there they went to the station and rushed into the trains – packing the inside, hanging from the railings, climbing onto the roofs – and went to Delhi, Calcutta, and Dhanbad to find work.

A month before the rains, the men came back from Dhanbad and Delhi and Calcutta, leaner, darker, angrier, but with money in their pockets. The women were waiting for them. They hid behind the door, and as soon as the men walked in, they pounced, like wildcats on a slab of flesh. There was fighting and wailing and shrieking. My uncles would resist, and managed to keep some of their money, but my father got peeled and skinned every time. 'I survived the city, but I couldn't survive the women in my home,' he would say, sunk into a corner of the room. The women would feed him after they fed the buffalo.

I would come to him, and play around with him, by climbing his back, and passing my palm over his fore-head – over his eyes – over his nose – and down to his neck, to the little depression at the pit of his neck. I would let my finger linger there – it still is my favourite part of the human body.

A rich man's body is like a premium cotton pillow, white and soft and blank. *Ours* are different. My father's spine was a knotted rope, the kind that women use in villages to pull water from wells; the clavicle curved around his neck in high relief, like a dog's collar; cuts and nicks and scars, like little whip marks in his flesh, ran down his chest and waist, reaching down below his hipbones into his buttocks. The story of a poor man's life is written on his body, in a sharp pen.

My uncles also did backbreaking work, but they did what everyone else did. Each year, as soon it began raining, they would go out to the fields with blackened sickles, begging one landlord or the other for some work. Then they cast seed, cut weeds, and harvested corn and paddy. My father could have worked with them; he could have worked with the landlords' mud, but he chose not to.

He chose to fight it.

Now, since I doubt that you have rickshaw-pullers in China – or in any other civilized nation on earth – you will have to see one for yourself. Rickshaws are not allowed inside the posh parts of Delhi, where foreigners might see them and gape. Insist on going to Old Delhi, or Nizamuddin – there you'll see the road full of them – thin, sticklike men, leaning forward from the seat of a bicycle, as they pedal along a carriage bearing a pyramid of middle-class flesh – some fat man with his fat wife and all their shopping bags and groceries.

And when you see these stick-men, think of my father.

Rickshaw-puller he may have been – a human beast of burden – but my father was a man with a plan.

I was his plan.

One day he lost his temper at home and began yelling

at the women. This was the day they told him that I had not been going to class. He did something he had never dared do before – he yelled at Kusum:

'How many times have I told you: Munna *must* read and write!'

Kusum was startled, but only for a moment. She yelled back:

'This fellow came running back from school – don't blame me! He's a coward, and he eats too much. Put him to work in the tea shop and let him make some money.'

My aunts and cousin-sisters gathered around her. I crawled behind my father's back as they told him the story of my cowardice.

Now, you may find it incredible that a boy in a village would be frightened of a lizard. Rats, snakes, monkeys, and mongooses don't bother me at all. On the contrary – I *love* animals. But lizards… each time I see one, no matter how tiny, it's as if I turn into a girl. My blood freezes.

There was a giant cupboard in my classroom, whose door was always slightly ajar – no one knew what it was there for. One morning, the door creaked open, and a lizard jumped out.

It was light green in colour, like a half-ripe guava. Its tongue flicked in and out of its mouth. It was at least two feet long.

The other boys barely noticed. Until someone saw my face. They gathered in a circle around me.

Two of them pinned my hands behind my back and held my head still. Someone caught the thing in his hands, and began walking toward me with slow, exaggerated steps. Making no noise – only flicking its red tongue in and out of its mouth – the lizard came closer and closer to my face. The laughter grew louder. I couldn't make a noise. The teacher was snoring at his desk behind me. The lizard's face came right up to my face; and then it opened its light green mouth, and then I fainted for the second time in my life.

I had not gone back to school since that day.

My father did not laugh when he heard the story. He took a deep breath; I felt his chest expanding against me.

'You let Kishan drop out of school, but I told you this fellow had to stay in school. His mother told me he'd be the one who made it through school. His mother said—'

'Oh, to hell with his mother!' Kusum shouted. 'She was a crazy one, and she's dead, and thank goodness. Now listen to me: let the boy go to the tea shop like Kishan, that's what I say.'

The next day my father came with me to my school, for the first and last time. It was dawn; the place was empty. We pushed the door open. A dim blue light filled the classroom. Now, our schoolteacher was a big *paan*-and-spit man – and his expectorate made a sort of low, red wallpaper on three walls around us. When he went to sleep, which he usually did by noon, we stole *paan* from his pockets; distributed it amongst ourselves and chewed on it; and then, imitating his spitting style – hands on hips, back arched slightly – took turns spitting at the three dirty walls.

A faded mural of the Lord Buddha surrounded by deer and squirrels decorated the fourth wall – it was the only wall that the teacher spared. The giant lizard the colour of a half-ripe guava was sitting in front of this wall, pretending to be one of the animals at the feet of the Lord Buddha.

It turned its head to us; I saw its eyes shine.

'Is this the monster?'

The lizard turned its head this way and that, looking for an exit. Then it began banging the wall. It was no different from me; it was terrified.

'Don't kill it, Daddy – just throw it out the window, please?'

The teacher was lying in one corner of the room, reeking of booze, snoring soundly. Near him was the pot of toddy he had emptied the previous night – my father picked it up.

The lizard ran, and he ran behind it, swinging the pot of toddy at it.

'Don't kill it, Daddy – please!'

But he wouldn't listen. He kicked the cupboard, and the lizard darted out, and he chased it again, smashing everything in his way, and yelling, 'Heeyaa! Heeyaa!' He pounded it with the pot of toddy until the pot broke. He smashed its neck with his fist. He stamped on its head.

The air became acrid: a stench of crushed flesh. He picked the dead lizard up and flung it out the door.

My father sat panting against the mural of the Lord Buddha surrounded by the gentle animals.

When he caught his breath, he said, 'My whole life, I have been treated like a donkey. All I want is that one son of mine – at least one – should live like a man.'

What it meant to live like a man was a mystery. I thought it meant being like Vijay, the bus conductor. The bus stopped for half an hour at Laxmangarh, and the passengers got off, and the conductor got down to have a cup of tea. Now, he was a man all of us who worked in that tea shop looked up to. We admired his bus-company-issue khaki uniform, his silver whistle and the red cord from which it hung down from his pocket. Everything about him said: he had made it in life.

Vijay's family were pigherds, which meant they were the lowest of the low, yet he had made it up in life. Somehow he had befriended a politician. People said he had let the politician dip his beak in his backside. Whatever he had to do, he had done: he was the first entrepreneur I knew of. Now he had a job, and a silver whistle, and when he blew it – just as the bus was leaving – all the boys in the village went crazy and ran after the bus, and banged on its sides, and begged to be taken along too. I wanted to be like Vijay – with a uniform, a pay cheque, a shiny whistle with a piercing sound, and people looking at me with eyes that said, *How important he looks*.

2 a.m. already, Mr Premier. I'll have to stop for tonight fairly soon. Let me put my finger on the laptop screen, and see if there is any other useful information here.

Leaving out a few inessential details...

... in the Dhaula Kuan area of New Delhi, on the night of 2 September, near the ITC Maurya Sheraton hotel...

Now, this hotel, the Sheraton, is the finest in Delhi – I've never been inside, but my ex-boss, Mr Ashok, used to do all his late-night drinking there. There's a restaurant in the basement that's supposed to be very good. You should visit it if you get the chance.

The missing man was employed as driver of a Honda City vehicle at the time of the alleged incident. In this regard a case, FIR No. 438/05, P. S. Dhaula Kuan, Delhi, has been registered. He is also believed to be in possession of a bag filled with a certain quantity of cash.

Red bag, they should have said. Without the colour, the information is all but useless, isn't it? No wonder I was never spotted.

Certain quantity of cash. Open any newspaper in this country, and it's always this crap: 'A *certain* interested party has been spreading rumours', or 'A *certain* religious community doesn't believe in contraception.' I *hate* that.

Seven hundred thousand rupees.

That was how much cash was stuffed into the red bag. And trust me, the police knew it too. How much this is in Chinese money, I don't know, Mr Jiabao. But it buys ten silver Macintosh laptops from Singapore.

There's no mention of my school in the poster, sir – that's a real shame. You always ought to talk about a man's education when describing him. They should have said something like, *The suspect was educated in a school with two-foot-long lizards the colour of half-ripe guavas hiding in its cupboards...*

If the Indian village is a paradise, then the school is a paradise within a paradise.

There was supposed to be free food at my school –

a government programme gave every boy three *rotis*, yellow *daal*, and pickles at lunchtime. But we never ever saw *rotis*, or yellow *daal*, or pickles, and everyone knew why: the schoolteacher had stolen our lunch money.

The teacher had a legitimate excuse to steal the money – he said he hadn't been paid his salary in six months.He was going to undertake a Gandhian protest to retrieve his missing wages – he was going to do nothing in class until his pay cheque arrived in the mail. Yet he was terrified of losing his job, because though the pay of any government job in India is poor, the incidental advantages are numerous. Once, a truck came into the school with uniforms that the government had sent for us; we never saw them, but a week later they turned up for sale in the neighbouring village.

No one blamed the schoolteacher for doing this. You can't expect a man in a dung heap to smell sweet. Everyone in the village knew that he would have done the same in his position. Some were even proud of him, for having got away with it so cleanly.

One morning a man wearing the finest suit I had seen in my life, a blue safari suit that looked even more impressive than a bus conductor's uniform, came walking down the road that led to my school. We gathered at the door to stare at his suit. He had a cane in his hand, which he began swishing when he saw us at the door. We rushed back into the class and sat down with our books.

This was a surprise inspection.

The man in the blue safari suit – the inspector – pointed his cane at holes in the wall, or the red discolourations, while the teacher cowered by his side and said, 'Sorry sir, sorry sir.'

'There is no duster in this class; there are no chairs; there are no uniforms for the boys. How much money have you stolen from the school funds, you sister-fucker?'

The inspector wrote four sentences on the board and pointed his cane at a boy:

'Read.'

One boy after the other stood up and blinked at the wall.

'Try Balram, sir,' the teacher said. 'He's the smartest of the lot. He reads well.'

So I stood up, and read, '*We live in a glorious land. The Lord Buddha received his enlightenment in this land. The River Ganga gives life to our plants and our animals and our people. We are grateful to God that we were born in this land.*'

'Good,' the inspector said. 'And who was the Lord Buddha?'

'An enlightened man.'

'An enlightened *god*.'

(Oops! Thirty-six million and five—!)

The inspector made me write my name on the blackboard; then he showed me his wristwatch and asked me to read the time. He took out his wallet, removed a small photo, and asked me, 'Who is this man, who is the most important man in all our lives?'

The photo was of a plump man with spiky white hair and chubby cheeks, wearing thick earrings of gold; the face glowed with intelligence and kindness.

'He's the Great Socialist.'

'Good. And what is the Great Socialist's message for little children?'

I had seen the answer on the wall outside the temple: a policeman had written it one day in red paint.

'Any boy in any village can grow up to become the prime minister of India. That is his message to little children all over this land.'

The inspector pointed his cane straight at me. 'You, young man, are an intelligent, honest, vivacious fellow in this crowd of thugs and idiots. In any jungle, what is the rarest of animals – the creature that comes along only once in a generation?'

I thought about it and said:

'The white tiger.'

'That's what you are, in *this* jungle.'

Before he left, the inspector said, 'I'll write to Patna asking them to send you a scholarship. You need to go to a real school – somewhere far away from here. You need a real uniform, and a real education.'

He had a parting gift for me – a book. I remember the title very well: *Lessons for Young Boys from the Life of Mahatma Gandhi.*

So that's how I became the White Tiger. There will be a fourth and a fifth name too, but that's late in the story.

Now, being praised by the school inspector in front of my teacher and fellow students, being called a 'White Tiger', being given a book, and being promised a scholarship: all this constituted good news, and the one infallible law of life in the Darkness is that good news becomes bad news – and soon.

My cousin-sister Reena got hitched off to a boy in the next village. Because we were the girl's family, we were screwed. We had to give the boy a new bicycle, and cash, and a silver bracelet, and arrange for a big wedding – which we did. Mr Premier, you probably know how we Indians enjoy our weddings – I gather that these days people come from other countries to get married Indian-style. Oh, we could have taught those foreigners a thing or two, I tell you! Film songs blasting out from a black tape recorder, and drinking and dancing all night! I got smashed, and so did Kishan, and so did everyone in the family, and for all I know, they probably poured hooch into the water buffalo's trough.

Two or three days passed. I was in my classroom, sitting at the back, with the black slate and chalk that my father had brought me from one of his trips to Dhanbad, working on the alphabet on my own. The boys were chatting or fighting. The teacher had passed out.

Kishan was standing in the doorway of the classroom. He gestured with his fingers.

'What is it, Kishan? Are we going somewhere?'

Still he said nothing.

'Should I bring my book along? And my chalk?'

'Why not?' he said. And then, with his hand on my head, he led me out.

The family had taken a big loan from the Stork so they could have a lavish wedding and a lavish dowry for my cousin-sister. Now the Stork had called in his loan. He wanted all the members of the family working for him and he had seen me in school, or his collector had. So they had to hand me over too.

I was taken to the tea shop. Kishan folded his hands and bowed to the shopkeeper. I bowed to the shopkeeper too.

'Who's this?' The shopkeeper squinted at me.

He was sitting under a huge portrait of Mahatma Gandhi, and I knew already that I was going to be in big trouble.

'My brother,' Kishan said. 'He's come to join me.'

Then Kishan dragged the oven out from the tea shop and told me to sit down. I sat down next to him. He brought a gunnysack; inside was a huge pile of coals. He took out a coal, smashed it on a brick, and then poured the black chunks into the oven.

'Harder,' he said, when I hit the coal against the brick. 'Harder, harder.'

Finally I got it right – I broke the coal against the brick. He got up and said, 'Now break every last coal in this bag like that.'

A little later, two boys came around from school to watch me. Then two more boys came; then two more. I heard giggling.

'What is the creature that comes along only once in a generation?' one boy asked loudly.

'The coal breaker,' another replied.

And then all of them began to laugh.

'Ignore them,' Kishan said. 'They'll go away on their own.'

He looked at me.

'You're angry with me for taking you out of school, aren't you?'

I said nothing.

'You hate the idea of having to break coals, don't you?'
I said nothing.

He took the largest piece of coal in his hand and squeezed it. 'Imagine that each coal is my skull: they will get much easier to break.'

He'd been taken out of school too. That happened after my cousin-sister Meera's wedding. That had been a big affair too.

*

Working in a tea shop. Smashing coals. Wiping tables. Bad news for me, you say?

To break the law of his land – to turn bad news into good news – is the entrepreneur's prerogative.

Tomorrow, Mr Jiabao, starting again at midnight I'll tell you how I gave myself a better education at the tea shop than I could have got at any school. Right now, though, it's time for me to stop staring at this chandelier and get to work. It is almost three in the morning. This is when Bangalore comes to life. The American workday is coming to an end, and mine is beginning in earnest. I have to be alert as all the call-centre girls and boys are leaving their offices for their homes. This is when I must be near the phone.

I don't keep a mobile phone, for obvious reasons – they corrode a man's brains, shrink his balls, and dry up his semen, as all of us know – so I have to stay in the office. In case there is a crisis.

I am the man people call when they have a crisis!
Let's see quickly if there's anything else...

... any person having any information or clue about this missing man may kindly inform at CBI Web site (http://cbi.nic.in) e-mail ID (diccbi@cbi.nic.in), Fax No. 011-23011334, T No. 011-23014046 (Direct) 011-23015229 and 23015218 Extn. 210 and to the undersigned at the following address or telephone number or numbers given below.

DP 3687/05
SHO – Dhaula Kuan, New Delhi
Tel: 28653200, 27641000

Set into the text of the notice, a photograph: blurred, blackened, and smudged by the antique printing press of some police office, and barely recognizable even when it was on the wall of the train station, but now, transferred onto the computer screen, reduced to pixels, just an abstract idea of a man's face: a small creature with large, popped-out eyes and a stubby moustache. He could be half the men in India.

Mr Premier, I leave you for tonight with a comment on the shortcomings of police work in India. Now, a busload of men in khaki – it was a sensational case, after all – must have gone to Laxmangarh when investigating my disappearance. They would have questioned the shopkeepers, bullied the rickshaw pullers, and woken up the schoolteacher. Did he steal as a child? Did he sleep with whores? They would have smashed up a grocery shop or two, and forced out 'confessions' from one or two people.

Yet I bet you they missed the most important clue of all, which was right in front of them:

I am talking of the Black Fort, of course.

I begged Kusum many times to take me to the top of the hill, and through the entranceway, and into the fort. But she said I was a coward, I would die of fright if I went up there: an enormous lizard, the biggest in the whole world, lived in the fort.

So I could only watch. The long loopholes in its wall turned into lines of burning pink at sunrise and burning gold at sunset; the blue sky shone through the slits in the stone, while the moon shone on the jagged ramparts, and the monkeys ran wild along the walls, shrieking and attacking each other, as if they were the spirits of the dead warriors reincarnated, refighting their final battles.

I wanted to go up there too.

Iqbal, who is one of the four best poets in the world – the others being Rumi, Mirza Ghalib, and a fourth fellow, also a Muslim, whose name I've forgotten – has written a poem where he says this about slaves:

They remain slaves because they can't see what is beautiful in this world.

That's the truest thing anyone ever said.

A great poet, this fellow Iqbal – even if he *was* a Muslim.

(By the way, Mr Premier: have you noticed that all four of the greatest poets in the world are Muslim? And yet all the Muslims you meet are illiterate or covered head to toe in black burkas or looking for buildings to blow up? It's a puzzle, isn't it? If you ever figure these people out, send me an e-mail.)

Even as a boy I could see what was beautiful in the world: I was destined not to stay a slave.

One day Kusum found out about me and the fort. She followed me all the way from our home to the pond with the stones, and saw what I was doing. That night she told my father, 'He just stood there gaping at the fort – just the way his mother used to. He is going to come to nothing good in life, I'll tell you that right now.'

When I was maybe thirteen I decided to go up to the fort on my own. I waded into the pond, got to the other side, and climbed up the hill; just as I was on the verge of going in, a black thing materialized in the entranceway. I spun around and ran back down the hill, too frightened even to cry.

It was only a cow. I could see this from a distance, but I was too shaken up to go back.

I tried many more times, yet I was such a coward that each time I tried to go up, I lost my nerve and came back.

At the age of twenty-four, when I was living in Dhanbad and working in Mr Ashok's service as a chauffeur, I returned to Laxmangarh when my master and his wife went there on an excursion. It was a very important trip for me, and one I hope to describe in greater detail when time permits. For now, all I want to tell you is this: while Mr Ashok and Pinky Madam were relaxing, having eaten lunch, I had nothing to do, so I decided to try again. I swam through the pond, walked up the hill, went into the doorway, and entered the Black Fort for the first time. There wasn't much around – just some broken walls and a bunch of frightened monkeys watching me from a distance. Putting my foot on the wall, I looked down on the village from there. My little Lax-mangarh. I saw the temple tower, the market, the glistening line of sewage, the landlords' mansions – and my own house, with that dark little cloud outside – the water buffalo. It looked like the most beautiful sight on earth.

I leaned out from the edge of the fort in the direction of my village – and then I did something too disgusting to describe to you.

Well, actually, I *spat*. Again and again. And then, whistling and humming, I went back down the hill.

Eight months later, I slit Mr Ashok's throat.

The Second Night

His Excellency Wen Jiabao
Now probably fast asleep in the
Premier's Office
In China

From the Desk of:

His Midnight Educator
On matters entrepreneurial:
'The White Tiger'

Mr Premier.

So.

What does my laughter sound like?

What do my armpits smell like?

And when I grin, is it true – as you no doubt imagine by now – that my lips widen into a devil's rictus?

Oh, I could go on and on about myself, sir. I could gloat that I am not just any murderer, but one who killed his own employer (who is a kind of second father), and also contributed to the probable death of all his family members. A virtual mass murderer.

But I don't want to go on and on about myself. You should hear some of these Bangalore entrepreneurs – my *start-up* has got this contract with American Express, my *start-up* runs the software in this hospital in London, blah blah. I hate that whole fucking Bangalore attitude, I tell you.

(But if you absolutely must find out more about me, just log on to *my* Web site: *www.whitetiger-technology drivers.com*. That's right! That's the URL of *my* start-up!)

So I'm sick of talking about myself, sir. Tonight, I want to talk about the other important man in my story.

My ex.

Mr Ashok's face reappears now in my mind's eye as it used to every day when I was in his service – reflected in my rearview mirror. It was such a handsome face that sometimes I couldn't take my eyes off it. Picture a six-foot-tall fellow, broad-shouldered, with a landlord's powerful, punishing forearms; yet always gentle (*almost* always – except for that time he punched Pinky Madam in the face) and kind to those around him, even his servants and driver.

Now another face appears, to the side of his, in memory's mirror. Pinky Madam – his wife. Every bit as good-looking as her husband; just as the image of the goddess in the Birla Hindu Temple in New Delhi is as fair as the god to whom she is married. She would sit in the back, and the two of them would talk, and I would drive them wherever they wanted, as faithfully as the servant-god Hanuman carried about his master and mistress, Ram and Sita.

Thinking of Mr Ashok is making me sentimental. I hope I've got some paper napkins here somewhere.

Here's a strange fact: murder a man, and you feel responsible for his life – *possessive*, even. You know more about him than his father and mother; they knew his foetus, but you know his corpse. Only you can complete the story of his life; only you know why his body has to be pushed into the fire before its time, and why his toes curl up and fight for another hour on earth.

Now, even though I killed him, you won't find me saying one bad thing about him. I protected his good name when I was his servant, and now that I am (in a sense) his master, I won't stop protecting his good name. I owe him so much. He and Pinky Madam would sit in the back of the car, chatting about life, about India, about America – mixing Hindi and English together – and by eavesdropping on them, I learned a lot about life, India, and America – and a bit of English too. (Perhaps a bit more than I've let on so far—!) Many of my best ideas are, in fact, borrowed from my ex-employer or his brother or someone else whom I was driving about. (I confess, Mr Premier: I am not an original thinker – but I am an original *listener*.) True, eventually Mr Ashok and I had a disagreement or two about an English term – *income tax* – and things began to sour between us, but that messy stuff comes later on in the story. Right now we're still on the best of terms: we've just met, far from Delhi, in the city called Dhanbad.

I came to Dhanbad after my father's death. He had been ill for some time, but there is no hospital in Laxmangarh, although there are three different foundation stones for a hospital, laid by three different politicians before three different elections. When he began spitting blood that morning, Kishan and I took him by boat across the river. We kept washing his mouth with water from the river, but the water was so polluted that it made him spit more blood.

47

There was a rickshaw-puller on the other side of the river who recognized my father; he took the three of us for free to the government hospital.

There were three black goats sitting on the steps to the large, faded white building; the stench of goat faeces wafted out from the open door. The glass in most of the windows was broken; a cat was staring out at us from one cracked window.

A sign on the gate said:

LOHIA UNIVERSAL FREE HOSPITAL
PROUNDLY INAUGURATED BY THE GREAT SOCIALIST
A HOLY PROOF THAT HE KEEPS HIS PROMISES

Kishan and I carried our father in, stamping on the goat turds which had spread like a constellation of black stars on the ground. There was no doctor in the hospital. The ward boy, after we bribed him ten rupees, said that a doctor might come in the evening. The doors to the hospital's rooms were wide open; the beds had metal springs sticking out of them, and the cat began snarling at us the moment we stepped into the room.

'It's not safe in the rooms – that cat has tasted blood.'

A couple of Muslim men had spread a newspaper on the ground and were sitting on it. One of them had an open wound on his leg. He invited us to sit with him and his friend. Kishan and I lowered Father onto the newspaper sheets. We waited there.

Two little girls came and sat down behind us; both of them had yellow eyes.

'Jaundice. *She* gave it to me.'

'I did not. *You* gave it to me. And now we'll both die!'

An old man with a cotton patch on one eye came and sat down behind the girls.

The Muslim men kept adding newspapers to the ground, and the line of diseased eyes, raw wounds, and delirious mouths kept growing.

'Why *isn't* there a doctor here, uncle?' I asked. 'This is the only hospital on either side of the river.'

'See, it's like this,' the older Muslim man said. 'There's a government medical superintendent who's meant to check that doctors visit village hospitals like this. Now, each time this post falls vacant, the Great Socialist lets all the big doctors know that he's having an open auction for that post. The going rate for this post is about four hundred thousand rupees these days.'

'That much!' I said, my mouth opened wide.

'Why not? There's good money in public service! Now, imagine that I'm a doctor. I beg and borrow the money and give it to the Great Socialist, while touching his feet. He gives me the job. I take an oath to God and the Constitution of India and then I put my boots up on my desk in the state capital.' He raised his feet onto an imaginary table. 'Next, I call all the junior government doctors, whom I'm supposed to supervise, into my office. I take out my big government ledger. I shout out, "Dr Ram Pandey."'

He pointed a finger at me; I assumed my role in the play.

I saluted him: 'Yes, sir!'

He held out his palm to me.

'Now, you – Dr Ram Pandey – will kindly put one-third of your salary in my palm. Good boy. In return, I do *this*.' He made a tick on the imaginary ledger. 'You can keep the rest of your government salary and go work in some private hospital for the rest of the week. Forget the village. Because according to this ledger you've *been* there. You've *treated* my wounded leg. You've *healed* that girl's jaundice.'

'Ah,' the patients said. Even the ward boys, who had gathered around us to listen, nodded their heads in appreciation. Stories of rottenness and corruption are always the best stories, aren't they?

When Kishan put some food into Father's mouth, he spat it out with blood. His lean black body began to convulse, spewing blood this way and that. The girls with the yellow eyes began to wail. The other patients moved away from my father.

'He's got tuberculosis, hasn't he?' the older Muslim man asked, as he swatted the flies away from the wound in his leg.

'We don't know, sir. He's been coughing for a while, but we didn't know what it was.'

'Oh, it's TB. I've seen it before in rickshaw-pullers. They get weak from their work. Well, maybe the doctor will turn up in the evening.'

He did not. Around six o'clock that day, as the government ledger no doubt accurately reported, my father was permanently cured of his tuberculosis. The ward boys made us clean up after Father before we could remove the body. A goat came in and sniffed as we were mopping the blood off the floor. The ward boys petted her and fed her a plump carrot as we mopped our father's infected blood off the floor.

Kishan's marriage took place a month after the cremation.

It was one of the *good* marriages. We had the boy, and we screwed the girl's family hard. I remember exactly what we got in dowry from the girl's side, and thinking about it even now makes my mouth fill up with water: five thousand rupees cash, all crisp new unsoiled notes fresh from the bank, plus a Hero bicycle, plus a thick gold necklace for Kishan.

After the wedding, Kusum Granny took the five thousand rupees and the Hero cycle and the thick gold necklace; Kishan got two weeks to dip his beak into his wife, and then he was packed off to Dhanbad. My cousin Dilip and I came along with him. We three found work in a tea shop in Dhanbad – the owner had heard good things about Kishan's work at the tea shop in Laxmangarh.

Luckily for us, he hadn't heard anything about me.

Go to a tea shop anywhere along the Ganga, sir, and look at the men working in that tea shop – men, I say, but better to call them human spiders that go crawling in between and under the tables with rags in their hands, crushed humans in crushed uniforms, sluggish, unshaven, in their thirties or forties or fifties but still 'boys'. But that is your fate if you do your job well – with honesty, dedication, and sincerity, the way Gandhi would have done it, no doubt.

I did my job with near total dishonesty, lack of dedication, and insincerity – and so the tea shop was a profoundly enriching experience.

Instead of wiping out spots from tables and crushing coals for the oven, I used my time at the tea shop in Laxmangarh to spy on every customer at every table, and overhear everything they said. I decided that this was how I would keep my education going forward – that's the one good thing I'll say for myself. I've always been a big believer in education – especially my own.

The owner of the shop sat up at the front, below the big photo of Gandhi, stirring a slow-boiling broth of sugar syrup. He knew what I was up to! Whenever he saw me loafing around a table or pretending to be doing a spot of wiping just so I could hear more of a conversation, he would shout, 'You thug!' then jump down from his seat, chase me around the tea shop with the ladle he had been using to stir the sugar, and whack me on the head with it. The burning syrup singed me wherever the ladle touched, and left a series of spots on my ears which people sometimes mistake for vitiligo or another skin disease; a network of pink by which you can still identify me, although the police, predictably, missed it.

Eventually I got sent home. No one else in Laxmangarh would hire me after that, even as a field hand. So it was mostly for my sake that Kishan and Dilip had come to Dhanbad – to give me a chance to start my career as a human spider afresh.

In his journey from village to city, from Laxmangarh to Delhi, the entrepreneur's path crosses any number of provincial towns that have the pollution and noise and traffic of a big city – without any hint of the true city's sense of history, planning, and grandeur. Half-baked cities, built for half-baked men.

There was money in the air in Dhanbad. I saw buildings with sides made entirely of glass, and men with gold in their teeth. And all this glass and gold – all of it came from the coal pits. Outside the town, there was coal, more coal than you would find anywhere else in the Darkness, maybe more coal than anywhere else in the world. Miners came to eat at my tea shop – I always gave them the best service, because they had the best tales to tell.

They said that the coal mines went on and on for miles and miles outside the town. In some places there were fires burning under the earth and sending smoke into the air – fires that had been burning continuously for a hundred years!

And it was at the tea shop in this city built by coal, while wiping a table and lingering to overhear a conversation, that my life changed.

'You know, sometimes I think I did the wrong thing in life, becoming a miner.'

'Then? What else can people like you and me become? Politicians?'

'Everyone's getting a car these days – and you know how much they pay their drivers? One thousand seven hundred rupees a month!'

I dropped my rag. I ran to Kishan, who was cleaning out the insides of an oven.

After my father's death, it was Kishan who took care of me. I don't attempt to hide his role in making me who I am today. But he had no entrepreneurial spunk at all. He would have been happy to let me sink in the mud.

'Nothing doing,' Kishan said. 'Granny said stick to the tea shop – and we'll stick to the tea shop.'

I went to all the taxi stands; down on my knees I begged random strangers; but no one would agree to teach me car-driving for free. It was going to cost me three hundred rupees, to learn how to drive a car.

Three hundred rupees!

Today, in Bangalore, I can't get enough people for my business. People come and people go. Good men never stay. I'm even thinking of advertising in the newspaper.

BANGALORE-BASED BUSINESS MAN SEEKS
SMART MEN FOR HIS BUSINESS
APPLY AT ONCE!
ATTRACTIVE REMUNERATION PACKAGES ON OFFER
LESSONS IN LIFE AND ENTERPRENEURSHIP
INCLUDED FOR FREE!

Go to any pub or bar in Bangalore with your ears open and it's the same thing you hear: can't get enough call-centre workers, can't get enough software engineers, can't get enough sales managers. There are twenty, twenty-five pages of job advertisements in the newspaper every week.

Things are different in the Darkness. There, every morning, tens of thousands of young men sit in the tea shops, reading the newspaper, or lie on a charpoy humming a tune, or sit in their rooms talking to a photo of a film actress. They have no job to do today. They know they won't get any job today. They've given up the fight.

They're the smart ones.

The stupid ones have gathered in a field in the centre

of the town. Every now and then a truck comes by, and all the men in the field rush to it with their hands outstretched, shouting, 'Take me! Take me!'

Everyone pushed me; I pushed back, but the truck scooped up only six or seven men and left the rest of us behind. They were off on some construction or digging job – the lucky bastards. Another half-hour of waiting. Another truck came. Another scramble, another fight. After the fifth or sixth fight of the day, I finally found myself at the head of the crowd, face-to-face with the truck driver. He was a Sikh, a man with a big blue turban. In one hand he held a wooden stick, and he swung the stick to drive back the crowd.

'Everyone!' he shouted. 'Take off your shirts! I've got to see a man's nipples before I give him a job!'

He looked at my chest; he squeezed the nipples – slapped my butt – glared into my eyes – and then poked the stick against my thigh: 'Too thin! Fuck off!'

'Give me a chance, sir – my body is small but there's a lot of fight in it – I'll dig for you, I'll haul cement for you, I'll–'

He swung his stick; it hit me on the left ear. I fell down, and others rushed to take my place.

I sat on the ground, rubbed my ear, and watched the truck leave in a big cloud of dust.

The shadow of an eagle passed over my body. I burst into tears.

'White Tiger! There you are!'

Kishan and Cousin Dilip lifted me up from the ground, big smiles on their faces. Great news! Granny had agreed to let them invest in my driving classes. 'There's only one thing,' Kishan said. 'Granny says you're a greedy pig. She wants you to swear by all the gods in heaven that you won't forget her once you get rich.'

'I swear.'

'Pinch your neck and swear – you'll send every rupee you make every month back to Granny.'

We went into the house where the taxi drivers lived. An old man in a brown uniform, which was like an ancient army outfit, was smoking a hookah that was warmed up by a bowl of live coals. Kishan explained the situation to him.

The old driver asked, 'What caste are you?'

'Halwai.'

'Sweet-makers,' the old driver said, shaking his head. 'That's what you people do. You make sweets. How can you learn to drive?' He pointed his hookah at the live coals. 'That's like getting coals to make ice for you. Mastering a car' – he moved the stick of an invisible gearbox – 'it's like taming a wild stallion – only a boy from the warrior castes can manage that. You need to have aggression in your blood. Muslims, Rajputs, Sikhs – they're fighters, they can become drivers. You think sweet-makers can last long in fourth gear?'

Coal was taught to make ice, starting the next morning at six. Three hundred rupees, plus a bonus, will do that. We practised in a taxi. Each time I made a mistake with the gears, he slapped me on the skull. 'Why don't you stick to sweets and tea?'

For every hour I spent in the car, he made me spend two or three under it – I was made a free repair mechanic for all the taxis in the stand; late every evening, I emerged from under a taxi like a pig from sewage, my face black with grease, my hands shiny with engine oil. I dipped into a Ganga of black – and came out a driver.

'Listen,' the old driver said when I was handing him over the hundred rupees he had been promised as a bonus. 'It's not enough to drive. You've got to become a *driver*. You've got to get the right attitude, understand? Anyone tries to overtake you on the road, do this' – he clenched his fist and shook it – 'and call him a sister-fucker a few times. The road is a jungle, get it? A good driver must roar to get ahead on it.'

He patted me on the back.

'You're better than I thought – you are a surprise package, little fellow. I've got a reward for you.'

He walked; I followed. It was evening. We went through dim streets and markets. We walked for half an hour, while everything around us grew dark – and then it was as if we had stepped out into fireworks.

The street was full of coloured doors and coloured windows, and in each door and each window, a woman was looking out at me with a big smile. Ribbons of red paper and silver foil glittered between the rooftops of the street; tea was being boiled in stalls by the sides of the road. Four men rushed at us at once. The old driver explained that they should keep away, since it was my first time. 'Let him enjoy the sights first. That's the best part of this game, isn't it – the looking!'

'Sure, sure,' the men said, and stepped back. 'That's what we want him to do – enjoy!'

I walked with the old driver, my mouth open, gaping at all the gorgeous women jeering and taunting me from behind their grilled windows – all of them begging me to dip my beak into them!

The old driver explained the nature of the wares on offer. Up in one building, sitting on a windowsill in such a way that we could see the full spread of their gleaming dark legs, were the 'Americans': girls in short skirts and high platform shoes, carrying pink handbags with names in English written on them in sequins. They were slim and athletic – for men who like the Western kind. In this corner, sitting in the threshold of an open house, the 'traditionals' – fat, chunky types in saris, for those who like value for their money. There were eunuchs in one window – teenagers in the next window. The face of a small boy appeared from between a woman's legs and then vanished.

A blinding flash of light: a blue door opened, and four light-skinned Nepali women, in gorgeous red petticoats, looked out.

'Them!' I shouted. 'Them! Them! Them!'

'Good,' the old driver said. 'I like that too – I always go for the foreign ones.'

We went in, and he picked a woman from the four, and I picked another woman, and we went into two rooms, and the woman I picked closed the door behind me.

My first time!

Half an hour later, when the old driver and I staggered back, drunk and happy, to his house, I put coals in his hookah. I brought him the hookah and watched as he took a deep, contented suck on the pipe. Smoke came out of his nostrils.

'What is it now? I've taught you to be a driver and a man – what more do you want?'

'Sir… can't you ask the taxi men if they need someone? I'll work for free at first. I need a job.'

The old driver laughed. 'I haven't had work in forty years, you nitwit. How the fuck can I help you? Now get lost.'

So, next morning, I was walking from house to house, knocking on gates and on front doors of the rich, asking if anyone wanted a driver – a good driver – an experienced driver – for their car.

Everyone said no. You didn't get a job that way. You had to know someone in the family to get a job. Not by knocking on the gate and asking.

There's no reward for entrepreneurship in most of India, Your Excellency. It's a sad fact.

Every evening I came home tired and close to tears, but Kishan said, 'Keep trying. Someone will say yes in the end.'

So I went looking, from house to house, house to house, house to house. Finally, after two weeks of asking and being told to get lost, I got to a house with ten-foot-high walls, and a cage of iron grilles around each window.

A sly, slant-eyed Nepali with a white moustache peered at me through the bars of the gate.

'What do you want?'

I didn't like the way he asked that one bit; I put a big smile on my face.

'Any need of a driver, sir? I've got four years' experience. My master recently died, so I—'

'Fuck off. We have a driver already,' the Nepali said. He twirled a big bunch of keys and grinned.

My heart sank, and I was about to turn away – when I saw a figure on the terrace, a fellow in long loose white clothes, walking around and around, lost deep in thought. I swear by God, sir – I swear by all 36,000,004 of them – the moment I saw his face, I knew: *This is the master for me.*

Some dark fate had tied his lifeline to mine, because at that very moment he looked down.

I knew he was coming down to save me. I just had to divert this Nepali fucker as long as possible.

'I'm a good driver, sir. I don't smoke, I don't drink, I don't steal.'

'Fuck off, don't you understand?'

'I don't disrespect God, I don't disrespect my family.'

'What's wrong with you? Get lost, at once—'

'I don't gossip about my masters, I don't steal, I don't blaspheme.'

Just then, the door of the house opened. But it was not the man on the terrace – it was an older man, with a big white moustache that was thick, and curved, and pointy at the tips.

'What is going on, Ram Bahadur?' he asked the Nepali.

'He's begging, sir. Begging for money.'

I banged on the gate. 'I am from your village, sir. I am from Laxmangarh! The village near the Black Fort! Your village!'

The old man was the Stork!

He stared at me for the longest time, and then he told the Nepali guard, 'Let the boy in.'

Swoosh! – As soon as the gate was open, I dived straight at the Stork's feet. No Olympic runner could have gone in as fast as I did through those gates; the Nepali had no chance at all of blocking me.

You should have seen me that day – what a performance of wails and kisses and tears! You'd think I'd been born into a caste of performing actors! And all the time, while clutching the Stork's feet, I was staring at his huge, dirty, uncut toenails, and thinking, *What is he doing in Dhanbad? Why isn't he back home, screwing poor fishermen of their money and humping their daughters?*

'Get up, boy,' he said – big, uncut toenails scratched my cheeks. Mr Ashok – the man on the terrace, of course – was by his side now.

'You're *really* from Laxmangarh?'

'Yes, sir. I used to work in the tea shop – the one with the big photo of Gandhi in it. I used to break coals there. You came once to have tea.'

'Ah… the old village.' He closed his eyes. 'Do people there still remember me? It's been three years since I was there.'

'Of course, sir – people say, "Our father is gone, Thakur Ramdev is gone, the best of the landlords is gone, who will protect us now?"'

The Stork enjoyed hearing that. He turned to Mr Ashok. 'Let's see how good he is. Call Mukesh too. Let's go for a spin.'

Only later did I understand how lucky I'd been. Mr Ashok had come back from America just the previous day; a car had been bought for him. A driver was needed for the car. And on that day I had turned up.

Now, there were two cars in the garage. One was your standard Maruti Suzuki – that little white car you see all over India – and the other was the Honda City. Now, the Maruti is a small, simple fellow, a perfect servant to the driver; the moment you turn the ignition key, he does exactly what the driver wants him to. The Honda City is a larger car, a more sophisticated creature, with a mind of his own; he has power steering, and an advanced engine, and he does what *he* wants to. Given that I was so nervous then, if the Stork had told me to take the driving test in the Honda City, that would have been the end of me, sir. But luck was on my side.

They made me drive the Maruti Suzuki.

The Stork and Mr Ashok got into the back; a small dark man – Mukesh Sir, the Stork's other son – got into the front seat and gave me orders. The Nepali guard watched with a darkened face as I took the car out of the gates – and into the city of Dhanbad.

They made me drive them around for half an hour, and then told me to head back.

'Not bad,' the old man said as he got out of the car. 'Fellow is cautious and good. What's your last name again?'

'Halwai.'

'Halwai...' He turned to the small dark man. 'What caste is that, top or bottom?'

And I knew that my future depended on the answer to this question.

*

I should explain a thing or two about caste. Even Indians get confused about this word, especially educated Indians in the cities. They'll make a mess of explaining it to you. But it's simple, really.

Let's start with me.

See: Halwai, my name, means 'sweet-maker'.

That's my caste – my destiny. Everyone in the Darkness who hears that name knows all about me at once. That's why Kishan and I kept getting jobs at sweetshops wherever we went. The owner thought, *Ah, they're Halwais, making sweets and tea is in their blood.*

But if we were Halwais, then why was my father not making sweets but pulling a rickshaw? Why did I grow up breaking coals and wiping tables, instead of eating *gulab jamuns* and sweet pastries when and where I chose to? Why was I lean and dark and cunning, and not fat and creamy-skinned and smiling, like a boy raised on sweets would be?

See, this country, in its days of greatness, when it was the richest nation on earth, was like a zoo. A clean, well-kept, orderly zoo. Everyone in his place, everyone happy. Goldsmiths here. Cowherds here. Landlords there. The man called a Halwai made sweets. The man called a cowherd tended cows. The untouchable cleaned faeces. Landlords were kind to their serfs. Women covered their heads with a veil and turned their eyes to the ground when talking to strange men.

And then, thanks to all those politicians in Delhi, on the fifteenth of August, 1947 – the day the British left – the cages had been let open; and the animals had attacked and ripped each other apart and jungle law replaced zoo law. Those that were the most ferocious, the hungriest, had eaten everyone else up, and grown big bellies. That was all that counted now, the size of your belly. It didn't matter whether you were a woman, or a Muslim, or an untouchable: anyone with a belly could rise up. My father's father must have been a real Halwai, a sweet-maker, but when he inherited the shop, a member of some other caste must have stolen it from him with the help of the police. My father had not had the belly to fight back. That's why he had fallen all the way to the mud, to the level of a rickshaw-puller. That's why I was cheated of my destiny to be fat, and creamy-skinned, and smiling.

To sum up – in the old days there were one thousand castes and destinies in India. These days, there are just two castes: Men with Big Bellies, and Men with Small Bellies.

And only two destinies: eat – or get eaten up.

*

Now, the dark man – Mukesh Sir, brother of Mr Ashok – did not know the answer – I told you that people in the cities know nothing much about the caste system, so the Stork turned to me and asked me directly.

'Are you from a top caste or bottom caste, boy?'

I didn't know what he wanted me to say, so I flipped both answers – I could probably have made a good case either way – and then said, 'Bottom, sir.'

Turning to Mukesh Sir, the old man said, 'All our employees are top caste. It won't hurt to have one or two bottom castes working for us.'

Mukesh Sir looked at me with narrowed eyes. He didn't know the village ways, but he had all the cunning of the landlords.

'Do you drink?'

'No, sir. In my caste, we never drink.'

'Halwai . ' Mr Ashok said with a grin. 'Are you a sweet-maker? Can you cook for us while you're not driving?'

'Certainly, sir. I cook very well. Very tasty sweets. *Gulab jamuns*, *laddoos*, anything you desire,' I said. 'I worked at a tea shop for many years.'

Mr Ashok seemed to find this amusing. 'Only in India,' he said. 'Your driver can also make sweets for you. Only in India. Start from tomorrow.'

'Not so fast,' Mukesh Sir said. 'First we have to ask about his family. How many are they, where they live, everything. And one more thing: how much do you want?'

Another test.

'Absolutely nothing, sir. You're like a father and mother to me, and how can I ask for money from my parents?'

'Eight hundred rupees a month,' he said.

'No, sir, please – it's too much. Give me half of that, it's enough. More than enough.'

'If we keep you beyond two months, it'll go to one thousand five hundred.'

Looking suitably devastated, I accepted the money from him.

Mukesh Sir was not yet convinced about me. He looked me up and down and said, 'He's young. Don't we want someone older?'

The Stork shook his head. 'Catch 'em young, and you can keep 'em for life. A driver in his forties, you get, what, twenty years of service, then his eyes fail. This fellow will last thirty, thirty-five years. His teeth are solid, he's got his hair, he's in good shape.'

He sucked on his betel juice, which was filling up his mouth, turned, and spat out a jet of red liquid to the side.

Then he told me to come back in two days.

He must have phoned his man in Laxmangarh. And then that man must have gone and spoken to Kusum, and asked the neighbours about us, and phoned back: 'He's got a good family. They've never made any trouble. Father died some years ago of TB. He was a rickshaw-puller. Brother is in Dhanbad too, a worker in the tea shops. No history of supporting Naxals or other terrorists. And they don't move about: we know *exactly* where they are.'

That last piece of information was *very* important. They had to know where my family was, at all times.

I have not told you yet, have I, about what the Buffalo did to his domestic servant. The one who was supposed to guard his infant son, who got kidnapped by the Naxals and then tortured and killed. The servant was one of our caste, sir. A Halwai. I had seen him once or twice when I was a boy.

The servant said he had nothing to do with the kidnapping; the Buffalo did not believe him and got four of his hired gunmen to torture the servant. Then they shot him through the head.

Fair enough. I would do the same to someone who let my son get kidnapped.

But then, because the Buffalo was sure that the man had deliberately let the child be kidnapped, for money, he also went after the servant's family. One brother was set upon while working in the fields; beaten to death there. That brother's wife was finished off by three men working together. A sister, still unmarried, was also finished off. Then the house where the family had lived was surrounded by the four henchmen and set on fire.

Now, who would want this to happen to his family, sir? Which inhuman wretch of a monster would consign his own granny and brother and aunt and nephews and nieces to death?

The Stork and his sons could count on my loyalty.

When I came back, the Nepali guard opened the gate without a word. I was inside the compound now.

As far as masters go, Mr Ashok, Mukesh Sir, and the Stork were better than nine in ten. There was always enough food in the house for the servants. On Sundays you even got a special dish, rice mixed with small red chunks of boneless chicken. I had never had a regular chicken dish in my life until then; it made you feel like a king, eating chicken Sunday after Sunday and then licking your fingers. I had a covered room to sleep in. True, I had to share it with the other driver, a grim-looking fellow named Ram Persad, and he had the nice big bed, while I had to sleep on the floor – still a covered room's a covered room, and much nicer than sleeping on the road, as Kishan and I had been doing all the time we were in Dhanbad. Above all, I got the thing that we who grow up in the Darkness value most of all. A uniform. A *khaki* uniform!

The next day I went to the bank – the one that had a wall made all of glass. I saw myself reflected in the glass panes – all in khaki. I walked back and forth in front of that bank a dozen times, just gaping at myself.

If only they had given me a silver whistle, I would have been in paradise!

Kishan came once a month to see me. Kusum had decided that I could keep ninety rupees a month for myself: the rest would go straight to Kishan – who would send it straight to her, in the village. I gave him the money every month through the black bars of the rear gate, and we would talk for a few minutes before the Nepali shouted, 'That's enough – the boy has work to do now!'

The work of a number two driver was simple. If the number one driver, Ram Persad, was busy driving the masters around town in the Honda City, and someone in the house wanted to go to the market, or to a coal mine, or to the train station, I got into the Maruti Suzuki and drove them there. Otherwise I had to stay around the house and make myself useful.

Now, I say they took me on as their 'driver'. I don't exactly know how you organize your servants in China. But in India – or, at least, in the Darkness – the rich don't have drivers, cooks, barbers, and tailors. They simply have servants.

What I mean is that anytime I was not driving the car, I had to sweep the floor of the courtyard, make tea, clean cobwebs with a long broom, or chase a cow out of the compound. There was one thing I was not allowed to do, and this was to touch the Honda City: Ram Persad alone had the right to drive it and clean it. In the evenings I'd watch him wash the sleek exterior of the car with a soft cloth. And I'd burn with envy.

I could see, even from outside, that this was a beautiful, modern car, with all the necessary comforts: a speaker system, A/C, nice glossy leather seats, and a big stainless-steel spittoon in the back. It must be like paradise to drive such a nice car. All I had was a battered old Maruti Suzuki.

One evening, as I was watching, Mr Ashok came and poked his nose around the car. I was discovering that he was a very inquisitive man.

'What's that for? That shiny thing in the back.'

'Spittoon, sir.'

'What?'

Ram Persad explained. This spittoon was for the Stork, who liked to chew *paan*. If he spat the *paan* out the window the *paan* might streak the sides of the car, so he spat near his feet, into the spittoon, which the driver washed and cleaned at the end of every ride.

'Disgusting,' Mr Ashok said.

He was asking about something else when Mukesh Sir's son Roshan came running up to us with a plastic bat and ball in his hand.

Ram Persad snapped his fingers for me.

(Playing cricket with any brat in the household who wanted to play – and letting him win, handsomely – was one of the prescribed duties of driver number two.)

Mr Ashok joined the game. He stood as the wicket-keeper while I bowled full tosses to the brat.

'I'm Azharuddin, captain of India!' the boy shouted every time he hit a six or a four.

'Call yourself Gavaskar. Azharuddin is a Muslim.'

It was the Stork. He had come into the courtyard to watch.

Mr Ashok said, 'Father, what a silly thing to say! Hindu or Muslim, what difference does it make?'

'Oh, you young people and your modern ideas!' the Stork said. He put his hands on me. 'I have to steal the driver, Roshan – I'm sorry, you'll have him back in an hour, okay?'

The Stork had a special use for driver number two. He had bad legs, with blue veins in them, and had been told by a doctor to sit in the courtyard in the evening with his feet in warm water and have them massaged by a servant.

I had to heat water on the stove, carry it into the courtyard, and then lift the old man's feet up one after the other and immerse them in the hot water and then massage them both gently; as I did this, he would close his eyes and moan.

After half an hour, he would say, 'The water's gone cold,' and then I had to lift his feet out, one at a time, from the bucket, and carry the bucket in to the toilet. The water in it was dark – dead hair and bits of skin floated on it. I had to fill the bucket with fresh hot water, and bring it back.

As I was massaging, the two sons pulled up chairs and sat down by their father to talk. Ram Persad would bring out a bottle full of a golden liquid, and pour it into three glasses, and drop ice cubes in their glasses, and hand one glass to each of them. The sons would wait for the father to take the first sip and say, 'Ah... whisky. How would we survive this country without it,' and then the talking would start. The more they talked, the faster I massaged. They talked about politics, coal, and about your country – China. Somehow these things – politics, coal, China – were linked to the family fortunes of the Stork; and dimly I understood that my own fate, since I was part of this family now, was linked into these three things as well. The chatter of coal and China got mixed up with the aroma of whisky from the glasses, the stench of sweat rising up from the Stork's feet dipped in the warm water, the flakiness of his skin, and the light jabs of the san-dalled feet of Mr Ashok or the Mongoose when they bumped into my back in the process of moving about. I absorbed everything – that's the amazing thing about entrepreneurs. We are like sponges – we absorb and grow.

A sharp blow landed on my head.

I looked up and saw the Stork, with his palm still raised over my skull, glaring at me.

'Know what that was for?'

'Yes, sir,' I said – with a big smile on my face.

'Good.'

A minute later he hit me on the head again.

'Tell him what it was for, Father. I don't think he knows. Fellow, you're pressing too hard. You're too ex-cited. Father is getting annoyed. Slow down.'

'Yes, sir.'

'Do you have to hit the servants, Father?'

'This is not America, son. Don't ask questions like that.'

'Why can't I ask questions?'

'They expect it from us, Ashok. Remember that – they respect us for it.'

Now, Pinky Madam never joined in these conversations. Except to play badminton with Ram Persad, which she did wearing dark glasses, she never left her room. I wondered what was going on with her – was she having a fight with her husband? Was he not sticking it to her well in bed?

When the Stork said, 'The water's gone cold,' for the second time, and took his feet out of the bucket, my work was done.

I splashed the cold water down the sink.

I washed my hands for ten minutes, and dried them, and washed them again, but it made no difference. No matter how much you wash your hands after you have massaged a man's foot, the smell of his old, flaky skin will stay on your skin for an entire day.

*

There was only one activity that servant number one and servant number two had to do together. At least once a week, around six o'clock, Ram Persad and I left the house and went down the main road, until we got to a store with a sign that said:

'JACKPOT' ENGLISH LIQUOR SHOP
INDIAN-MADE FOREIGN LIQUOR SOLD HERE

I should explain to you, Mr Jiabao, that in this country we have two kinds of men: 'Indian' liquor men and 'English' liquor men. 'Indian' liquor was for village boys like me – toddy, arrack, country hooch. 'English' liquor, naturally, is for the rich. Rum, whisky, beer, gin – anything the English left behind. (Is there a 'Chinese' liquor, Mr Premier? I'd love to take a sip.)

One of the most important duties of driver number one was to come to Jackpot once a week and buy a bottle of the most expensive whisky for the Stork and his sons. It was part of servant protocol, though don't ask me why, that the junior driver accompany him on this outing. I guess I was supposed to make sure he did not run away with the bottle.

Coloured bottles of various sizes were stacked up on Jackpot's shelves, and two teenagers behind the counter struggled to take orders from the men shouting at them. On the white wall to the side of the shop, there were hundreds of names of liquor brands, written in a dripping red paint and subdivided into five categories, BEER, RUM, WHISKY, GIN, and VODKA.

PRICE LIST 'JACKPOT' ENGLISH LIQUOR SHOP

OUR WHISKY
WHISKY FIRST CLASS

	Quarter	Half	Full Bottle
BLACK DOG	–	–	1330
TEACHER'S	–	530	1230
VAT 69	–	–	1210

WHISKY SECOND CLASS

	Quarter	Half	Full Bottle
ROYAL CHALLENGE	110	220	390
ROYAL STAG	110	219	380
BAGPIPER	84	200	288

WHISKY THIRD CLASS

	Quarter	Half	Full Bottle
ROYAL CHOICE	61	110	200
WILD HORSE	44	120	200

(EVEN CHEAPER WHISKY IS AVAILABLE: ASK AT THE COUNTER.)

OUR VODKA
VODKA FIRST CLASS...

It was a small store, and at least fifty men were crammed into the ten feet of space in front of the counter, each yelling at the top of his voice, while waving rupee notes of the higher denominations:

'Kingfisher Strong One Litre!'
'Old Monk Half Bottle!'
'Thunderbolt! Thunderbolt!'

They were not going to be drinking this liquor; I could tell from their torn and dirty shirts that they were only servants, like Ram Persad and me, come to buy English liquor for their masters. If we came after eight o'clock on a weekend night to Jackpot, it was like a civil war in front of the counter; I had to keep the men at bay, while Ram Persad shoved his way to the counter and yelled:

'Black Dog! Full Bottle!'

Black Dog was the first name in the first-class category of whisky. It was the only thing that the Stork and his sons drank.

Ram Persad would get the liquor; and then I would swat at the other servants and fight for some space for us to get out, while he cradled the bottle in his arms. It was the only time we were ever like a team.

On our way back to the house, Ram Persad would always stop by the side of the road and slide the Black Dog out of its cardboard box. He said this was to check that Jackpot hadn't cheated us. I knew he was lying. He just wanted to hold the bottle. He wanted to hold the full, virgin bottle of first-class whisky in his hand. He wanted to imagine that he was buying it for himself. Then he would slide the bottle back into the cardboard box and return to the house, me behind him, my eyes still dazzled by the sight of so much English liquor.

At night, while Ram Persad snored from his bed, I lay on the floor with my head resting on my palms.

I was staring at the ceiling.

And thinking how the Stork's two sons were as different from each other as night and day.

Mukesh Sir was small, and dark, and ugly, and very shrewd. We would have called him 'the Mongoose' back at home. He had been married for some years, to a homely wife who was turning fat on schedule, after having two children, both boys. This fellow, this Mongoose, did not have his father's body – but he had his father's mind. If he ever saw me waste even one moment, he would shout, 'Driver, don't loiter there! Clean the car.'

'Cleaned it already, sir.'

'Then take a broom and sweep the courtyard.'

Mr Ashok had his father's body; he was tall, and broad, and handsome, like a landlord's son should be. In the evenings, I saw him play badminton with his wife in the compound of the house. She wore trousers; I gaped.

Who had ever seen a woman dressed in trousers before – except in the movies? I assumed at first she was an American, one of those magical things he had brought home from New York, like his accent and the fruit-flavoured perfume he put on his face after shaving.

Two days later, Ram Persad and the slanty-eyed Nepali were gossiping. I took a broom, began sweeping the courtyard, and edged closer and closer to them.

'She's a Christian, did you know?'

'No way.'

'Yes!'

'And he married her?'

'They married in America. When we Indians go there, we lose all respect for caste,' the Nepali said.

'The old man was dead set against the marriage. Her people were not happy either.'

'So – how did it happen?'

The Nepali glared at me. 'Hey, are you eavesdropping on us?'

'No, sir.'

*

One morning there was a knocking on the door of the drivers' quarters, and when I went out, Pinky Madam was standing with two rackets in her hand.

A net had been tied between two poles in one corner of the courtyard; she got on one side of the net and I got on the other side. She hit the shuttle – it rose up, and then fell near my foot.

'Hey! Move! Hit it back!'

'Sorry, madam. I'm so sorry.'

I'd never played this game before. I hit the shuttle back to her, and it went straight into the net.

'Oh, you're *useless*. Where is that other driver?'

Ram Persad dashed up to the net at once. He had been watching the game all the time from the side. He knew *exactly* how to play badminton.

I watched him hit the shuttle cleanly over the net and match her shot for shot, and my belly burned.

Is there any hatred on earth like the hatred of the number two servant for the number one?

Though we slept in the same room, just a few feet apart, we never said a word to each other – never a *Hello*, or *How's your mother doing*, nothing. I could feel heat radiate out from him all night – I knew he was cursing me and putting spells on me in his sleep. See, he began every day by bowing in front of at least twenty pictures of various gods he kept in his side of the room, and saying, 'Om, om, om.' As he did this, he looked at me through the corner of his eye, as if to say, *Don't you pray? What are you, a Naxal?*

One evening I went to the market and bought two dozen of the cheapest idols of Hanuman and Ram I could find and brought them back and packed them into the room. So both of us now had the same number of gods in the room; and we drowned out each other's prayers in the morning while bowing before our respective deities.

The Nepali was hand in hand with Ram Persad. One day he burst into my room and put a big plastic bucket down on the floor with a thud.

'Do you like dogs, village boy?' he asked with a big smile.

There were two white Pomeranians in the house – Cuddles and Puddles. The rich expect their dogs to be treated like humans, you see – they expect their dogs to be pampered, and walked, and petted, and even washed! And guess who had to do the washing? I got down on my knees and began scrubbing the dogs, and then lathering them, and foaming them, and then washing them down, and taking a blow dryer and drying their skin. Then I took them around the compound on a chain while the king of Nepal sat in a corner and shouted, 'Don't pull the chain so hard! They're worth more than you are!'

By the time I was done with Puddles and Cuddles, I walked back, sniffing my hands – the only thing that can take the smell of dog skin off a servant's hands is the smell of his master's skin.

Mr Ashok was standing outside my room.

I ran up to him and bowed low. He went into the room; I followed, still crouched over. He bent low to make his way through the doorway – the doorway was built for undernourished servants, not for a tall, well-fed master like him. He looked at the ceiling dubiously.

'How awful,' he said.

Until then I had never noticed how the paint on the ceiling was peeling off in large flakes, and how there were spiderwebs in every corner. I had been so happy in this room until now.

'Why is there such a smell? Open the windows.'

He sat down on Ram Persad's bed and poked it with his fingertips. It felt hard. I immediately stopped being jealous of Ram Persad.

(And so I saw the room with *his* eyes; smelled it with

his nose; poked it with *his* fingers – I had already begun to digest my master!)

He looked in my direction, but avoided my gaze, as if he were guilty about something.

'You and Ram Persad will both get a better room to sleep in. And separate beds. And some privacy.'

'Please don't do that, sir. This place is like a palace for us.'

That made him feel better. He looked at me.

'You're from Laxmangarh, aren't you?'

'Yes, sir.'

'I was born in Laxmangarh. But I haven't seen it since. Were you born there too?'

'Yes, sir. Born and raised there.'

'What's it like?'

Before I could answer, he said, 'It must be so nice.'

'Like paradise, sir.'

He looked me up and down, from head to toe, the way I had been looking at him ever since I had come to the house.

His eyes seemed full of wonder: how could two such contrasting specimens of humanity be produced by the same soil, sunlight, and water?

'Well, I want to go there today,' he said, getting up from the bed. 'I want to see my birthplace. You'll drive me.'

'Yes, sir!'

Going home! And in my uniform, driving the Stork's car, chatting up his son and daughter-in-law!

I was ready to fall at his feet and kiss them!

The Stork had wanted to come along with us, and that

would really make it a grand entry for me into the village – but at the last minute he decided to stay back. In the end, it was just Mr Ashok and Pinky Madam whom I was taking in the Honda City, out into the countryside, towards Laxmangarh.

It was the first time I was driving the two of them – Ram Persad had had the privilege until now. I still wasn't used to the Honda City, which is a moody car with a mind of its own, as I've said. I just prayed to the gods – all of them – not to let me make a mistake.

They said nothing for half an hour. Sometimes you can feel as a driver when there is tension in the car; it raises the temperature inside. The woman inside the car was very angry.

'Why are we going to this place in the middle of no-where, Ashoky?' Her voice, breaking the silence at last.

'It's my ancestral village, Pinky. Wouldn't you like to see it? I was born there – but Father sent me away as a boy. There was some trouble with the Communist guerrillas then. I thought we could—'

'Have you decided on a return date?' she asked suddenly. 'I mean to New York.'

'No. Not yet. We'll get one soon.'

He was silent for a minute; my ears were really wide open now. If they went back to America – would they no longer need a second driver in the home?

She said nothing; but I swear, I could hear teeth gritting.

Mr Ashok had no clue, though – he began humming a film song, until she said, 'What a fucking joke.'

'What was that?'

'You lied about returning to America, didn't you, Ashok – you're never going back, are you?'

'There's a driver in the car, Pinky – I'll explain every-thing later.'

'Oh, what does he matter! He's only the driver. And you're just changing the topic again!'

A lovely fragrance filled the car – and I knew that she must have moved about and adjusted her clothes.

'Why do we even need a driver? Why can't you drive, like you used to?'

'Pinky, that was New York – you can't drive in India, just look at this traffic. No one follows any rules – people run across the road like crazy – look – look at that—'

A tractor was coming down the road at full speed, belching out a nice thick plume of black diesel from its exhaust pipe.

'It's on the wrong side of the road! The driver of that tractor hasn't even noticed!'

I hadn't noticed either. Well, I suppose you are meant to drive on the left side of the road, but until then I had never known anyone to get agitated over this rule.

'And just look at the diesel it's spewing out. If I drive here, Pinky, I'll go completely mad.'

We drove along a river, and then the tar road came to an end and I took them along a bumpy track, and then through a small marketplace with three more or less iden-tical shops, selling more or less identical items of kerosene, incense, and rice. Everyone stared at us. Some children began running alongside the car. Mr Ashok waved at them, and tried to get Pinky Madam to do the same.

The children disappeared; we had crossed a line they

could not follow us beyond. We were in the landlords' quarter.

The caretaker was waiting at the gate of the Stork's mansion; he opened the door of the car even before I had brought it to a full stop, and touched Mr Ashok's feet.

'Little prince, you're here at last! You're here at last!'

The Wild Boar came to have lunch with Mr Ashok and Pinky Madam – he was their uncle, after all. As soon as I saw him enter the mansion for lunch, I went to the kitchen and told the caretaker, 'I love Mr Ashok so much you must let me serve him lunch!' The cook agreed – and I got to take my first good look at the Wild Boar in years. He was older than I remembered, and more bent over, but his teeth were exactly the same: sharp and blackened and with two distinctive hooked ones curving up by the side. They ate in the dining room – a magnificent place, with high ceilings, heavy, old-fashioned furniture all around, and a huge chandelier.

'It's a lovely old mansion,' Mr Ashok said. 'Everything's gorgeous in here.'

'Except the chandelier – it's a bit tacky,' she said.

'Your father *loves* chandeliers,' the Wild Boar said. 'He wanted to put one up in the bathroom here, did you know that? I'm serious!'

When the caretaker brought out the dishes and put them on the table, Mr Ashok looked at them and said, 'Don't you have anything vegetarian? I don't eat meat.'

'I've never heard of a landlord who was vegetarian,' the Wild Boar said. 'It's not natural. You need meat to toughen you up.' He opened his lips and showed his curved teeth.

'I don't believe in killing animals needlessly. I knew vegetarians in America, and I think they're right.'

'What crazy ideas do you boys pick up?' the old man said. 'You're a landlord. It's the Brahmins who are vegetarian, not us.'

After lunch I washed the dishes; I helped the caretaker make tea. My master was taken care of; now it was time to see my family. I went out of the mansion by the back door.

Well, they had beaten me to it. My family had all come to the mansion, and they were around the Honda City, staring at it with pride, though too frightened to touch it.

Kishan raised his hand. I hadn't seen him since he left Dhanbad and came back home to work in the fields – that was three months ago. I bent down and touched his feet, and held on to them for seconds longer than needed, because I knew the moment I let go he would bugger me badly – I hadn't sent any money home for the past two months.

'Oh, so now he remembers his family at last!' he said, shaking me off his feet. 'Has he thought about us at all?'

'Forgive me, brother.'

'You've not sent any money for months. You forgot our arrangement.'

'Forgive me, forgive me.'

But they weren't really angry. For the first time I can remember, I got more attention than the water buffalo. Most lavish in her fussing, naturally, was sly old Kusum, who kept grinning at me and rubbing her forearms.

'Oh, how I used to stuff your mouth with sweets as a child,' she said, trying to squeeze my cheeks. She was too frightened of my uniform to try and touch me any-where else.

They almost carried me on their backs to the old house, I tell you. The neighbours were waiting there to see my uniform.

I was shown the children that had been born in the family since I had left, and forced to kiss them on the forehead. My aunt Laila had had two children when I was gone. Cousin Pappu's wife, Leela, had had a child. The family was larger. The needs were more. I was chas-tized by all for not sending money each month.

Kusum beat her head with her fist; she wailed into the neighbours' house. 'My grandson has a job, and he still forces me to work. This is the fate of an old woman in this world.'

'Marry him off!' the neighbours yelled. 'That's the only way to tame the wild ones like him!'

'Yes,' Kusum said. 'Yes, that's a good idea.' She grinned, and rubbed her forearms. 'A very good idea.'

Kishan had a lot of news for me – and since this was the Darkness, all of it was bad news. The Great Socialist was as corrupt as ever. The fighting between the Naxal terrorists and the landlords was getting bloodier. Small people like us were getting caught in between. There were private armies on each side, going around to shoot and torture people suspected of sympathizing with the other.

'Life has become hell here,' he said. 'But we're so happy you're out of this mess – you've got a uniform, and a good master.'

Kishan had changed. He was thinner, and darker – his

neck tendons were sticking out in high relief above the deep clavicles. He had become, all of a sudden, my father.

I saw Kusum grinning and rubbing her forearms and talking of my marriage. She served me lunch herself. As she ladled the curry onto my plate – she had made chicken, just for me – she said, 'We'll fix up the wedding for later this year, okay? We've already found someone for you – a nice plump duck. The moment she has her menstrual cycle, she can come here.'

There was red, curried bone and flesh in front of me – and it seemed to me that they had served me flesh from Kishan's own body on that plate.

'Granny,' I said, looking at the large piece of red, curried meat, 'give me some more time. I'm not ready to be married.'

Her jaw dropped. 'What do you mean, not yet? You'll do what we want.' She smiled. 'Now eat it, dear. I made chicken just for you.'

I said, 'No.'

'Eat it.'

She pushed the plate closer to me.

Everyone in the household stopped to look at our tussle.

Granny squinted. 'What are you, a Brahmin? Eat, eat.'

'No!' I pushed the plate so hard it went flying to a corner and hit the wall and spilled the red curry on the floor. 'I said, I'm *not* marrying!'

She was too stunned even to yell. Kishan got up and tried to stop me as I left, but I pushed him to the side – he fell down hard – and I just walked out of the house.

The children ran along with me outside, little dirty brats born to one aunt or the other whose names I did not want to know, whose hair I did not want to touch. Gradually they got the message and went back.

I left behind the temple, the market, the pigs, and the sewage. Then I was alone at the pond – the Black Fort on the hill up in front of me.

Near the water's edge I sat down, gnashing my teeth.

I couldn't stop thinking of Kishan's body. They were eating him alive in there! They would do the same thing to him that they did to Father – scoop him out from the inside and leave him weak and helpless, until he got tuberculosis and died on the floor of a government hospital, waiting for some doctor to see him, spitting blood on this wall and that!

There was a splashing noise. The water buffalo in the pond lifted its water-lily-covered head – it peeked at me. A crane stood watching me on one leg.

I walked until the water came up to my neck, and then swam – past lotuses and water lilies, past the water buffalo, past tadpoles and fish and giant boulders fallen from the fort.

Up on the broken ramparts, the monkeys gathered to look at me: I had started climbing up the hill.

*

You are familiar already with my love of poetry – and especially of the works of the four Muslim poets acknowledged to be the greatest of all time. Now, Iqbal, who is one of the four, has written this remarkable poem in which he imagines that he is the Devil, standing up for his rights at a moment when God tries to bully him. The Devil, according to the Muslims, was once God's sidekick, until he fought with Him and went freelance, and ever since, there has been a war of brains between God and the Devil. This is what Iqbal writes about. The exact words of the poem I can't remember, but it goes something like this.

God says: *I am powerful. I am huge. Become my servant again.*

Devil says: *Ha!*

When I remember Iqbal's Devil, as I do often, lying here under my chandelier, I think of a little black figure in a wet khaki uniform who is climbing up the entranceway to a black fort.

There he stands now, one foot on the ramparts of the Black Fort, surrounded by a group of amazed monkeys.

Up in the blue skies, God spreads His palm over the plains below, showing this little man Laxmangarh, and its little tributary of the Ganga, and all that lies beyond: a million such villages, a billion such people. And God asks this little man:

Isn't it all wonderful? Isn't it all grand? Aren't you grateful to be my servant?

And then I see this small black man in the wet khaki uniform start to shake, as if he has gone mad with anger, before delivering to the Almighty a gesture of thanks for having created the world this particular way, instead of all the other ways it could have been created.

I see the little man in the khaki uniform *spitting* at God again and again, as I watch the black blades of the midget fan slice the light from the chandelier again and again.

*

Half an hour later, when I came down the hill, I went straight to the Stork's mansion. Mr Ashok and Pinky Madam were waiting for me by the Honda City.

'Where the hell have you been, driver?' she yelled. 'We've been waiting.'

'Sorry, madam,' I said, grinning to her. 'I'm very sorry.'

'Have a heart, Pinky. He was seeing his family. You know how close they are to their families in the Darkness.'

Kusum, Luttu Auntie, and all the other women were gathered by the side of the road as we drove out. They gaped at me – stunned that I wasn't coming to apologize: I saw Kusum clench her gnarled fist at me.

I put my foot down on the accelerator and drove right past all of them.

We went through the market square – I took a look at the tea shop: the human spiders were at work at the tables, the rickshaws were arranged in a line at the back, and the cyclist with the poster for the daily pornographic film on the other side of the river had just begun his rounds.

I drove through the greenery, through the bushes and the trees and the water buffaloes lazing in muddy ponds; past the creepers and the bushes; past the paddy fields; past the coconut palms; past the bananas; past the neems and the banyans; past the wild grass with the faces of the water buffaloes peeping through. A small, half-naked boy was riding a buffalo by the side of the road; when he saw us, he pumped his fists and shouted in joy – and I wanted to shout back at him: *Yes, I feel that way too! I'm never going back there!*

'Can you talk now, Ashoky? Can you answer my question?'

'All right. Look, when I came back, I really thought it was going to be for two months, Pinky. But… things have changed so much in India. There are so many more things I could do here than in New York now.'

'Ashoky, that's bullshit.'

'No, it's not. Really, it's not. The way things are changing in India now, this place is going to be like America in ten years. Plus, I like it better here. We've got people to take care of us here – our drivers, our watchmen, our masseurs. Where in New York will you find someone to bring you tea and sweet biscuits while you're still lying in bed, the way Ram Bahadur does for us? You know, he's been in my family for thirty years – we call him a servant, but he's part of the family. Dad found this Nepali wandering about Dhanbad one day with a gun in his hand and said—'

He stopped talking all at once.

'Did you see that, Pinky?'

'What?'

'Did you see what the driver did?'

My heart skipped a beat. I had no idea what I had just done. Mr Ashok leaned forward and said, 'Driver, you just touched your finger to your eye, didn't you?'

'Yes, sir.'

'Didn't you see, Pinky – we just drove past a temple' –
Mr Ashok pointed to the tall, conical structure with the
black intertwining snakes painted down the sides that
we had left behind – 'so the driver...'

He touched me on the shoulder.

'What is your name?'

'Balram.'

'So Balram here touched his eye as a mark of respect.
The villagers are so religious in the Darkness.'

That seemed to have impressed the two of them, so I
put my finger to my eye a moment later, again.

'What's that for, driver? I don't see any temples
around.'

'Er... we drove past a sacred tree, sir. I was offering
my respects.'

'Did you hear that? They worship nature. It's beautiful, isn't it?'

The two of them kept an eye open for every tree or
temple we passed by, and turned to me for a reaction of
piety – which I gave them, of course, and with growing
elaborateness: first just touching my eye, then my neck,
then my clavicle, and even my nipples.

They were convinced I was the most religious servant
on earth. (Take *that*, Ram Persad!)

Our way back into Dhanbad was blocked. There was a
truck parked on the road. It was full of men with red
headbands shouting slogans.

'Rise against the rich! Support the Great Socialist.
Keep the landlords out!'

Soon another set of trucks drove by: the men in them
wore green headbands and shouted at the men in the

other truck. A fight was about to break out.

'What's going on?' Pinky Madam asked in an alarmed tone of voice.

'Relax,' he said. 'It's election time, that's all.'

Now, to explain to you what was going on with all this shouting from the trucks, I will have to tell you all about democracy – something that you Chinese, I am aware, are not very familiar with. But that will have to wait for tomorrow, Your Excellency.

It's 2:44 a.m.

The hour of degenerates, drug addicts – and Bangalore-based entrepreneurs.

The Fourth Morning

But we don't really need these formalities any more, do we, Mr Jiabao?

We know each other by now. Plus we don't have the time for formalities, I'm afraid.

It'll be a short session today, Mr Premier – I was listening to a programme on the radio about this man called Castro who threw the rich out of his country and freed his people. I love listening to programmes about great men – and before I knew it, it had turned to 2 a.m.! I wanted to hear more about this Castro, but for your sake, I've turned the radio off. I'll resume the story exactly where we left off.

O, democracy!

Now, Mr Premier, the little take-home pamphlet that you will be given by the prime minister will no doubt contain a very large section on the splendour of democracy in India – the awe-inspiring spectacle of one billion people casting their votes to determine their own future, in full freedom of franchise, and so on and so forth.

I gather you yellow-skinned men, despite your triumphs in sewage, drinking water, and Olympic gold medals, still don't have democracy. Some politician on the radio was saying that that's why we Indians are going to beat you: we may not have sewage, drinking water, and Olympic gold medals, but we *do* have democracy.

If I were making a country, I'd get the sewage pipes first, then the democracy, then I'd go about giving pamphlets and statues of Gandhi to other people, but what do I know? I'm just a murderer!

I've got no problem with democracy, Mr Jiabao. Far from it, I owe democracy a lot – even my birthday, in fact. This was back in the days when I was smashing coals and wiping tables at the tea shop in Laxmangarh. There was a clapping from the direction of the portrait of Gandhi – the old tea shop owner began shouting that all his workers had to leave whatever they were doing and march to the school.

A man in a government uniform sat at the teacher's desk in the schoolroom, with a long book and a black pen, and he was asking everyone two questions.

'Name.'

'Balram Halwai.'

'Age.'

'No age.'

'No date of birth?'

'No, sir, my parents didn't make note of it.'

He looked at me and said, 'I think you're eighteen. I think you turned eighteen today. You just forgot, didn't you?'

I bowed to him. 'That's correct, sir. I forgot. It was my birthday today.'

'Good boy.'

And then he wrote that down in his book and told me to go away. So I got a birthday from the government.

I had to be eighteen. All of us in the tea shop had to be eighteen, the legal age to vote. There was an election coming up, and the tea shop owner had already sold us. He had sold our fingerprints – the inky fingerprints which the illiterate person makes on the ballot paper to indicate his vote. I had overheard this from a customer. This was supposed to be a close election; he had got a good price for each one of us from the Great Socialist's party.

Now, the Great Socialist had been the boss of the Darkness for a decade at the time of this election. His party's symbol, a pair of hands breaking through handcuffs – symbolizing the poor shaking off the rich – was imprinted in black stencils on the walls of every government office in the Darkness. Some of the customers at the tea shop said the Great Socialist started off as a good man. He had come to clean things up, but the mud of Mother Ganga had sucked him in. Others said he was dirty from the start, but he had just fooled everyone and only now did we see him for what he was. Whatever the case was, no one seemed able to vote him out of power. He had ruled the Darkness, winning election after election, but now his rule was weakening.

You see, a total of ninety-three criminal cases – for murder, rape, grand larceny, gun-smuggling, pimping, and many other such minor offences – are pending against the Great Socialist and his ministers at the present moment. Not easy to get convictions when the judges are judging in Darkness, yet three convictions have been delivered, and three of the ministers are currently in jail, but continue to be ministers. The Great Socialist himself is said to have embezzled one billion rupees from the Darkness, and transferred that money into a bank account in a small, beautiful country in Europe full of white people and black money.

Now that the date for the elections had been set, and declared on radio, election fever had started spreading again. These are the three main diseases of this country, sir: typhoid, cholera, and election fever. This last one is the worst; it makes people talk and talk about things that they have no say in. The Great Socialist's enemies seemed to be stronger this election than at the last one. They had made pamphlets, and went about on buses and trucks with microphones, and announced they were going to topple him over and drag the River Ganga and everyone who lived on its banks out of the Darkness and into the Light.

At the tea shop, the gossip grew furious. People sipped their tea and discussed the same things again and again.

Would they do it this time? Would they beat the Great Socialist and win the elections? Had they raised enough money of their own, and bribed enough policemen, and bought enough fingerprints of their own, to win? Like eunuchs discussing the Kama Sutra, the voters discuss the elections in Laxmangarh.

One morning I saw a policeman writing a slogan on the wall outside the temple with a red paintbrush:

DO YOU WANT GOOD ROADS, CLEAN WATER, GOOD HOSPITALS? THEN VOTE OUT THE GREAT SOCIALIST!

For years there was a deal between the landlords and the Great Socialist – everyone in the village knew about this – but this year something had gone wrong with the deal, so the four Animals had joined together and started a party of their own.

And below the slogan the policeman wrote:

ALL INDIA SOCIAL PROGRESSIVE FRONT (LENINIST FACTION)

Which was the name of the landlords' party.

In the weeks before the elections, trucks bumped up and down the dirty street of Laxmangarh, full of young men holding microphones: 'Stand up to the rich!'

Vijay, the bus conductor, was always on one of these trucks. He had quit his old job and joined politics now. That was the thing about Vijay; each time you saw him he had done better for himself. He was a born politician. He wore a red headband to show that he was one of the Great Socialist's supporters, and made speeches every morning in front of the tea shop. The landlords brought in trucks full of their own supporters in retaliation. And from these trucks men shouted out, 'Roads! Water! Hospitals! Vote out the Great Socialist!'

A week before the elections, both sides stopped sending out their trucks. I heard what had happened while cleaning up a table.

The Animals' bluff had worked. The Great Socialist had agreed to cut a deal with them.

Vijay bowed down and touched the feet of the Stork at a big rally in front of the tea shop. It seemed that all differences had been patched up, and the Stork had been named the president of the Laxmangarh branch of the Great Socialist's party. Vijay was to be his deputy.

Now the rallies were done. The priest celebrated a special *pooja* to pray for the Great Socialist's victory; mutton *biryani* was distributed on paper plates in front of the temple; and in the evening, there was free booze for all.

Lots of dust and policemen came into the village next morning. One officer read out voting instructions in the marketplace.

Whatever was being done, was being done for our own good. The Great Socialist's enemies would try and steal the election from us, the poor, and take the power away from us, the poor, and put those shackles back on our hands that he, the Great Socialist, had so lovingly taken off our hands. Did we understand? And then, in a cloud of dust, the police drove off.

'It's the way it always is,' my father told me that night. 'I've seen twelve elections – five general, five state, two local – and someone else has voted for me twelve times. I've heard that people in the other India get to vote for themselves – isn't that something?'

On the day of the election, one man went mad.

This happens every time, at every election in the Darkness.

One of my father's colleagues, a small dark-skinned man whom no one had taken any notice of until now, was surrounded by a mob of rickshaw-pullers, including my father. They were trying to dissuade him, but only halfheartedly.

They had seen this thing happening before. They wouldn't be able to stop this man now.

Every now and then, even in a place like Laxmangarh, a ray of sunlight will break through. All these posters and speeches and slogans on the wall, maybe they get into a man's head. He declares himself a citizen of the democracy of India and he wants to cast his vote. That was where this rickshaw-puller had got to. He declared himself free of the Darkness: he had made his Benaras that day.

He began walking straight to the voting booth at the school. 'I'm supposed to stand up to the rich, aren't I?' he shouted. 'Isn't that what they keep telling us?'

When he got there, the Great Socialist's supporters had already put up the tally of votes outside on a blackboard: they had counted 2,341 votes in that booth. Everyone had voted for the Great Socialist. Vijay the bus conductor was up on a ladder, hammering into the wall a banner with the Great Socialist's symbol (the hands breaking their shackles). The slogan on the banner said:

CONGRATULATIONS TO THE GREAT SOCIALIST ON HIS UNANIMOUS VICTORY FROM LAXMANGARH!

Vijay dropped the hammer, the nails, and the banner when he saw the rickshaw-puller.

'What are you doing here?'

'Voting,' he shouted back. 'Isn't it the election today?'

I cannot confirm what happened next, even though I was only a few feet behind him. A big crowd had gathered to watch him from a distance, but when the policeman charged at us, we turned and ran in a stampede. So I never saw what they did to that brave, mad man.

I heard about it the next day, while pretending to

scratch a dirty spot out of a tabletop. Vijay and a police-man had knocked the rickshaw-puller down, and they had begun beating him; they hit him with their sticks, and when he thrashed at them they kicked him. They took turns. Vijay hit him and the policeman stamped on his face and then Vijay did it again. And after a while the body of the rickshaw-puller stopped wriggling and fight-ing back, but they kept stamping on him, until he had been stamped back into the earth.

If I may go back for a moment to that WANTED poster, Your Excellency. Being called a murderer: fine, I have no objection to that. It's a fact: I am a sinner, a fallen human. But to be called a murderer by the police!

What a fucking joke.

Here's a little souvenir of your Indian visit to keep with you. Balram Halwai is a vanished man, a fugitive, someone whose whereabouts are unknown to the police, right?

Ha!

The police know exactly where to find me. They will find me dutifully voting on election day at the voting booth in the school compound in Laxmangarh in Gaya District, as I have done in every general, state, and local election since I turned eighteen.

I am India's most faithful voter, and I still have not seen the inside of a voting booth.

*

Now, though the elections were due soon in Dhanbad, life went on as ever within the high walls of the Stork's house. He sighed as his legs were pressed in warm water; games of cricket and badminton went on around him; and I washed and cleaned the two Pomeranian dogs faithfully.

Then one day a familiar face turned up at the gate. Vijay, the bus conductor from Laxmangarh. My childhood hero had a new uniform this time. He was dressed all in white, and wore a white Nehru cap on his head, and had rings of solid gold on eight of his fingers!

Public service had been good to him.

I waited by the gate and watched. The Stork himself came out to see Vijay, and bowed down before him – a landlord bowing before a pigherd's son! The marvels of democracy!

Two days later, the Great Socialist came to the house.

The entire household was abuzz because of the visit. Mr Ashok stood at the gate, waiting with a garland of jasmine flowers. His brother and his father were by his side.

A car came to the gate, its door opened, and then the face I had seen on a million election posters since I was a boy emerged – I saw the puffy cheeks, the spiky white hair, the thick gold earrings.

Vijay was wearing his red headband today, and holding up the flag with the breaking-shackles symbol. He shouted, 'Long live the Great Socialist!'

The great man folded his palms and bowed all around him. He had one of those either/or faces that all great Indian politicians have. This face says that it is now at peace – and you can be at peace too if you follow the owner of that face. But the same face can also say, with a little twitch of its features, that it has known the opposite

103

of peace: and it can make this other fate yours too, if it so wishes.

Mr Ashok put the garland on the great man's thick, bull-like neck.

'My son,' the Stork said. 'Returned from America recently.'

The Great Socialist squeezed Mr Ashok's cheeks. 'Good. We need more boys to come back and build India into a superpower.'

And then they went into the house, and all the doors and windows were closed. After a while, the Great Socialist came out into the courtyard, followed by the old man, the Mongoose, and Mr Ashok.

I was trying to overhear them, and so pretended to be sweeping the ground, while inching closer and closer to them. I had swept myself right into hearing distance when the Great Socialist tapped me on the back.

'What's your name, son?' he asked.

Then he said, 'Your employers are trying to bugger me, Balram. What do you say to this?'

Mr Ashok looked stunned. The Stork simpered.

'A million and a half is a lot, sir. We'll be happy to come to a settlement with you.'

The Great Socialist waved his hands as if dismissing that plea.

'Bullshit. You've got a good scam going here – taking coal for free from the government mines. You've got it going because I let it happen. You were just some little village landlord when I found you – I brought you here – I made you what you are today: and by God, you cross me, and you'll go back there into that village. I said a million and a fucking half, and I *mean* a million and…'

He had to stop – he had been chewing *paan*, and now his mouth had filled up with red spittle, which was beginning to dribble out. He turned to me and made the shape of a bowl with his hands. I rushed to the Honda City to get the spittoon.

When I came back with the spittoon, he coolly turned to the Mongoose and said, 'Son, won't you hold the spittoon for me?'

The Mongoose refused to move, so the Great Socialist took the spittoon from my hands and held it out.

'Take it, son.'

The Mongoose took it.

Then the Great Socialist spat into the spittoon, three times.

The Mongoose's hands trembled; his face turned black with shame.

'Thank you for that, son,' the Great Socialist said, wiping his lips. He turned to me and tickled his forehead. 'Where was I, now?'

There you have it. That was the positive side of the Great Socialist. He humiliated all our masters – that's why we kept voting him back in.

That night, on the pretext again of sweeping the courtyard, I got close to the Stork and his sons; they were sitting on a bench, holding glasses of golden liquor and talking. Mukesh Sir had just finished; the old man shook his head.

'We can't do that, Mukesh. We need him.'

'I'm telling you, Father. We don't any more. We can go straight to Delhi. We know people there now.'

'I agree with Mukesh, Father. We shouldn't let him treat us like this any more – like we're his slaves.'

'Quiet, Ashok. Let Mukesh and me discuss this.'

I swept the courtyard twice over, and listened. Then I began tightening Pinky Madam's sagging badminton net, so I could stay near them.

But a pair of suspicious Nepali eyes spotted me: 'Don't loiter in the courtyard. Go and sit in your room and wait for the masters to call you.'

'All right.'

Ram Bahadur glared at me, so I said, 'All right, sir.'

(Servants, incidentally, are obsessed with being called 'sir' by other servants, sir.)

The next morning, when I was blow-drying Puddles and Cuddles after having shampooed them, Ram Bahadur came up to me, and said, 'Have you ever been to Delhi?

I shook my head.

'They're going to Delhi in a week. Mr Ashok and Pinky Madam. They're going to leave for three months.'

I got down on my knees and directed the blow-drier under Cuddles's legs, pretending not to be interested, and asked, as casually as I could, 'Why?'

The Nepali shrugged. Who knew? We were just servants. One thing, though, he did know.

'Only one driver will be taken along. And this driver will get three thousand rupees a month – that's how much they'll pay him in Delhi.'

The blow-drier fell out of my hand. 'Seriously? Three thousand?'

'Yes.'

'Will they take me along, sir?' I got up and asked pleadingly, 'Can't you make them take me?'

'They'll take Ram Persad,' he said with a sneer of his Nepali lips. 'Unless…'

'Unless?'

He minted coins with his fingers.

Five thousand rupees – and he would tell the Stork that I was the man to be taken along to Delhi.

'Five thousand – where will I get such money? My family steals my whole pay cheque!'

'Oh, well. In that case, it'll be Ram Persad. As for you' – he pointed to Cuddles and Puddles – 'you'll be cleaning the dogs for the rest of your life, I guess.'

*

I woke up, both nostrils burning.

It was still dark.

Ram Persad was up. He was sitting on his bed, chopping onions on a wooden board: I heard the *tack, tack, tack* of his knife hitting the board.

What the hell is he chopping onions so early for? I thought, turning onto my side and closing my eyes again. I wanted to go back to sleep, but the *tack, tack, tack* of the knife hitting the board insisted:

This man has a secret.

I stayed awake, while the man on the bed chopped onions. I tried to figure it out.

What had I noticed about Ram Persad in the past few days?

For one thing, his breath had gone bad. Even Pinky Madam complained. He had suddenly stopped eating with us, either inside the house or outside. Even on Sundays, when there would be chicken, Ram Persad would refuse to eat with us, saying he had already done so, or he wasn't hungry, or…

The chopping of the onions continued, and I kept adding thought to thought in the dark.

I watched him all day. Towards evening, as I was expecting, he began moving to the gate.

From my conversation with the cook, I had learned that Ram Persad had started to head out of the house at the same time every evening. I followed at a distance. He went into a part of the city I had never seen before, and walked around a few alleys. At one point I distinctly saw him turn around, as if to make sure no one was following him; then he darted.

He had stopped in front of a two-storey building. The wall had a large metal grille divided into square units; a series of small black taps jutted out from the wall below the grille. He bent down to a tap, washed his face and gargled and spat. Then he took off his sandals. Shoes and sandals had been folded and stuffed into the squares of the grille – he did the same with his sandals. Then he went into the building and closed the door.

I slapped my forehead.

What a fool I'd been! 'It's Ramadan! They can't eat and drink during the day.'

I ran back to the house and found the Nepali. He was standing at the gate, rubbing his teeth with a twig broken from a neem tree – which is what many poor people in my country do, Mr Premier, when they want to clean their teeth.

'I just saw a film, sir.'

'Fuck off.'

'A great film, sir. Lots of dancing. Hero was a Muslim. Name of Mohammad Mohammad.'

'Don't waste my time, boy. Go clean the car if you've got nothing to do.'

'Now, this Mohammad Mohammad was a poor, honest, hardworking Muslim, but he wanted a job at the home of an evil, prejudiced landlord who didn't like Muslims – so, just to get a job and feed his starving family, he claimed to be a Hindu! And took the name of Ram Persad.'

The twig fell out of the Nepali's mouth.

'And you know how he managed to pull this off? Because the Nepali guard at this house, whom the masters trusted absolutely, and who was supposed to check up on Ram Persad's background, was *in* on the scam!'

Before he could run, I caught him by the collar. Technically, in these servant-versus-servant affairs, that is all you need to do to indicate: 'I have won.' But if you're going to do these things, it's better to do them in style, right? So I slapped him too.

I was servant number one from now on in this household.

I ran back to the mosque. *Namaz* must have ended by now. And indeed, Ram Persad – or Mohammad or whatever his name really was – came out of the mosque, took his sandals down from the window, slapped them on the ground, wriggled his feet into them, and began walking out. He saw me – I winked at him – and he knew that the game was up.

I did the needful in a few precise words.

Then I went back to the house. The Nepali was watching me from behind the black bars. I took his key chain from him and put it in my pocket. 'Get me some tea. And biscuits.' I pinched his shirt. 'And I want your uniform too. Mine is getting old.'

I slept in the bed that night.

In the morning someone came into the room. It was ex–driver number one. Without a word to me, he began packing. All his things fitted into one small bag.

I thought, *What a miserable life he's had, having to hide his religion, his name, just to get a job as a driver – and he is a good driver, no question of it, a far better one than I will ever be.* Part of me wanted to get up and apologize to him right there and say, *You go and be a driver in Delhi. You never did anything to hurt me. Forgive me, brother.*

I turned to the other side, farted, and went back to sleep.

When I woke up, he was gone – he had left all his images of gods behind, and I scooped them into a bag. You never know when those things can come in handy.

In the evening, the Nepali came to me with a grin on his face – the same fake servant's grin he showed to the Stork all day long. He told me that, since Ram Persad had left their service without a word, I would be driving Mr Ashok and Pinky Madam to Delhi. He had personally – and forcefully – recommended my name to the Stork.

I went back to my bed – all mine now – stretched out on it, and said, 'Great. Now clean those webs off the ceiling, won't you?'

He glared at me, but said nothing, and went away to get a broom. I shouted:

'Sir!'

From then on, every morning, it was hot Nepali tea, and some nice sugar biscuits, on a porcelain platter.

Kishan came to the gate that Sunday and heard the news from me. I thought he was going to bugger me for how abruptly I had left them at the village, but he was overcome with joy – his eyes were full of tears. Someone in his family was going to make it out of the Darkness and into New Delhi!

'It's just like our mother always said. She knew you were going to make it.'

Two days later, I was driving Mr Ashok, the Mongoose, and Pinky Madam to Delhi in the Honda City. It wasn't hard to find the way – I just had to follow the buses. For there were buses and jeeps all along the road – and they were bursting with passengers who packed the insides, and hung out of the doors, and even got on the roofs. They were all headed from the Darkness to Delhi. You'd think the whole world was migrating.

Each time we passed by one of these buses, I had to grin; I wished I could roll down the window and yell at them, *I'm going to Delhi in a car – an* air-conditioned *car!*

But I'm sure they saw the words in my eyes.

Around noon, Mr Ashok tapped me on the shoulder.

From the start, sir, there was a way in which I could understand what he wanted to say, the way dogs understand their masters. I stopped the car, and then moved to my left, and he moved to his right, and our bodies passed each other (so close that the stubble on his face scraped my cheeks like the shaving brush that I use every morning, and the cologne from his skin – a lovely, rich, fruity cologne – rushed into my nostrils for a heady instant, while the smell of my servant's sweat rubbed off onto his face), and then he became driver and I became passenger.

He started the car.

The Mongoose, who had been reading a newspaper the whole time, now saw what had happened.

'Don't do this, Ashok.'

He was an old-school master, the Mongoose. He knew right from wrong.

'You're right – this feels weird,' Mr Ashok said.

The car came to a stop. Our bodies crossed each other again, our scents were exchanged once more, and I was again the driver and servant, and Mr Ashok was again the passenger and master.

We reached Delhi late at night.

It is not yet three, I could go on a little while longer. But I want to stop, because from here on I have to tell you a new kind of story.

Remember, Mr Premier, the first time, perhaps as a boy, when you opened the bonnet of a car and looked into its entrails? Remember the coloured wires twisting from one part of the engine to the other, the black box full of yellow caps, enigmatic tubes hissing out steam and oil and grease everywhere – remember how mysterious and magical everything seemed? When I peer into the portion of my story that unfolds in New Delhi, I feel the same way. If you ask me to explain how one event connects to another, or how one motive strengthens or weakens the next, or how I went from thinking *this* about my master to thinking *that* – I will tell you that I myself don't understand these things. I cannot be certain that the story, as I will tell it, is the right story to tell. I cannot be certain that I know exactly why Mr Ashok died.

It will be good for me to stop here.

When we meet again, at midnight, remind me to turn the chandelier up a bit. The story gets much darker from here.

The Fourth Night

I should talk a little more about this chandelier.

Why not? I've got no family any more. All I've got is chandeliers.

I have a chandelier here, above my head in my office, and then I have two in my apartment in Raj Mahal Villas Phase Two. One in the drawing room, and a small one in the toilet too. It must be the only toilet in Bangalore with a chandelier!

I saw all these chandeliers one day, tied to the branch of a big banyan tree near Lalbagh Gardens; a boy from a village was selling them, and I bought all of them on the spot. I paid some fellow with a bullock cart to bring them home and we went riding through Bangalore, me and this fellow and four chandeliers, on a limousine powered by bulls!

It makes me happy to see a chandelier. Why not, I'm a free man, let me buy all the chandeliers I want. For one thing, they keep the lizards away from this room. It's the truth, sir. Lizards don't like the light, so as soon as they see a chandelier, they stay away.

I don't understand why other people don't buy chandeliers all the time, and put them up everywhere. Free people don't know the value of freedom, that's the problem.

Sometimes, in my apartment, I turn on both chandeliers, and then I lie down amid all that light, and I just start laughing. A man in hiding, and yet he's surrounded by chandeliers!

There – I'm revealing the secret to a successful escape. The police searched for me in darkness: but I hid myself in light.

In Bangalore!

Now, among the many uses of a chandelier, this most unsung and unloved object, is that, when you forget something, all you have to do is stare at the glass pieces shining in the ceiling long enough, and within five minutes you'll remember exactly what it is you were trying to remember.

See, I'd forgotten where we left off the story last night, so I had to go on about chandeliers for a while, keeping you busy, but now I remember where we were.

Delhi – we had got to Delhi last night when I stopped the narrative.

The capital of our glorious nation. The seat of Parliament, of the president, of all ministers and prime ministers. The pride of our civic planning. The showcase of the republic.

That's what *they* call it.

Let a driver tell you the truth. And the truth is that Delhi is a crazy city.

See, the rich people live in big housing colonies like Defence Colony or Greater Kailash or Vasant Kunj, and inside their colonies the houses have numbers and letters, but this numbering and lettering system follows no known system of logic. For instance, in the English alphabet, A is next to B, which everyone knows, even people like me who don't know English. But in a colony, one house is called A 231, and then the next is F 378. So one time Pinky Madam wanted me to take her to Greater Kailash E 231, I tracked down the houses to E 200, and just when I thought we were almost there, E Block vanished completely. The next house was S something.

Pinky Madam began yelling. 'I told you not to bring this yokel from the village!'

And then another thing. Every road in Delhi has a name, like Aurangazeb Road, or Humayun Road, or Archbishop Makarios Road. And no one, masters or servants, knows the name of the road. You ask someone, 'Where's Nikolai Copernicus Marg?'

And he could be a man who lived on Nikolai Copernicus Marg his whole life, and he'll open his mouth and say, '*Hahn?*'

Or he'll say, 'Straight ahead, then turn left,' even though he has no idea.

And all the roads look the same, all of them go around and around grassy circles in which men are sleeping or eating or playing cards, and then four roads shoot off from that grassy circle, and then you go down one road, and you hit another grassy circle where men are sleeping or playing cards, and then four more roads go off from it. So you just keep getting lost, and lost, and lost in Delhi.

Thousands of people live on the sides of the road in Delhi. They have come from the Darkness too – you can tell by their thin bodies, filthy faces, by the animal-like way they live under the huge bridges and overpasses, making fires and washing and taking lice out of their hair while the cars roar past them. These homeless people are a particular problem for drivers. They never wait for a red light – simply dashing across the road on impulse. And each time I braked to avoid slamming the car into one of them, the shouting would start from the passenger's seat.

But I ask you, who built Delhi in this crazy way? Which geniuses were responsible for making F Block come after A Block and House Number 69 come after House Number 12? Who was so busy partying and drinking English liquor and taking their Pomeranian dogs for walks and shampoos that they gave the roads names that no one could remember?

'Are you lost again, driver?'

'Don't go after him again.'

'Why do you always defend him, Ashok?'

'Don't we have more serious things to discuss? Why are we always talking about this driver?'

'All right, let's discuss the other things, then. First let's discuss your wife, and her temper tantrums.'

'Do you really think that's more important than the tax thing? I keep asking you what are we doing about it, and you keep changing the topic. I think it's *insane*, how much they're asking us to pay.'

'I told you. It's a political thing. They're harassing us because Father is trying to distance himself from the Great Socialist.'

'I don't know why he ever got involved with that rogue.'

'He got into politics because he had to, Ashok – you don't have a choice in the Darkness. And don't panic, we can deal with this income tax charge. This is India, not America. There's always a way out here. I told you, we have someone here who works for us – Ramanathan. He's a good fixer.'

'Ramanathan is a sleazy, oily *cretin*. We need a new tax lawyer, Mukesh! We need to go to the newspapers and tell them we're being raped by these politicians!'

'Listen' – the Mongoose raised his voice – 'you just got back from America. Even this man driving our car knows more about India than you do right now. We need a *fixer*. He'll get us the interview with a minister that we need. That's how Delhi works.'

The Mongoose leaned forward and put his hand on my shoulder. 'Lost again? Do you think you could find your way home this time without getting lost a dozen times?'

He sighed and fell back on his seat. 'We shouldn't have brought him here, he's hopeless. Ram Bahadur got it all wrong about this fellow. Ashok.'

'Hm?'

'Look up from your phone a minute. Have you told Pinky that you're staying back for good?'

'Hm. Yes.'

'What does the Queen say?'

'Don't call her that. She's your sister-in-law, Mukesh. She'll be happy in Gurgaon, it's the most American part of the city.'

Now, Mr Ashok's thinking was smart. Ten years ago, they say, there was nothing in Gurgaon, just water buffaloes and fat Punjabi farmers. Today it's the *modernest* suburb of Delhi. American Express, Microsoft, all the big American companies have offices there. The main road is full of shopping malls – each mall has a cinema inside! So if Pinky Madam missed America, this was the best place to bring her.

'This moron,' the Mongoose said, 'see what he's done. He's got lost again.'

He stretched his hand and smacked my skull with it. 'Take a left from the fountain, you idiot! Don't you know how to get to the house from here?'

I began apologizing, but a voice from behind me said, 'It's all right, Balram. Just get us home.'

'See – you're defending him again.'

'Just put yourself in his place, Mukesh. Can you imagine how confusing Delhi must be to him? It must be like getting to New York for the first time was for me.'

The Mongoose switched to English – and I didn't catch what he said – but Mr Ashok replied in Hindi, 'Pinky thinks the same too. That's the only thing you and she agree on, but I won't have it, Mukesh. We don't know who's who in Delhi. This fellow, we can trust him. He's from home.'

At that moment I looked at the rearview mirror, and I caught Mr Ashok's eyes looking at me: and in those master's eyes, I saw the most unexpected emotion.

Pity.

*

'How much are they paying you, Country-Mouse?'

'Enough. I'm happy.'

'Not telling me, eh, Country-Mouse? Good boy. A loyal servant to the end. Liking Delhi?'

'Yes.'

'Ha! Don't lie to me, sister-fucker. I know you're completely lost here. You must hate it!'

He tried to put his hand on me, and I squirmed and moved back. He had a skin disease – vitiligo had turned his lips bright pink in the middle of a pitch-black face. I'd better explain about this skin disease, which afflicts so many poor people in our country. I don't know why you get it, but once you do, your skin changes colour from brown to pink. Nine cases out of ten, it's a few bright pink spots on a boy's nose or cheeks like a star exploding on his face, or a rash of pink on the fore-arm like someone burned him with boiling water there, but sometimes a fellow's whole body has changed colour, and as you walk past, you think, *An American!* You stop to gape; you want to go near and touch. Then you realize it's just one of ours, with that horrible condition.

In the case of this driver, since the flash of pink had completely discoloured his lips – and nothing else – he looked like a clown at the circus with painted lips. My stomach churned just to see his face. Still, he was the only one of the drivers who was being nice to me, so I stayed close to him.

We were outside the mall. We – a dozen or so chauf-feurs – were waiting for our masters to finish their shopping. We weren't allowed inside the mall, of course – no one had to tell us these things. We had made a ring by the side of the car park, and we were smoking and chatting – every now and then someone would emit a red jet of *paan* from his mouth.

On account of the fact that he too was from the Darkness – he had of course guessed my origin at once – the driver with the diseased lips gave me a course on how to survive Delhi and make sure I wasn't sent back to the Darkness on the top of a bus.

'The main thing to know about Delhi is that the roads are good, and the people are bad. The police are *totally* rotten. If they see you without a seat belt, you'll have to bribe them a hundred rupees. Our masters are not such a great lot, either. When they go for their late-night parties, it's hell for us. You sleep in the car, and the mosquitoes eat you alive. If they're malaria mosquitoes it's all right, you'll just be raving for a couple of weeks, but if it's the dengue mosquitoes, then you're in deep shit, and you'll die for sure. At two in the morning, he comes back, banging on the windows and shouting for you, and he's reeking of beer, and he farts in the car all the way back. The cold gets really bad in January. If you know he's having a late-night party, take along a blanket so you can cover yourself in the car. Keeps the mosquitoes away too. Now, you'll get bored sitting in the car and waiting for him to come back from his parties – I knew one driver who went nuts from the waiting – so you need something to read. You *can* read, can't you? Good. This is the absolutely best thing to read in the car.'

He gave me a magazine with a catchy cover – a woman in her underwear was lying on a bed, cowering from the shadow of a man.

MURDER WEEKLY
RUPEES 4.50
EXCLUSIVE TRUE STORY:
'A GOOD BODY NEVER GOES TO WASTE'
MURDER. RAPE. REVENGE.

Now I have to tell you about this magazine, *Murder Weekly*, since our prime minister certainly won't tell you anything about it. It's sold in every newsstand in the city, alongside the cheap novels, and it is very popular reading among all the servants of the city – whether they be cooks, children's maids, or gardeners. Drivers are no different. Every week when this magazine comes out, with a cover image of a woman cowering from her would-be murderer, some driver has bought the magazine and is passing it around to the other drivers.

Now, don't panic at this information, Mr Premier – no beads of chill sweat need form on your yellow brow. Just because drivers and cooks in Delhi are reading *Murder Weekly*, it doesn't mean that they are all about to slit their masters' necks. Of course, they'd *like* to. Of course, a billion servants are secretly fantasizing about strangling their bosses – and that's why the government of India publishes this magazine and sells it on the streets for just four and a half rupees so that even the poor can buy it. You see, the murderer in the magazine is so mentally disturbed and sexually deranged that not one reader would want to be like him – and in the end he always gets caught by some honest, hardworking police officer (ha!), or goes mad and hangs himself by a bedsheet after writing a sentimental letter to his mother or primary school teacher, or is chased, beaten, buggered, and garroted by the brother of the woman he has done in. So if your driver is busy flicking through the pages of *Murder Weekly*, relax. No danger to you. Quite the contrary.

It's when your driver starts to read about Gandhi and the Buddha that it's time to wet your pants, Mr Jiabao.

After showing it to me, Vitiligo-Lips closed the magazine and threw it into the circle where the other drivers were sitting; they made a grab for it, like a bunch of dogs rushing after a bone. He yawned and looked at me.

'What does your boss do for a living, Country-Mouse?'

'I don't know.'

'Being loyal or being stupid, Country-Mouse? Where is he from?'

'Dhanbad.'

'He's into coal, then. Probably here to bribe ministers. It's a rotten business, coal.' He yawned again. 'I used to drive a man who sold coal. Bad, bad business. But my current boss is into steel, and he makes the coal men look like saints. Where does he live?'

I told him the name of our apartment block.

'My master lives there too! We're neighbours!'

He sidled right up to me; without moving away – that would have been rude – I tilted my body as far as I could from his lips.

'Country-Mouse – does your boss' – he looked around, and dropped his voice to a whisper – '*need* anything?'

'What do you mean?'

'Does your boss like foreign wine? I have a friend who works at a foreign embassy as a driver. He's got contacts there. You know the foreign-wine foreign-embassy scam?'

I shook my head.

'The scam is this, Country-Mouse. Foreign wine is very expensive in Delhi, because it's taxed. But the embassies get it in for free. They're supposed to drink their wine, but they sell it on the black market. I can get him other stuff too. Does he want golf balls? I've got people in the US Consulate who will sell me that. Does he want women? I can get that too. If he's into boys, no problem.'

'My master doesn't do these things. He's a good man.'

The diseased lips opened up into a smile. 'Aren't they all?'

He began whistling some Hindi film song. One of the drivers had begun reading out a story from the magazine; all the others had gone silent. I looked at the mall for a while.

I turned to the driver with the horrible pink lips and said, 'I've got a question to ask you.'

'All right. Ask. You know I'll do anything for you, Country-Mouse.'

'This building – the one they call a mall – the one with the posters of women hanging on it – it's for shopping, right?'

'Right.'

'And that' – I pointed to a shiny glass building to our left – 'is that also a mall? I don't see any posters of women hanging on it.'

'That's not a mall, Country-Mouse. That's an office building. They make calls from there to America.'

'What kind of calls?'

'I don't know. My master's daughter works in one of those buildings too. I drop her off at eight o'clock and she comes back at two in the morning. I know she makes pots and pots of money in that building, because she spends it all day in the malls.' He leaned in close – the pink lips were just centimetres from mine. 'Between the two of us, I think it's rather odd – girls going into buildings late at night and coming out with so much cash in the morning.'

He winked at me. 'What else, Country-Mouse? You're a curious fellow.'

I pointed to one of the girls coming out of the mall.

'What about her, Country-Mouse? You like her?'

I blushed. 'Tell me,' I said, 'don't the women in cities – like her – have hair in their armpits and on their legs like women in our villages?'

*

After half an hour, Mukesh Sir and Mr Ashok and Pinky Madam came out of the mall with shopping bags; I ran ahead to take their bags from them, and put them in the back of the car, and then closed the back and jumped into the driver's seat of the Honda City and drove them to their new home, which was up on the thirteenth floor of a gigantic apartment building. The name of the apartment building was Buckingham Towers B Block. It was next to another huge apartment building, built by the same housing company, which was Buckingham Towers A Block. Next to that was Windsor Manor A Block. And there were apartment blocks like this, all shiny and new, and with nice big English names, as far as the eye could see. Buckingham Towers B Block was one of the best – it had a nice big lobby, and a lift in the lobby that all of us took up to the thirteenth floor.

Personally, I didn't like the apartment much – the whole place was the size of the kitchen in Dhanbad. There were nice, soft, white sofas inside, and on the wall above the sofas, a giant framed photo of Cuddles and Puddles. The Stork had not allowed them to come with us to the city.

I couldn't stand to look at those creatures, even in a photograph, and kept my eyes to the carpet the whole time I was in the room – which had the additional benefit of giving me the look of a *pucca* servant.

'Leave the bags anywhere you want, Balram.'

'No. Put them down next to the table. Put them down *exactly* there,' the Mongoose said.

After putting the bags down, I went into the kitchen to see if any cleaning needed to be done – there was a servant just to take care of the apartment, but he was a sloppy fellow, and as I said, they didn't really have a 'driver', just a servant who drove the car sometimes. I knew without being told I also had to take care of the apartment. Any cleaning there was to be done, I would do, and then come back and wait near the door with folded hands until Mukesh Sir said, 'You can go now. And be ready at 8 a.m. No hanky-panky just because you're in the city, understand?'

Then I went down in the lift, got out of the building, and went down the stairs to the servants' quarters in the basement.

I don't know how buildings are designed in your country, but in India every apartment block, every house, every hotel is built with a servants' quarters – sometimes at the back, and sometimes (as in the case of Buckingham Towers B Block) underground – a warren of inter-connected rooms where all the drivers, cooks, sweepers, maids, and chefs of the apartment block can rest, sleep, and wait. When our masters wanted us, an electric bell began to ring throughout the quarters – we would rush to a board and find a red light flashing next to the number of the apartment whose servant was needed upstairs.

I walked down two flights of stairs and pushed open the door to the servants' quarters.

The moment I got there, the other servants screamed – they yelled – they howled with laughter.

The vitiligo-lipped driver was sitting with them, howling the hardest. He had told them the question I had asked him. They could not get over their amuse-ment; each one of them had to come up to me, and force his fingers through my hair, and call me a 'village idiot', and slap me on the back too.

Servants need to abuse other servants. It's been bred into us, the way Alsatian dogs are bred to attack strangers. We attack anyone who's familiar.

There and then I resolved never again to tell anyone in Delhi *anything* I was thinking. Especially not another servant.

They kept teasing all evening long, and even in the night, when we all went to the dormitory to sleep. Some-thing about my face, my nose, my teeth, I don't know, it got on their nerves. They even teased me about my uniform. See, in cities the drivers do not wear uniforms. They said I looked like a monkey in that uniform. So I changed into a dirty shirt and trousers like the rest of them, but the teasing, it just went on all night long.

There was a man who swept the dormitory, and in the morning I asked him, 'Isn't there somewhere a man can be alone here?'

'There's one empty room on the other side of the quarters, but no one wants it,' he told me. 'Who wants to live alone?'

It was horrible, this room. The floor had not been finished, and there was a cheap whitish plaster on the walls in which you could see the marks of the hand that had applied the plaster. There was a flimsy little bed, barely big enough even for me, and a mosquito net on top of it.

It would do.

The second night, I did not sleep in the dormitory – I went to the room. I swept the floor, tied the mosquito net to four nails on the wall, and went to sleep. In the middle of the night, I understood why the mosquito net had been left there. Noises woke me up. The wall was covered with cockroaches, which had come to feed on the minerals or the limestone in the plaster; their chewing made a continuous noise, and their antennae trembled from every spot on the wall. Some of the cockroaches landed on top of the net; from inside, I could see their dark bodies against its white weave. I folded in the fibre of the net and crushed one of them. The other cockroaches took no notice of this; they kept landing on the net – and getting crushed. *Maybe everyone who lives in the city gets to be slow and stupid like this*, I thought, and smiled, and went to sleep.

'Had a good night among the roaches?' they teased when I came to the common toilet.

Any thought I had of rejoining the dormitory ended there. The room was full of roaches, but it was mine, and no one teased me. One disadvantage was that the electric bell did not penetrate this room – but that was a kind of advantage too, I discovered in time.

In the morning, after waiting my turn at the common toilet, and then my turn at the common sink, and then my turn at the common bathroom, I went up one flight of stairs, pushed open the door to the car park, and walked to the spot where the Honda City was parked. The car had to be wiped with a soft, wet cloth, inside and outside; a stick of incense had to be placed at the small statue of the goddess Lakshmi, goddess of wealth, which sat above the dashboard – this had the double advantage of getting rid of the mosquitoes that had sneaked in at night, and scenting the insides with an aroma of religion. I wiped the seats – nice, plush leather seats; I wiped the dials; I lifted the leather mats on the floor and slapped the dust out of them. There were three magnetic stickers with images of the mother-goddess Kali on the dashboard – I had put them there, throwing out Ram Persad's magnetic stickers; I wiped them all. There was also a small fluffy ogre with a red tongue sticking out of its mouth hung by a chain from the rearview mirror. It was supposed to be a lucky charm, and the Stork liked to see it bob up and down as we drove. I punched the ogre in the mouth – then I wiped it clean. Next came the business of checking the box of paper tissues in the back of the car – it was elaborately carved and gilded, like something that a royal family had owned, though it was actually made of cardboard. I made sure there were fresh tissues in the box. Pinky Madam used dozens of tissues each time we went out – she said the pollution in Delhi was so bad. She had left her crushed and crumpled used tissues near the box, and I had to pick them up and throw them out.

The electric buzzer sounded through the car park. A voice over the lobby microphone said, 'Driver Balram. Please report to the main entrance of Buckingham B Block with the car.'

And so it was that I would get into the Honda City, drive up a ramp, and come out to see my first sunlight of the day.

The brothers were dressed in posh suits – they were standing at the door to the building, chatting and chirruping; when they got in, the Mongoose said, 'The Congress Party headquarters, Balram. We went there the other day – I hope you remember it and don't get lost again.'

I'm not going to let you down today, sir.

Rush hour in Delhi. Cars, scooters, motorbikes, auto-rickshaws, black taxis, jostling for space on the road. The pollution is so bad that the men on the motorbikes and scooters have a handkerchief wrapped around their faces – each time you stop at a red light, you see a row of men with black glasses and masks on their faces, as if the whole city were out on a bank heist that morning.

There was a good reason for the face masks; they say

the air is so bad in Delhi that it takes ten years off a man's life. Of course, those in the cars don't have to breathe the outside air – it is just nice, cool, clean, air-conditioned air for us. With their tinted windows up, the cars of the rich go like dark eggs down the roads of Delhi. Every now and then an egg will crack open – a woman's hand, dazzling with gold bangles, stretches out of an open window, flings an empty mineral water bottle onto the road – and then the window goes up, and the egg is resealed.

I was taking my particular dark egg right into the heart of the city. To my left I saw the domes of the President's House – the place where all the important business of the country is done. When the air pollution is really bad, the building is completely blotted out from the road; but today it shone beautifully.

In ten minutes, I was at the headquarters of the Congress Party. Now, this is an easy place to find, because there are always two or three giant cardboard billboards with the face of Sonia Gandhi outside.

I stopped the car, ran out, and opened the door for Mr Ashok and the Mongoose; as he got out, Mr Ashok said, 'We'll be back in half an hour.'

This confused me; they never told me in Dhanbad when they'd be back. Of course it meant nothing. They could take two hours to come back, or three. But it was a kind of courtesy that they apparently now had to give me because we were in Delhi.

A group of farmers came to the headquarters, and weren't allowed inside, and shouted something or other, and left. A TV van came to the headquarters and honked; they were let in at once.

I yawned. I punched the little black ogre in its red mouth, and it bobbed back and forth. I turned my head around, from side to side.

I looked at the big poster of Sonia Gandhi. She was holding a hand up in the poster, as if waving to me – I waved back.

I yawned, closed my eyes, and slithered down my seat. With one eye open, I looked at the magnetic sticker of the goddess Kali – who is a very fierce black-skinned goddess, holding a scimitar, and a garland of skulls. I made a note to myself to change that sticker. She looked too much like Granny.

Two hours later, the brothers returned to the car.

'We're going to the President's House, Balram. Up the hill. You know the place?'

'Yes, sir, I've seen it.'

Now, I'd already seen most of the famous sights of Delhi – the House of Parliament, the Jantar Mantar, the Qutub – but I'd not yet been to this place – the most important one of all. I drove toward Raisina Hill, and then all the way up the hill, stopping each time a guard put his hand out and checked inside the car, and then stopping right in front of one of the big domed buildings around the President's House.

'Wait in the car, Balram. We'll be back in thirty minutes.'

For the first half an hour, I was too frightened to get out of the car. I opened the door – I stepped out – I took a look around. Somewhere inside these domes and towers that were all around me, the big men of this country – the prime minister, the president, top ministers and bureaucrats – were discussing things, and writing them out, and stamping papers. Someone was saying, 'There, five hundred million rupees for that dam!', and someone was saying, 'Fine, attack Pakistan, then!'

I wanted to run around shouting: 'Balram is here too! Balram is here too!'

I got back into the car to make sure I didn't do anything stupid and get arrested for it.

It was getting dark when the two brothers came out of the building; a fat man walked out with them, and talked to them for a while, outside the car, and then shook their hands and waved goodbye to us.

Mr Ashok was dark and sullen when he got in. The Mongoose asked me to drive them back home – 'without making any mistakes again, understand?'

'Yes, sir.'

They sat in silence, which confused me. If I had just gone into the President's House, I'd roll down the windows and shout it aloud to everyone on the road!

'Look at that.'

'What?'

'That statue.'

I looked out of the window to see a large bronze statue of a group of men – this is a well-known statue, which you will no doubt see in Delhi: at the head is Mahatma Gandhi, with his walking stick, and behind him follow the people of India, being led from darkness to light.

The Mongoose squinted at the statue.

'What about it? I've seen it before.'

'We're driving past Gandhi, after just having given

a bribe to a minister. It's a *fucking joke*, isn't it.'

'You sound like your wife now,' the Mongoose said. 'I don't like swearing – it's not part of our traditions here.'

But Mr Ashok was too red in the face to keep quiet.

'It is a *fucking joke* – our political system – and I'll keep saying it as long as I like.'

'Things are complicated in India, Ashok. It's not like in America. Please reserve your judgement.'

*

There was a fierce jam on the road to Gurgaon. Every five minutes the traffic would tremble – we'd move a foot – hope would rise – then the red lights would flash on the cars ahead of me, and we'd be stuck again. Everyone honked. Every now and then, the various horns, each with its own pitch, blended into one continuous wail that sounded like a calf taken from its mother. Fumes filled the air. Wisps of blue exhaust glowed in front of every headlight; the exhaust grew so fat and thick it could not rise or escape, but spread horizontally, sluggish and glossy, making a kind of fog around us. Matches were continually being struck – the drivers of autorickshaws lit cigarettes, adding tobacco pollution to petrol pollution.

A man driving a buffalo cart had stopped in front of us; a pile of empty car engine oil cans fifteen feet high had been tied by rope to his cart. His poor water buffalo! To carry all that load – while sucking in this air!

The autorickshaw driver next to me began to cough violently – he turned to the side and spat, three times in a row. Some of the spit flecked the side of the Honda

City. I glared – I raised my fist. He cringed, and *namast-ed* me in apology.

'It's like we're in a concert of spitting!' Mr Ashok said, looking at the autorickshaw driver.

Well, if you were out there breathing that acid air, you'd be spitting like him too, I thought.

The cars moved again – we gained three feet – then the red lights flashed and everything stopped again.

'In Beijing apparently they've got a dozen ring roads. Here we have *one*. No wonder we keep getting jams. Nothing is *planned*. How will we ever catch up with the Chinese?'

(By the way, Mr Jiabao – a *dozen* ring roads? Wow.)

Dim streetlights were glowing down onto the pavement on either side of the traffic; and in that orange-hued half-light, I could see multitudes of small, thin, grimy people squatting, waiting for a bus to take them somewhere, or with nowhere to go and about to unfurl a mattress and sleep right there. These poor bastards had come from the Darkness to Delhi to find some light – but they were still in the darkness. Hundreds of them, there seemed to be, on either side of the traffic, and their life was entirely unaffected by the jam. Were they even aware that there was a jam? We were like two separate cities – inside and outside the dark egg. I knew I was in the right city. But my father, if he were alive, would be sitting on that pavement, cooking some rice gruel for dinner, and getting ready to lie down and sleep under a streetlamp, and I couldn't stop thinking of that and recognizing his features in some beggar out there. So I was in some way out of the car too, even while I was driving it.

After an hour of thrashing through the traffic, we got home at last to Buckingham B Block. But the torture wasn't over.

As he was getting out of the car, the Mongoose tapped his pockets, looked confused for a moment, and said, 'I've lost a rupee.'

He snapped his fingers at me.

'Get down on your knees. Look for it on the floor of the car.'

I got down on my knees. I sniffed in between the mats like a dog, all in search of that one rupee.

'What do you mean, it's not there? Don't think you can steal from us just because you're in the city. I want that rupee.'

'We've just paid half a million rupees in a bribe, Mukesh, and now we're screwing this man over for a single rupee. Let's go up and have a scotch.'

'That's how you corrupt servants. It starts with one rupee. Don't bring your American ways here.'

Where that rupee coin went remains a mystery to me to this day, Mr Premier. Finally, I took a rupee coin out of my shirt pocket, dropped it on the floor of the car, picked it up, and gave it to the Mongoose.

'Here it is, sir. Forgive me for taking so long to find it!'

There was a childish delight on his dark master's face. He put the rupee coin in his hand and sucked his teeth, as if it were the best thing that had happened to him all day.

I took the lift up with the brothers, to see if any work was to be done in the apartment.

Pinky Madam was on the sofa watching TV; as soon as

we got in, she said, 'I've eaten already,' turned the TV off, and went into another room. The Mongoose said he didn't want dinner, so Mr Ashok would have to eat alone at the dinner table. He asked me to heat some of the vegetables in the fridge for him, and I went into the kitchen to do so.

Casting a quick look back as I opened the fridge door, I saw that he was on the verge of tears.

*

When you're the driver, you never see the whole picture. Just flashes, glimpses, bits of conversation – and then, just when the masters are coming to the crucial part of their talk – it always happens.

Some moron in a white jeep almost hits you while trying to overtake a car on the wrong side of the road. You swerve to the side, glare at the moron, curse him (silently) – and by the time you're eavesdropping again, the conversation in the backseat has moved on... and you never know how that sentence ended.

I knew something was wrong, but I hadn't realized how bad the situation had become until the morning Mr Ashok said to me, 'Today you'll drop Mukesh Sir at the railway station, Balram.'

'Yes, sir.' I hesitated. I wanted to ask, *Just him?*

Did that mean he was going back for good? Did that mean Pinky Madam had finally got rid of him with her door-slamming and tart remarks?

At six o'clock, I waited with the car outside the entranceway. I drove the brothers to the railway station. Pinky Madam did not come along.

I carried the Mongoose's bags to the right carriage of the train, then went to a stall and bought a *dosa*, wrapped in paper, for him. That was what he always liked to eat on the train. But I unwrapped the *dosa* and removed the potatoes, flinging them onto the rail tracks, because potatoes made him fart, and he didn't like that. A servant gets to know his master's intestinal tract from end to end – from lips to anus.

The Mongoose told me, 'Wait. I have instructions for you.'

I squatted in a corner of the railway carriage.

'Balram, you're not in the Darkness any longer.'

'Yes, sir.'

'There is a law in Delhi.'

'Yes, sir.'

'You know those bronze statues of Gandhi and Nehru that are everywhere? The police have put cameras inside their eyes to watch for the cars. They see everything you do, understand that?'

'Yes, sir.'

Then he frowned, as if wondering what else to say. He said, 'The air conditioner should be turned off when you are on your own.'

'Yes, sir.'

'Music should not be played when you are on your own.'

'Yes, sir.'

'At the end of each day you must give us a reading of the meter to make sure you haven't been driving the car on your own.'

'Yes, sir.'

The Mongoose turned to Mr Ashok and touched him on the forearm. 'Take some interest in this, Ashok Brother, you'll have to check up on the driver when I'm gone.'

But Mr Ashok was playing with his mobile phone. He put it down and said, 'The driver's honest. He's from Laxmangarh. I saw his family when I went there.' Then he went back to his mobile.

'Don't talk like that. Don't make a joke of what I'm saying,' the Mongoose said.

But he was paying no attention to his brother – he kept punching the buttons on his mobile: 'One minute, one minute, I'm talking to a friend in New York.'

Drivers like to say that some men are *first-gear* types. Mr Ashok was a classic *first-gear man*. He liked to start things, but nothing held his attention for long.

Looking at him, I made two discoveries, almost simultaneously. Each filled me with a sense of wonder. Firstly, you could 'talk' on a mobile phone – to someone in New York – just by punching on its buttons. The wonders of modern science never cease to amaze me!

Secondly, I realized that this tall, broad-shouldered, handsome, foreign-educated man, who would be my only master in a few minutes, when the long whistle blew and this train headed off towards Dhanbad, was weak, helpless, absentminded, and completely unprotected by the usual instincts that run in the blood of a landlord.

If you were back in Laxmangarh, we would have called you the Lamb.

'Why are you grinning like a donkey?' the Mongoose snapped at me, and I almost fell over apologizing to him.

That evening, at eight o'clock, Mr Ashok sent a

message to me through another servant: 'Be ready in half an hour, Balram. Pinky Madam and I will be going out.'

And the two of them did come down, about two and three-quarter hours later.

The moment the Mongoose left, I swear, the skirts became even shorter.

When she sat in the back, I could see half her boobs hanging out of her clothes each time I had to look in the rearview mirror.

This put me in a very bad situation, sir. For one thing, my beak was aroused, which is natural in a healthy young man like me. On the other hand, as you know, master and mistress are like father and mother to you, so how can you get excited by the mistress?

I simply avoided looking at the rearview mirror. If there was a crash, it wouldn't be my fault.

Mr Premier, maybe when you have been driving, in the thick traffic, you have stopped your car and lowered your window; and then you have felt the hot, panting breath of the exhaust pipe of a truck next to you. Now be aware, Mr Premier, that there is a hot panting diesel engine just in front of your own nose.

Me.

Each time she came in with that low black dress, my beak got big. I hated her for wearing that dress; but I hated my beak even more for what it was doing.

*

At the end of the month, I went up to the apartment. He was sitting there, alone, on the couch beneath the framed photo of the two Pomeranians.

'Sir?'

'Hm. What's up, Balram?'

'It's been a month.'

'So?'

'Sir... my wages.'

'Ah, yes. Three thousand, right?' He whipped out his wallet – it was fat with notes – and flicked out three notes onto the table. I picked them up and bowed. Something of what his brother had been saying must have got to him, because he said, 'You're sending some of it home, aren't you?'

'All of it, sir. Just what I need to eat and drink here – the rest goes home.'

'Good, Balram. Good. Family is a good thing.'

At ten o'clock that night I walked down to the market just around the corner from Buckingham Towers B Block. It was the last shop in the market; on a billboard above it, huge black letters in Hindi said:

'Action' English Liquor Shop
Indian-made foreign Liquor sold here

It was the usual civil war that you find in a liquor shop in the evenings: men pushing and straining at the counter with their hands outstretched and yelling at the top of their voices. The boys behind the counter couldn't hear a word of what was being said in that din, and kept getting orders mixed up, and that led to more yelling and fighting. I pushed through the crowd – got to the counter, banged my fist, and yelled, 'Whisky! The cheapest kind! Immediate service – or someone will get hurt, I swear!'

It took me fifteen minutes to get a bottle. I stuffed it down my trousers, for there was nowhere else to hide it, and went back to Buckingham.

*

'Balram. You took your time.'

'Forgive me, madam.'

'You look ill, Balram. Are you all right?'

'Yes, madam. I have a headache. I didn't sleep well last night.'

'Now make some tea. I hope you can cook better than you can drive?'

'Yes, madam.'

'I hear you're a Halwai, your family are cooks. Do you know some special traditional type of ginger tea?'

'Yes, madam.'

'Then make it.'

I had no idea what Pinky Madam wanted, but at least her boobs were covered – that was a relief.

I got the tea kettle ready and began making tea. I had just got the water boiling when the kitchen filled up with perfume. She was watching from the threshold.

My head was still spinning from last night's whisky. I had been chewing aniseed all morning so no one would notice the stench of booze on my breath, but I was still worried, so I turned away from her as I washed a chunk of ginger under the tap.

'What are you doing?' she shouted.

'Washing ginger, madam.'

'That's with your right hand. What's your left hand doing?'

145

'Madam?'

I looked down.

'Stop scratching your groin with your left hand!'

'Don't be angry, madam. I'll stop.'

But it was no use. She would not stop shouting:

'You're so filthy! Look at you, look at your teeth, look at your clothes! There's red *paan* all over your teeth, and there are red spots on your shirt. It's disgusting! Get out – clean up the mess you've made in the kitchen and get out.'

I put the piece of ginger back in the fridge, turned off the boiling water, and went downstairs.

I got in front of the common mirror and opened my mouth. The teeth were red, blackened, rotting from *paan*. I washed my mouth out, but the lips were still red.

She was right. The *paan* – which I'd chewed for years, like my father and like Kishan and everyone else I knew – was discolouring my teeth and corroding my gums.

The next evening, Mr Ashok and Pinky Madam came down to the entranceway fighting, got into the car fighting, and kept fighting as I drove the Honda City from Buckingham Towers B Block onto the main road.

'Going to the mall, sir?' I asked, the moment they were quiet.

Pinky Madam let out a short, high laugh.

I expected such things from her, but not from him – yet he joined in too.

'It's not *maal*, it's a mall,' he said. 'Say it again.'

I kept saying '*maal*', and they kept asking me to repeat it, and then giggled hysterically each time I did so. By the end they were holding hands again. So some good came out of my humiliation – I was glad for that, at least.

They got out of the car, slammed the door, and went into the mall; a guard saluted as they came close, then the glass doors opened by themselves and swallowed the two of them in.

I did not get out of the car: it helped me concentrate my mind better if I was here. I closed my eyes.

Moool.

No, that wasn't it.

Mowll.

Malla.

'Country-Mouse! Get out of the car and come here!'

A little group of drivers crouched in a circle outside the car park in the mall. One of them began shouting at me, waving a copy of a magazine in his hand.

It was the driver with the diseased lips. I put a big smile on my face and went up to him.

'Any more questions about city life, Country-Mouse?' he asked. Cannonades of laughter all around him.

He put a hand on me and whispered, 'Have you thought about what I said, sweetie pie? Does your master need anything? Ganja? Girls? Boys? Golf balls – good-quality American golf balls, duty-free?'

'Don't offer him all these things now,' another driver said. This one was crouching on his knees, swinging a key chain with the keys to his master's car like a boy with a toy. 'He's raw from the village, still pure. Let city life corrupt him first.' He snatched the magazine – *Murder Weekly*, of course – and began reading out loud. The gossip stopped. All the drivers drew closer.

'*It was a rainy night. Vishal lay in bed, his breath smelling of liquor, his eyes glancing out of the window. The woman next door had come home, and was about to remove her—*'

The man with the vitiligo lips shouted, 'Look there! It's happening today too—'

The driver with the magazine, annoyed at this disturbance, kept reading – but the others were standing up now, looking in the direction of the mall.

What was happening, Mr Premier, was one of those incidents that were so common in the early days of the shopping mall, and which were often reported in the daily newspapers under the title 'Is There No Space for the Poor in the Malls of New India?'

The glass doors had opened, but the man who wanted to go into them could not do so. The guard at the door had stopped him. He pointed his stick at the man's feet and shook his head – the man had sandals on his feet. All of us drivers too had sandals on our feet. But everyone who was allowed into the mall had shoes on their feet.

Instead of backing off and going away – as nine in ten in his place would have done – the man in the sandals exploded, 'Am I not a human being too?'

He yelled it so hard that the spit burst from his mouth like a fountain and his knees were trembling. One of the drivers let out a whistle. A man who had been sweeping the outer compound of the mall put down his broom and watched.

For a moment the man at the door looked ready to hit the guard – but then he turned around and walked away.

'That fellow has balls,' one of the drivers said. 'If all of us were like that, we'd rule India, and *they* would be polishing our boots.'

Then the drivers got back into their circle. The reading of the story resumed.

I watched the keys circling in the key chain. I watched the smoke rising from the cigarettes. I watched the *paan* hit the earth in red diagonals.

The worst part of being a driver is that you have hours to yourself while waiting for your employer. You can spend this time chit-chatting and scratching your groin. You can read murder and rape magazines. You can develop the chauffeur's habit – it's a kind of yoga, really – of putting a finger in your nose and letting your mind go blank for hours (they should call it the 'bored driver's *asana*'). You can sneak a bottle of Indian liquor into the car – boredom makes drunks of so many honest drivers.

But if the driver sees his free time as an opportunity, if he uses it to think, then the worst part of his job becomes the best.

That evening, while driving back to the apartment, I looked into the rearview mirror. Mr Ashok was wearing a T-shirt.

It was like no T-shirt I would ever choose to buy at a store. The larger part of it was empty and white and there was a small design in the centre. I would have bought something very colourful, with lots of words and designs on it. Better value for the money.

Then one night, after Mr Ashok and Pinky Madam had gone up, I went out to the local market. Under the glare of naked yellow lightbulbs, men squatted on the road, selling basketfuls of glassy bangles, steel bracelets, toys, head scarves, pens, and key chains. I found the fellow selling T-shirts.

'No,' I kept saying to each shirt he showed me – until I found one that was all white, with a small word in English in the centre. Then I went looking for the man selling black shoes.

I bought my first toothpaste that night. I got it from the man who usually sold me *paan*; he had a side business in toothpastes that cancelled out the effects of *paan*.

SHAKTI WHITENER

WITH CHARCOAL AND CLOVES

TO CLEAN YOUR TEETH

ONLY ONE RUPEE FIFTY PAISE!

As I brushed my teeth with my finger, I noticed what my left hand was doing: it had crawled up to my groin without my noticing – the way a lizard goes stealthily up a wall – and was about to scratch.

I waited. The moment it moved, I seized it with the right hand.

I pinched the thick skin between the thumb and the index finger, where it hurts the most, and held it like that for a whole minute. When I let go, a red welt had formed on the skin of the palm.

There.

That's your punishment for groin-scratching from now on.

In my mouth, the toothpaste had thickened into a milky foam; it began dripping down the sides of my lips. I spat it out.

Brush. Brush. Spit.

Brush. Brush. Spit.

Why had my father never told me not to scratch my groin? Why had my father never taught me to brush my teeth in milky foam? Why had he raised me to live like an animal? Why do all the poor live amid such filth, such ugliness?

Brush. Brush. Spit.

Brush. Brush. Spit.

If only a man could spit his past out so easily.

*

Next morning, as I drove Pinky Madam to the mall, I felt a small parcel of cotton pressing against my shoe-clad feet. She left, slamming the door; I waited for ten minutes. And then, inside the car, I changed.

I went to the gateway of the mall in my new white T-shirt. But there, the moment I saw the guard, I turned around – went back to the Honda City. I got into the car and punched the ogre three times. I touched the stickers of the goddess Kali, with her long red tongue, for good luck.

This time I went to the rear entrance.

I was sure the guard in front of the door would challenge me and say, *No, you're not allowed in*, even with a pair of black shoes and a T-shirt that is mostly white with just one English word on it. I was sure, until the last moment, that I would be caught, and called back, and slapped and humiliated there.

Even as I was walking inside the mall, I was sure someone would say, *Hey! That man is a paid driver! What's he doing in here?* There were guards in grey uniforms on every floor – all of them seemed to be watching me. It was my first taste of the fugitive's life.

I was conscious of a perfume in the air, of golden light, of cool, air-conditioned air, of people in T-shirts and jeans who were eyeing me strangely. I saw a lift going up and down that seemed made of pure golden glass. I saw shops with walls of glass, and huge photos of handsome European men and women hanging on each wall. If only the other drivers could see me now!

Getting out was as tricky as getting in, but again the guards didn't say a word to me, and I walked back to the car park, got into the car, and changed back into my usual, richly coloured shirt, and left the rich man's plain T-shirt in a bundle near my feet.

I came running out to where the other drivers were sitting. None of them had noticed me going in or coming out. They were too occupied with something else. One of the drivers – it was the fellow who liked to twirl his key chain all the time – had a mobile phone with him. He forced me to take a look at his phone.

'Do you call your wife with this thing?'

'You can't talk to anyone with it, you fool – it's a one-way phone!'

'So what's the point of a phone you can't talk to your family with?'

'It's so that my master can call me and give me instructions on where to pick him up. I just have to keep it here – in my pocket – wherever I go.'

He took the phone back from me, rubbed it clean, and put it in his pocket. Until this evening, his status in the drivers' circle had been low: his master drove only a

Maruti–Suzuki Zen, a small car. Today he was being as bossy as he wanted. The drivers were passing his mobile from hand to hand and gazing at it like monkeys gaze at something shiny they have picked up. There was the smell of ammonia in the air; one of the drivers was pissing not far from us.

Vitiligo-Lips was watching me from a corner.

'Country-Mouse,' he said. 'You look like a fellow who wants to say something.'

I shook my head.

*

The traffic grew worse by the day. There seemed to be more cars every evening. As the jams grew worse, so did Pinky Madam's temper. One evening, when we were just crawling down M.G. Road into Gurgaon, she lost it completely. She began screaming.

'Why can't we go back, Ashoky? Look at this fucking traffic jam. It's like this every other day now.'

'Please don't begin that again. Please.'

'Why not? You promised me, Ashoky, we'll be in Delhi just three months and get some paperwork done and go back. But I'm starting to think you only came here to deal with this income-tax problem. Were you lying to me the whole time?'

It wasn't his fault, what happened between them – I will insist on that, even in a court of law. He was a good husband, always coming up with plans to make her happy. On her birthday, for instance, he had me dress up as a maharaja, with a red turban and dark cooling glasses, and serve them their food in this costume. I'm not talking of any ordinary home cooking, either – he got me to serve her some of that stinking stuff that comes in cardboard boxes and drives all the rich absolutely crazy.

She laughed and laughed and laughed when she saw me in my costume, bowing low to her with the cardboard box. I served them, and then, as Mr Ashok had instructed, stood near the portrait of Cuddles and Puddles with folded hands and waited.

'Ashok,' she said. 'Now hear this. Balram, what is it we're eating?'

I knew it was a trap, but what could I do? – I answered. The two of them burst into giggles.

'Say it again, Balram.'

They laughed again.

'It's not piJJA. It's piZZa. Say it properly.'

'Wait – you're mispronouncing it too. There's a *T* in the middle. *Peet. Zah.*'

'Don't correct *my* English, Ashok. There's no *T* in pizza. Look at the box.'

I had to hold my breath as I stood there waiting for them to finish. The stuff smelled so awful.

'He's cut the pizza so badly. I just don't understand how he can come from a caste of cooks.'

'You've just dismissed the cook. Please don't fire this fellow too – he's an honest one.'

When they were done, I scraped the food off the plates and washed them. From the kitchen window, I could see the main road of Gurgaon, full of the lights of the shopping malls. A new mall had just opened up at the end of the road, and the cars were streaming into its gates.

I pulled the window blind down and went back to washing dishes.

'Pijja.'

'Pzijja.'

'Zippja.'

'Pizja.'

I wiped the sink with my palm and turned off the lights.

The two of them had gone into their bedroom. I heard shouting from inside. On tiptoe, I went to the closed door. I put my ear to the wood.

Shouting rose from both sides – followed by a scream – followed by the sound of man's flesh slapping woman's flesh.

About time you took charge, O Lamb-that-was-born-from-the-loins-of-a-landlord. I locked the door behind me and took the lift down.

Half an hour later, just when I was about to fall asleep, another of the servants came and yelled for me. The bell was ringing! I put on my trousers, washed my hands again and again at the common tap, and drove the car up to the entrance of the building.

'Drive us into the city.'

'Yes, sir. Where in the city?'

'Any place you want to go, Pinky?'

No word from her.

'Take us to Connaught Place, Balram.'

Neither husband nor wife talked as I drove. I still had the maharaja outfit on. Mr Ashok looked at Pinky Madam nervously half a dozen times.

'You're right, Pinky,' he said in a husky voice. 'I didn't

mean to challenge you on what you said. But I told you, there's only one thing wrong with this place – we have this fucked-up system called parliamentary democracy. Otherwise, we'd be just like China–'

'Ashok. I have a headache. Please.'

'We'll have some fun tonight. There's a good T.G.I. Friday's here. You'll like it.'

When we got to Connaught Place, he made me stop in front of a big red neon light.

'Wait for us here, Balram. We'll be back in twenty minutes.'

They had been gone for an hour and I was still inside the car, watching the lights of Connaught Place.

I punched the fluffy black ogre a dozen times. I looked at the magnetic stickers of goddess Kali with her skulls and her long red tongue – I stuck my tongue out at the old witch. I yawned.

It was well past midnight and very cold.

I would have loved to play some music to pass the time, but of course the Mongoose had forbidden that.

I opened the door of the car: there was an acrid smell in the air. The other drivers had made a fire for themselves, which they kept going by shoving bits of plastic into it.

The rich of Delhi, to survive the winter, keep electrical heaters, or gas heaters, or even burn logs of wood in their fireplaces. When the homeless, or servants like night watchmen and drivers who are forced to spend time outside in winter, want to keep warm, they burn whatever they find on the ground. One of the best things to put in the fire is Cellophane, the kind used to wrap fruits, vegetables, and business books in: inside the flame, it changes its nature and melts into a clear fuel. The only problem is that while burning, it gives off a white smoke that makes your stomach churn.

Vitiligo-Lips was feeding bags of Cellophane into the fire; with his free hand he waved to me.

'Country-Mouse, don't sit there by yourself! That leads to bad thoughts!'

The warmth was so tempting.

But no. My mouth would tickle if I went near them, and I would ask for *paan*.

'Look at the snob! He's even dressed like a maharaja today!'

'Come join us, maharaja of Buckingham!'

Away from the warmth, away from temptation I walked, down the pathways of Connaught Place, until the smell of churned mud filled the air.

There is construction work in any direction you look in Delhi. Glass skeletons being raised for malls or office blocks; rows of gigantic T-shaped concrete supports, like a line of anvils, where the new bridges or overpasses are coming up; huge craters being dug for new mansions for the rich. And here too, in the heart of Connaught Place, even in the middle of the night, under the glare of immense spotlights, construction went on. A giant pit had been excavated. Machines were rumbling from inside it.

I had heard of this work: they were putting a railway under the ground of Delhi. The pit they had made for this work was as large as any of the coal mines I'd seen in Dhanbad. Another man was watching the pit with me – a well-dressed man in a shirt and tie and trousers with nice pleats. Normally his kind would never talk to me, but maybe my maharaja tunic confused him.

'This city is going to be like Dubai in five years, isn't it?'

'Five?' I said contemptuously. 'In *two* years!'

'Look at that yellow crane. It's a monster.'

It *was* a monster, sitting at the top of the pit with huge metal jaws alternately gorging and disgorging immense quantities of mud. Like creatures that had to obey it, men with troughs of mud on their heads walked in circles around the machine; they did not look much bigger than mice. Even in the winter night the sweat had made their shirts stick to their glistening black bodies.

It was freezing cold when I returned to the car. All the other drivers had left. Still no sign of my masters. I closed my eyes and tried to remember what I had had for dinner.

A nice hot curry with juicy chunks of dark meat. Big puddles of red oil in the gravy.

Nice.

They woke me up by banging on my window. I scrambled out and opened the doors for them. Both were loud and happy, and reeked of some English liquor: whatever it was, I hadn't yet tried it at the shop.

I tell you, they were going at it like animals as I drove them out of Connaught Place. He was pushing his hand up and down her thigh, and she was giggling. I watched one second too long. He caught me in the mirror.

I felt like a child that had been watching his parents through a slit in their bedroom door. My heart began to sweat – I half expected him to catch me by the collar, and fling me to the ground, and stamp me with his boots, the way his father used to do to fishermen in Laxmangarh.

But this man, as I've told you, was different – he was capable of becoming someone better than his father. My eyes had touched his conscience; he nudged Pinky Madam and said, 'We're not alone, you know.'

She became grumpy at once, and turned her face to the side. Five minutes passed in silence. Reeking of English liquor, she leaned towards me.

'Give me the steering wheel.'

'No, Pinky, don't, you're drunk, let him—'

'What a fucking joke! Everyone in India drinks and drives. But you won't let *me* do it?'

'Oh, I hate this.' He slumped on his seat. 'Balram, remember never to marry.'

'Is he stopping at the traffic signal? Balram, why are you stopping? Just drive!'

'It is a traffic signal, Pinky. Let him stop. Balram, obey the traffic rules. I command you.'

'I command you to drive, Balram! Drive!'

Completely confused by this time, I compromised – I took the car five feet in front of the white line, and then came to a stop.

'Did you see what he did?' Mr Ashok said. 'That was pretty clever.'

'Yes, Ashok. He's a fucking genius.'

The timer next to the red light said that there were still thirty seconds to go before the light changed to green. I was watching the timer when the giant Buddha materialized on my right. A beggar child had come up to the

Honda City holding up a beautiful plaster-of-paris statue of the Buddha. Every night in Delhi, beggars are always selling something by the roadside, books or statues or strawberries in boxes – but for some reason, perhaps because my nerves were in such a bad state, I gazed at this Buddha longer than I should have.

... It was just a tilt of my head, just a thing that happened for half a second, but she caught me out.

'Balram appreciates the statue,' she said.

Mr Ashok chuckled.

'Sure, he's a connoisseur of fine art.'

She cracked the egg open – she lowered the window and said, 'Let's see it,' to the beggar child.

He – or she, you can never tell with beggar children – pushed the Buddha into the Honda.

'Do you want to buy the sculpture, driver?'

'No, madam. I'm sorry.'

'Balram Halwai, maker of sweets, driver of cars, connoisseur of sculpture.'

'I'm sorry, madam.'

The more I apologized, the more amused the two of them got. At last, putting an end to my agony, the light changed to green, and I drove away from the wretched Buddha as fast as I could.

She reached over and squeezed my shoulder. 'Balram, stop the car.' I looked at Mr Ashok's reflection – he said nothing.

I stopped the car.

'Balram, get out. We're leaving you to spend the night with your Buddha. The maharaja and the Buddha, together for the night.'

She got into the driver's seat, started the car, and drove away, while Mr Ashok, dead drunk, giggled and waved goodbye at me. If he hadn't been drunk, he never would have allowed her to treat me like this – I'm *sure* of that. People were always taking advantage of him. If it were just me and him in that car, nothing bad would ever have happened to either of us.

There was a traffic island separating the two sides of the road, and trees had been planted in the island. I sat down under a tree.

The road was dead – then two cars went by, one behind the other, their headlights making a continuous ripple on the leaves, like you see on the branches of trees that grow by a lake. How many thousands of such beautiful things there must be to see in Delhi. If you were just free to go wherever you wanted, and do whatever you wanted.

A car was coming straight towards me, flashing its headlights on and off and sounding its horns. The Honda City had done a U-turn – an illegal U-turn, mind you – down the road, and was charging right at me, as if to plough me down. Behind the wheel I saw Pinky Madam, grinning and howling, while Mr Ashok, next to her, was smiling.

Did I see a wrinkle of worry for my fate on his forehead – did I see his hand reach across and steady the steering wheel so that the car wouldn't hit me?

I like to think so.

The car stopped half a foot in front of me, with a screech of burning rubber. I cringed: how my poor tyres had suffered, because of this woman.

Pinky Madam opened the door and popped her grinning face out.

'Thought I had really left you behind, Mr Maharaja?'

'No, madam.'

'You're not angry, are you?'

'Not at all.' And then I added, to make it more believable, 'Employers are like mother and father. How can one be angry with them?'

I got into the backseat. They did another U-turn across the middle of the avenue, and then drove off at top speed, racing through one red light after the other. The two of them were shrieking, and pinching each other, and making giggling noises, and, helpless to do anything, I was just watching the show from the backseat, when the small black thing jumped into our path, and we hit it and knocked it over and rolled the wheels of the car over it.

From the way the wheels crunched it completely, and from how there was no noise when she stopped the car, not even a whimper or a barking, I knew at once what had happened to the thing we had hit.

She was too drunk to brake at once – by the time she had, we had hurtled on another two or three hundred yards, and then we came to a complete stop. In the middle of the road. She had kept her hands on the wheel; her mouth was open.

'A dog?' Mr Ashok asked me. 'It was a dog, wasn't it?'

I nodded. The streetlights were too dim, and the object – a large black lump – was too far behind us already to be seen clearly. There was no other car in sight. No other living human being in sight.

As if in slow motion, her hands moved back from the wheel and covered her ears.

'It wasn't a dog! It wasn't a—'

Without a word between us, Mr Ashok and I acted as a team. He grabbed her, put a hand on her mouth, and pulled her out of the driver's seat; I rushed out of the back. We slammed the doors together; I turned the ignition key and drove the car at full speed all the way back to Gurgaon.

Halfway through she quietened down, but then, as we got closer to the apartment block, she started up again. She said, 'We have to go back.'

'Don't be crazy, Pinky. Balram will get us back to the apartment block in a few minutes. It's all over.'

'We hit something, Ashoky.' She spoke in the softest of voices. 'We have to take that thing to the hospital.'

'No.'

Her mouth opened again – she was going to scream again in a second. Before she could do that, Mr Ashok gagged her with his palm – he reached for the box of facial tissues and stuffed the tissues into her mouth; while she tried to spit them out, he tore the scarf from around her neck, tied it tightly around her mouth, and shoved her face into his lap and held it down there.

When we got to the apartment, he dragged her to the lift with the scarf still around her mouth.

I got a bucket and washed the car. I wiped it down thoroughly, and scrubbed out every bit of blood and flesh – there was a bit of both around the wheels.

When he came down, I was washing the tyres for the fourth time.

'Well?'

I showed him a piece of bloodied green fabric that had got stuck to the wheel.

'It's cheap stuff, sir, this green cloth,' I said, rubbing the rough material between my fingers. 'It's what they put on children.'

'And do you think the child...' He couldn't say the word.

'There was no sound at all, sir. No sound at all. And the body didn't move even a bit.'

'God, Balram, what will we do now – what will we—' He slapped his hand to his thigh. 'What are these children doing, walking about Delhi at one in the morning, with no one to look after them?'

When he had said this, his eyes lit up.

'Oh, she was one of *those* people.'

'Who live under the flyovers and bridges, sir. That's my guess too.'

'In that case, will anyone miss her...?'

'I don't think so, sir. You know how those people in the Darkness are: they have eight, nine, ten children – sometimes they don't know the names of their own children. Her parents – if they're even here in Delhi, if they even know where she is tonight – won't go to the police.'

He put a hand on my shoulder, the way he had been touching Pinky Madam's shoulder earlier in the night.

Then he put a finger on his lips.

I nodded. 'Of course, sir. Now sleep well – it's been a difficult night for you and Pinky Madam.'

I removed the maharaja tunic, and then I went to

sleep. I was tired as hell – but on my lips there was the big, contented smile that comes to one who has done his duty by his master even in the most difficult of moments.

The next morning, I wiped the seats of the car as usual – I wiped the stickers with the face of the goddess – I wiped the ogre – and then I lit up the incense stick and put it inside so that the seats would smell nice and holy. I washed the wheels one more time, to make sure there was not a spot of blood I had missed in the night.

Then I went back to my room and waited. In the evening one of the other drivers brought a message that I was wanted in the lobby – without the car. The Mongoose was waiting for me up there. I don't know how he got to Delhi this fast – he must have rented a car and driven all night. He gave me a big smile and patted me on the shoulder. We went up to the apartment in the lift.

He sat down on the table, and said, 'Sit, sit, make yourself comfortable, Balram. You're part of the family.'

My heart filled up with pride. I crouched on the floor, happy as a dog, and waited for him to say it again. He smoked a cigarette. I had never before seen him do that. He looked at me with narrowed eyes.

'Now, it's important that you stay here in Buckingham Towers B Block and not go anywhere else – not even to A Block – for a few days. And not say a word to anyone about what happened.'

'Yes, sir.'

He looked at me for a while, smoking. Then he said again, 'You're part of the family, Balram.'

'Yes, sir.'

'Now go downstairs to the servants' quarters and wait there.'

'Yes, sir.'

An hour passed, and then I got called upstairs again.

This time there was a man in a black coat sitting at the dinner table next to the Mongoose. He was looking over a printed piece of paper and reading it silently with his lips, which were stained red with *paan*. Mr Ashok was on the phone in his room; I heard his voice through the closed door. The door to Pinky Madam's room was closed too. The whole house had been handed over to the Mongoose.

'Sit down, Balram. Make yourself comfortable.'

'Yes, sir.'

I squatted and made myself uncomfortable again.

'Would you like some *paan*, Balram?' the Mongoose asked.

'No, sir.'

He smiled. 'Don't be shy, Balram. You chew *paan*, don't you?' He turned to the man in the black coat. 'Give him something to chew, please.'

The man in the black coat reached into his pocket and held out a small green *paan*. I stuck my palm out. He dropped it into my palm without touching me.

'Put it in your mouth, Balram. It's for you.'

'Yes, sir. It's very good. Chewy. Thank you.'

'Let's go over all this slowly and clearly, okay?' the man in the black suit said. The red juice almost dripped out of his mouth as he spoke.

'All right.'

'The judge has been taken care of. If your man does

what he is to do, we'll have nothing to worry about.'

'My man will do what he is to do, no worries about that. He's part of the family. He's a good boy.'

'Good, good.'

The man in the black coat looked at me and held out a piece of paper.

'Can you read, fellow?'

'Yes, sir.' I took the paper from his hand and read:

TO WHOMSOEVER IT MAY CONCERN,

I, Balram Hawai, son of Vikram Halwai, of Laxmangarh village in the district of Gaya, do make the following statement of my own free will and intention:

That I drove the car that hit an unidentified person, or persons, or person and objects, on the night of January 23rd this year. That I then panicked and refused to fulfil my obligations to the injured party or parties by taking them to the nearest hospital emergency ward. That there were no other occupants of the car at the time of the accident. That I was alone in the car, and alone responsible for all that happened.

I swear by almighty God that I make this statement under no duress and under instruction from no one.

Signature or thumb print:

(Balram Halwai)

**Statement made in the presence of
the following witnesses:**

**Kusum Halwai, of Laxmangarh village, Gaya
District**

Chamandas Varma, Advocate, Delhi High Court

Smiling affectionately at me, the Mongoose said,
'We've already told your family about it. Your granny,
what's her name?'

'...'

'I didn't hear that.'

'...m.'

'Yes, that's it. Kusum. I drove down to Laxmangarh –
it's a bad road, isn't it? – and explained everything to her
personally. She's quite a woman.'

He rubbed his forearms and made a big grin, so I
knew he was telling the truth.

'She says she's so proud of you for doing this. She's
agreed to be a witness to the confession as well. That's
her thumbprint on the page, Balram. Just below the spot
where you're going to sign.'

'If he's illiterate, he can press his thumb,' the man in
the black coat said. 'Like this.' He pressed his thumb
against the air.

'He's literate. His grandmother told me he was the
first in the family to read and write. She said you always
were a smart boy, Balram.'

I looked at the paper, pretending to read it again, and
it began to shake in my hands.

What I am describing to you here is what happens to

drivers in Delhi every day, sir. You don't believe me – you think I'm making all this up, Mr Jiabao?

When you're in Delhi, repeat the story I've told you to some good, solid middle-class man of the city. Tell him you heard this wild, extravagant, impossible story from some driver about being framed for a murder his master committed on the road. And watch as your good, solid middle-class friend's face blanches. Watch how he swallows hard – how he turns away to the window – watch how he changes the topic at once.

The jails of Delhi are full of drivers who are there behind bars because they are taking the blame for their good, solid middle-class masters. We have left the villages, but the masters still own us, body, soul, and arse.

Yes, that's right: we all live in the world's greatest democracy here.

What a fucking joke.

Doesn't the driver's family protest? Far from it. They would actually go about bragging. Their boy Balram had taken the fall, gone to Tihar Jail for his employer. He was loyal as a dog. He was the perfect servant.

The judges? Wouldn't they see through this obviously forced confession? But they are in the racket too. They take their bribe, they ignore the discrepancies in the case. And life goes on.

For everyone but the driver.

That is all for tonight, Mr Premier. It's not yet 3 a.m., but I've got to end here, sir. Even to think about this again makes me so angry I might just go out and cut the throat of some rich man right now.

The Fifth Night

Mr Jiabao.

Sir.

When you get here, you'll be told we Indians invented everything from the Internet to hard-boiled eggs to space-ships before the British stole it all from us.

Nonsense. The greatest thing to come out of this country in the ten thousand years of its history is the Rooster Coop.

Go to Old Delhi, behind the Jama Masjid, and look at the way they keep chickens there in the market. Hundreds of pale hens and brightly coloured roosters, stuffed tightly into wire-mesh cages, packed as tightly as worms in a belly, pecking each other and shitting on each other, jostling just for breathing space; the whole cage giving off a horrible stench – the stench of terrified, feathered flesh. On the wooden desk above this coop sits a grinning young butcher, showing off the flesh and organs of a recently chopped-up chicken, still oleaginous with a coating of dark blood. The roosters in the coop smell the blood from above. They see the organs of their brothers lying around them. They know they're next. Yet they do not rebel. They do not try to get out of the coop.

The very same thing is done with human beings in this country.

Watch the roads in the evenings in Delhi; sooner or later you will see a man on a cycle-rickshaw, pedalling down the road, with a giant bed, or a table, tied to the cart that is attached to his cycle. Every day furniture is delivered to people's homes by this man – the delivery-man. A bed costs five thousand rupees, maybe six thousand. Add the chairs, and a coffee table, and it's ten or fifteen thousand. A man comes on a cycle-cart, bringing you this bed, table, and chairs, a poor man who may make five hundred rupees a month. He unloads all this furniture for you, and you give him the money in cash – a fat wad of cash the size of a brick. He puts it into his pocket, or into his shirt, or into his underwear, and cycles back to his boss and hands it over without touching a single rupee of it! A year's salary, two years' salary, in his hands, and he never takes a rupee of it.

Every day, on the roads of Delhi, some chauffeur is driving an empty car with a black suitcase sitting on the backseat. Inside that suitcase is a million, two million rupees; more money than that chauffeur will see in his lifetime. If he took the money he could go to America, Australia, anywhere, and start a new life. He could go inside the five-star hotels he has dreamed about all his life and only seen from the outside. He could take his family to Goa, to England. Yet he takes that black suitcase where his master wants. He puts it down where he is meant to, and never touches a rupee. Why?

Because Indians are the world's most honest people, like the prime minister's booklet will inform you?

No. It's because 99.9 per cent of us are caught in the Rooster Coop just like those poor guys in the poultry market.

The Rooster Coop doesn't always work with minuscule sums of money. Don't test your chauffeur with a rupee coin or two – he may well steal that much. But leave a million dollars in front of a servant and he won't touch a penny. Try it: leave a black bag with a million dollars in a Mumbai taxi. The taxi driver will call the police and return the money by the day's end. I guarantee it. (Whether the police will give it to you or not is another story, sir!) Masters trust their servants with diamonds in this country! It's true. Every evening on the train out of Surat, where they run the world's biggest diamond-cutting and polishing business, the servants of diamond merchants are carrying suitcases full of cut diamonds that they have to give to someone in Mumbai. Why doesn't that servant take the suitcase full of diamonds? He's no Gandhi, he's human, he's you and me. But he's in the Rooster Coop. The trustworthiness of servants is the basis of the entire Indian economy.

The Great Indian Rooster Coop. Do you have something like it in China too? I doubt it, Mr Jiabao. Or you wouldn't need the Communist Party to shoot people and a secret police to raid their houses at night and put them in jail like I've heard you have over there. Here in India we have no dictatorship. No secret police.

That's because we have the coop.

Never before in human history have so few owed so much to so many, Mr Jiabao. A handful of men in this country have trained the remaining 99.9 per cent – as strong, as talented, as intelligent in every way – to exist in perpetual servitude; a servitude so strong that you can put the key of his emancipation in a man's hands and he will throw it back at you with a curse.

You'll have to come here and see it for yourself to believe it. Every day millions wake up at dawn – stand in dirty, crowded buses – get off at their masters' posh houses – and then clean the floors, wash the dishes, weed the garden, feed their children, press their feet – all for a pittance. I will never envy the rich of America or England, Mr Jiabao: they have no servants there. They cannot even *begin* to understand what a good life is.

Now, a thinking man like you, Mr Premier, must ask two questions.

Why does the Rooster Coop work? How does it trap so many millions of men and women so effectively?

Secondly, can a man break out of the coop? What if one day, for instance, a driver took his employer's money and ran? What would his life be like?

I will answer both for you, sir.

The answer to the first question is that the pride and glory of our nation, the repository of all our love and sacrifice, the subject of no doubt considerable space in the pamphlet that the prime minister will hand over to you, *the Indian family*, is the reason we are trapped and tied to the coop.

The answer to the second question is that only a man who is prepared to see his family destroyed – hunted, beaten, and burned alive by the masters – can break out of the coop. That would take no normal human being, but a freak, a pervert of nature.

It would, in fact, take a White Tiger. You are listening to the story of a social entrepreneur, sir.

*

To go back to my story.

There is a sign in the National Zoo in New Delhi, near the cage with the white tiger, which says: Imagine yourself in the cage.

When I saw that sign, I thought, *I can do that – I can do that with no trouble at all.*

For a whole day I was down there in my dingy room, my legs pulled up to my chest, sitting inside that mosquito net, too frightened to leave the room. No one asked me to drive the car. No one came down to see me.

My life had been written away. I was to go to jail for a killing I had not done. I was in terror, and yet not once did the thought of running away cross my mind. Not once did the thought, *I'll tell the judge the truth*, cross my mind. I was trapped in the Rooster Coop.

What would jail be like? That was all I could think about. What kinds of strategies would I follow to escape the big, hairy, dirty men I would find in there?

I remembered a story from *Murder Weekly* in which a man sent to jail pretended to have AIDS so that no one would bugger him. Where was that copy of the magazine – if only I had it with me now, I could copy his exact words, his exact gestures! But if I said I had AIDS, would they assume I was a professional bugger – and bugger me even more?

I was trapped. Through the perforations of my net, I sat staring at the impressions of the anonymous hand that had applied the white plaster to the walls of the room.

'Country-Mouse!'

Vitiligo-Lips had come to the threshold of my room.

'Your boss is ringing the bell like crazy.'

I put my head on the pillow.

He came into the room and pressed his black face and pink lips against the net. 'Country-Mouse, are you ill? Is it typhoid? Cholera? Dengue?'

I shook my head. 'I'm fine.'

'Good to hear that.'

With a big smile of his diseased lips, he left.

I went up like a man to his hanging – up the stairs, and into the apartment building, and then up the elevator to the thirteenth floor.

The Mongoose opened the door. There was no smile on his face this time – not a hint of what he had planned for me.

'You took your time coming. Father is here. He wants to have a word with you.'

My heart raced. The Stork was here! *He* would save me! He wasn't useless, like his two sons. He was an old-fashioned master. He knew he had to protect his servants.

He was on the sofa, with his pale legs stretched out. As soon as he saw me his face broke open in a big smile, and I thought, *He's smiling because he's saved me!* But the old landlord wasn't thinking of me at all. Oh, no, he was thinking of things far more important than my life. He pointed to those two important things.

'Aah, Balram, my feet really need a good massage. It was a long trip by train.'

My hand shook as it turned on the hot-water tap in the

bathroom. The water hit the bottom of the bucket and splashed all over my legs, and when I looked down I saw that they were almost rattling. A trickle of urine was running down them.

A minute later, a big smile on my face, I came to where the Stork was sitting and placed the bucket of hot water near him.

'Put your feet in, sir.'

'Oh,' he said, and closed his eyes; his lips parted and he began to make little moans, sir, and the sound of those moans drove me to press his feet harder and harder; my body began rocking as I did so and my head knocked the sides of his knees.

The Mongoose and Mr Ashok were sitting in front of a TV screen, playing a computer game together.

The door to the bedroom opened, and Pinky Madam came out. She had no makeup on, and her face was a mess – black skin under her eyes, lines on her forehead. The moment she saw me, she got excited.

'Have you people told the driver?'

The Stork said nothing. Mr Ashok and the Mongoose kept playing the game. 'Has no one told *him*? What a fucking joke! He's the one who was going to go to jail!'

Mr Ashok said, 'I suppose we should tell him.' He looked at his brother, who kept his eyes on the TV screen.

The Mongoose said, 'Fine.'

Mr Ashok turned to me.

'We have a contact in the police – he's told us that no one has reported seeing the accident. So your help won't be needed, Balram.'

I felt such tremendous relief that I moved my hands abruptly, and the bucket of warm water spilled over, and then I scrambled to put the bucket upright. The Stork opened his eyes, smacked me on the head with his hand, and then closed his eyes.

Pinky Madam watched; her face changed. She ran into her room and slammed the door. (Who would have thought, Mr Jiabao, that of this whole family, this lady with the short skirts would be the one with a conscience?)

The Stork watched her go into her room and said, 'She's gone crazy, that woman. Wanting to find the family of the child and give them compensation – craziness. As if we were all murderers here.' He looked sternly at Mr Ashok. 'You need to control that wife of yours better, son. The way we do it in the village.'

Then he gave me a light tap on the head and said, 'The water's gone cold.'

I massaged his feet every morning for the next three days. One morning he had a little pain in his stomach, so the Mongoose made me drive him down to Max, which is one of Delhi's most famous private hospitals. I stood outside and watched as the Mongoose and the old man went inside the beautiful big glass building. Doctors walked in and out with long white coats, and stethoscopes in their pockets. When I peeped in from outside, the hospital's lobby looked as clean as the inside of a five-star hotel.

The day after the hospital trip, I drove the Stork and the Mongoose down to the railway station, bought them the snacks they would need for their trip home, waited for the train to leave, and then drove the car back, wiped it down, went to a nearby Hanuman temple to say a prayer of thanks, came back to my room and fell inside the mosquito net, dead tired.

When I woke up, someone was standing in my room, turning the lights on and off.

It was Pinky Madam.

'Get ready. You're going to drive me.'

'Yes, madam,' I said, rubbing my eyes. 'What time is it?'

She put a finger to her lips.

I put on a shirt, and then got the car out, and drove it to the front of the building. She had a bag in her hand.

'Where to?' I asked. It was two in the morning.

She told me, and I asked, 'Isn't Sir coming?'

'Just drive.'

I drove her to the airport, I asked no questions.

When she got out at the airport, she pushed a brown envelope into my window – then slammed her door and left.

And that was how, Your Excellency, my employer's marriage came to an end.

Other drivers have techniques to prolong the marriages of their masters. One of them told me that whenever the fighting got worse he drove fast, so they would get home quickly; whenever they got romantic he let the car slow down. If they were shouting at each other he asked them for directions; if they were kissing he turned the music up. I feel some part of the responsibility falls on me, that their marriage broke up while I was the driver.

The following morning, Mr Ashok called me to the

apartment. When I knocked on the door, he caught me by the collar of my shirt and pulled me inside.

'Why didn't you tell me?' he said, tightening his hold on the collar, almost choking me. 'Why didn't you wake me up at once?'

'Sir... she said... she said... she said...'

He grabbed me and pushed me against the balcony of the apartment. The landlord inside him wasn't dead, after all.

'Why did you drive her there, sister-fucker?'

I turned my head – behind me I saw all the shiny towers and shopping malls of Gurgaon.

'Did you want to ruin my family's reputation?'

He pushed me harder against the balcony; my head and chest were over the edge now, and if he pushed me even a bit more I was in real danger of flying over. I gathered my legs and kicked him in the chest – he staggered back and hit the sliding glass door between the house and the balcony. I slid down against the edge of the balcony; he sat down against the glass door. The two of us were panting.

'You can't blame me, sir!' I shouted. 'I'd never heard of a woman leaving her husband for good! I mean, yes, on TV, but not in real life! I just did what she told me to.'

A crow sat down on the balcony and cawed. Both of us turned and stared at it.

Then his madness was over. He covered his face in his hands and began to sob.

I ran down to my room. I got into the mosquito net and sat on the bed. I counted to ten to make sure he hadn't followed me. Then, reaching under the bed, I took out the brown envelope and opened it again.

It was full of one-hundred-rupee notes.

Forty-seven of them.

I shoved the envelope under the bed: someone was coming towards my room. Four of the drivers walked in.

'Tell us all about it, Country-Mouse.'

They took positions around me.

'Tell you what?'

'The gatekeeper spilled the beans. There are no secrets around here. You drove the woman somewhere at night and came back alone. Has she left him?'

'I don't know what you're talking about.'

'We know they've been fighting, Country-Mouse. And you drove her somewhere at night. The airport? She's gone, isn't she? It's a divorce – every rich man these days is divorcing his wife. These rich people...' He shook his head. His lips curled up in scorn, exposing his reddish, rotting, *paan*-decayed canines. 'No respect for God, for marriage, family – nothing.'

'She just went out for some fresh air. And I brought her back. That gatekeeper has gone blind.'

'Loyal to the last. They don't make servants like you any more.'

I waited all morning for the bell to ring – but it did not. In the afternoon, I went up to the thirteenth floor, and rang the bell and waited. He opened his door, and his eyes were red.

'What is it?'

'Nothing, sir. I came to... make lunch.'

'No need for that.' I thought he was going to apologize for almost killing me, but he said nothing about it.

'Sir, you must eat. It's not good for your health to starve... Please, sir.'

With a sigh, he let me in.

Now that she was gone, I knew that it was my duty to be like a wife to him. I had to make sure he ate well, and slept well, and did not get thin. I made lunch, I served him, I cleaned up. Then I went down and waited for the bell. At eight o'clock, I took the lift up again. Pressing my ear against the door, I listened.

Nothing. Not a sound.

I rang the bell: no response. I knew he couldn't be out – I was his driver, after all. Where could he go without me?

The door was open. I walked in.

He lay beneath the framed photo of the two Pomeranians, a bottle on the mahogany table in front of him, his eyes closed.

I sniffed the bottle. Whisky. Almost all of it gone. I put it to my lips and emptied the dregs.

'Sir,' I said, but he did not wake up. I gave him a push. I slapped him on the face. He licked his lips, sucked his teeth. He was waking up, but I slapped him a second time anyway.

(A time-honoured servants' tradition. Slapping the master when he's asleep. Like jumping on pillows when masters are not around. Or urinating into their plants. Or beating or kicking their pet dogs. Innocent servants' pleasures.)

I dragged him into his bedroom, pulled the blanket over him, turned the lights off, and went down. There was going to be no driving tonight, so I headed off to the

'Action' English Liquor Shop. My nose was still full of Mr Ashok's whisky.

The same thing happened the next night too.

The third night he was drunk, but awake.

'Drive me,' he said. 'Anywhere you want. To the malls. To the hotels. Anywhere.'

Around and around the shiny malls and hotels of Gurgaon I drove him, and he sat slouched in the back-seat – not even talking on the phone, for once.

When the master's life is in chaos, so is the servant's. I thought, *Maybe he's sick of Delhi now. Will he go back to Dhanbad? What happens to me then?* My belly churned. I thought I would crap right there, on my seat, on the gearbox.

'Stop the car,' he said.

He opened the door of the car, put his hand on his stomach, bent down, and threw up on the ground. I wiped his mouth with my hand and helped him sit down by the side of the road. The traffic roared past us. I patted his back.

'You're drinking too much, sir.'

'Why do men drink, Balram?'

'I don't know, sir.'

'Of course, in your caste you don't... Let me tell you, Balram. Men drink because they are sick of life. I thought caste and religion didn't matter any longer in today's world. My father said, "No, don't marry her, she's of another..." I...'

Mr Ashok turned his head to the side, and I rubbed his back, thinking he might throw up again, but the spasm passed.

'Sometimes I wonder, Balram. I wonder what's the point of living. I really wonder...'

The point of living? My heart pounded. *The point of your living is that if you die, who's going to pay me three and a half thousand rupees a month?*

'You must believe in God, sir. You must go on. My granny says that if you believe in God, then good things will happen.'

'That's true, it's true. We must believe,' he sobbed.

'Once there was a man who stopped believing in God, and you know what happened?'

'What?'

'His buffalo died at once.'

'I see.' He laughed. 'I see.'

'Yes, sir, it really happened. The next day he said, "God, I'm sorry, I believe in You," and guess what happened?'

'His buffalo came back to life?'

'Exactly!'

He laughed again. I told him another story, and this made him laugh some more.

Has there ever been a master–servant relationship like this one? He was so powerless, so lost, my heart just had to melt. Whatever anger I had against him for trying to pin Pinky Madam's hit-and-run killing on me passed away that evening. That was *her* fault. Mr Ashok had nothing to do with it. I forgave him entirely.

I talked to him about the wisdom of my village – half repeating things I remembered Granny saying, and half making things up on the spot – and he nodded. It was a scene to put you in mind of that passage in the Bhagavad

Gita, when our Lord Krishna – another of history's famous chauffeurs – stops the chariot he is driving and gives his passenger some excellent advice on life and death. Like Krishna I philosophized – I joked – I even sang a song – all to make Mr Ashok feel better.

Baby, I thought, rubbing his back as he heaved and threw up one more time, *you big, pathetic baby*.

I put my hand out and wiped the vomit from his lips, and cooed soothing words to him. It squeezed my heart to see him suffer like this – but where my genuine concern for him ended and where my self-interest began, I could not tell: no servant can ever tell what the motives of his heart are.

Do we loathe our masters behind a facade of love – or do we love them behind a facade of loathing?

We are made mysteries to ourselves by the Rooster Coop we are locked in.

The next day I went to a roadside temple in Gurgaon. I put a rupee before the two resident pairs of divine arses and prayed that Pinky Madam and Mr Ashok should be reunited and given a long and happy life together in Delhi.

*

A week passed like this, and then the Mongoose turned up from Dhanbad and Mr Ashok and I went together to the station to collect him.

The moment he arrived, everything changed for me. The intimacy was over between me and Mr Ashok.

Once again, I was only the driver. Once again, I was only the eavesdropper.

'I spoke to her last night. She's not coming back to India. Her parents are happy with her decision. This can end only one way.'

'Don't worry about it, Ashok. It's okay. And don't call her again. I'll handle it from Dhanbad. If she makes any noise about wanting your money, I'll just gently bring up that matter of the hit-and-run, see?'

'It's not the money I'm worried about, Mukesh—'

'I know, I know.'

The Mongoose put his hand on Mr Ashok's shoulder – just the way Kishan had put his hand on my shoulder so many times.

We were driving past a slum: one of those series of makeshift tents where the workers at some construction site were living. The Mongoose was saying something, but Mr Ashok wasn't paying attention – he was looking out of the window.

My eyes obeyed his eyes. I saw the silhouettes of the slum dwellers close to one another inside the tents; you could make out one family – a husband, a wife, a child – all huddled around a stove inside one tent, lit up by a golden lamp. The intimacy seemed so complete – so crushingly complete. I understood what Mr Ashok was going through.

He lifted his hand – I prepared for his touch – but he wrapped it around the Mongoose's shoulder.

'When I was in America, I thought family was a burden, I don't deny it. When you and Father tried to stop me from marrying Pinky because she wasn't a Hindu I was furious with you, I don't deny it. But without family, a man is nothing. Absolutely nothing. I had nothing but this driver in front of me for five nights. Now at last I have someone real by my side: you.'

I went up to the apartment with them; the Mongoose wanted me to make a meal for them, and I made a *daal* and *chapattis*, and a dish of okra. I served them, and then I cleaned the utensils and plates.

During dinner, the Mongoose said, 'If you're getting depressed, Ashok, why don't you try yoga and meditation? There's a yoga master on TV, and he's very good – this is what he does every morning on his programme.' He closed his eyes, breathed in, and then exhaled slowly, saying, 'Ooooooom.'

When I came out of the kitchen, wiping my hands on the sides of my trousers, the Mongoose said, 'Wait.'

He took a piece of paper from his pocket and dangled it with a big grin, as if it were a prize for me.

'You have a letter from your granny. What is her name?' He began to cut the letter open with a thick black finger.

'Kusum, sir.'

'Remarkable woman,' he said, and rubbed his fore-arms up and down.

I said, 'Sir, don't bother yourself. I can read.'

He cut the letter open. He began reading it aloud.

Mr Ashok spoke in English – and I guessed what he said: 'Doesn't he have the right to read his own letters?'

And his brother replied in English, and again I guessed, rather than understood, his meaning: 'He won't mind a thing like this. He has no sense of *privacy*. In the villages there are no separate rooms so they just lie together at night and fuck like that. Trust me, he doesn't mind.'

He turned so that the light was behind him and began to read aloud:

'*Dear grandson. This is being written by Mr Krishna, the schoolteacher. He remembers you fondly and refers to you by your old nickname, the White Tiger. Life has become hard here. The rains have failed. Can you ask your employer for some money for your family? And remember to send the money home.*'

The Mongoose put the letter down.

'That's all these servants want. Money, money, money. They're called your servants, but they suck the lifeblood out of you, don't they?'

He continued reading the letter.

'*With your brother Kishan I said, "Now is the time", and he did it – he married. With you, I do not order. You are different from all the others. You are deep, like your mother. Even as a boy you were so; when you would stop near the pond and stare at the Black Fort with your mouth open, in the morning, and evening, and night. So I do not order you to marry. But I tempt you with the joys of married life. It is good for the community. Every time there is a marriage there is more rain in the village. The water buffalo will get fatter. It will give more milk. These are known facts. We are all so proud of you, being in the city. But you must stop thinking only about yourself and think about us too. First you must visit us and eat my chicken curry. Your loving Granny. Kusum.*'

The Mongoose was about to give me the letter, but Mr Ashok took it from him and read it again.

'Sometimes they express themselves so movingly, these villagers,' he said, before flinging the letter on the

190

table for me to pick up.

In the morning, I drove the Mongoose to the railway station, and got him his favourite snack, the *dosa*, once again, from which I removed the potatoes, flinging them on the tracks, before handing it over to him. I got down onto the platform and waited. He chomped on the dosa in his seat; down below on the tracks, a mouse nibbled on the discarded potatoes.

I drove back to the apartment block. I took the lift to the thirteenth floor. The door was open.

'Sir!' I shouted, when I saw what was going on in the living room. 'Sir, this is madness!'

He had put his feet in a plastic bucket and was massaging them himself.

'You should have told me, I would have massaged you!' I shouted, and reached down to his feet.

He shrieked. 'No!'

I said, 'Yes, sir, you must – I'm failing in my duty if I let you do it yourself!' and forced my hands into the dirty water in the bucket, and squeezed his feet.

'No!'

Mr Ashok kicked the bucket, and the water spilled all over the floor.

'How *stupid* can you people get?' He pointed to the door. 'Get out! Can you leave me alone for just five minutes in a day? Do you think you can manage that?'

*

That evening I had to drive him to the mall again. I stayed inside the car after he got out; I did not mix with any of the other drivers.

Even at night, the construction work goes on in Gurgaon – big lights shine down from towers, and dust rises from pits, scaffolding is being erected, and men and animals, both shaken from their sleep and bleary and insomniac, go around and around carrying concrete rubble or bricks.

A man from one of these construction sites was leading an ass; it wore a bright red saddle, and on this saddle were two metal troughs, filled to the brim with rubble. Behind this ass, two smaller ones, of the same colour, were also saddled with metal troughs full of rubble. These smaller asses were walking slower, and the lead ass stopped often and turned to them, in a way that made you think it was their mother.

At once I knew what was troubling me.

I did not want to obey Kusum. She was blackmailing me; I understood why she had sent that letter through the Mongoose. If I refused, she would blow the whistle on me – tell Mr Ashok I hadn't been sending money home.

Now, it had been a long time since I had dipped my beak into anything, sir, and the pressure had built up. The girl would be so young – seventeen or eighteen – and you know what girls taste like at that age, like watermelons. Any diseases, of body or mind, get cured when you penetrate a virgin. These are known facts. And then there was the dowry that Kusum would screw out of the girl's family. All that twenty-four-carat gold, all that cash fresh from the bank. At least some of it I'd keep for myself. All these were sound arguments in favour of marriage.

But on the other hand.

See, I was like that ass now. And all I would do, if I had children, was teach them to be asses like me, and carry rubble around for the rich.

I put my hands on the steering wheel, and my fingers tightened into a strangling grip.

The way I had rushed to press Mr Ashok's feet, the moment I saw them, even though he hadn't asked me to! Why did I feel that I had to go close to his feet, touch them and press them and make them feel good – why? Because the desire to be a servant had been bred into me: hammered into my skull, nail after nail, and poured into my blood, the way sewage and industrial poison are poured into Mother Ganga.

I had a vision of a pale stiff foot pushing through a fire.

'No,' I said.

I pulled my feet up onto the seat, got into the lotus position, and said, 'Om', over and over again. How long I sat that evening in the car with my eyes closed and legs crossed like the Buddha I don't know, but the giggling and scratching noise made me open my eyes. All the other drivers had gathered around me – one of them was scratching the glass with his fingernails. Someone had seen me in the lotus position inside the locked car. They were gaping at me as if I were something in a zoo.

I scrambled out of the lotus position at once. I put a big grin on my face – I got out of the car to a volley of thumps and blows and shrieks of laughter, all of which I meekly accepted, while murmuring, 'Just trying it out, yoga – they show it on TV all the time, don't they?'

The Rooster Coop was doing its work. Servants have

to keep other servants from becoming innovators, exper-
imenters, or entrepreneurs.

Yes, that's the sad truth, Mr Premier.

The coop is guarded from the inside.

Mr Premier, you must excuse me – the phone is ringing. I'll be back in a minute.

*

Alas: I'll have to stop this story for a while. It's only 1:32
in the morning, but we'll have to break off here. Something has come up, sir – an emergency. I'll be back, trust
me.

The Sixth Morning

Pardon me, Your Excellency, for the long intermission. It's now 6:20, so I've been gone five hours. Unfortunately, there was an incident that threatened to jeopardize the reputation of an outsourcing company I work with.

A fairly serious incident, sir. A man has lost his life in this incident. (No: don't misunderstand. I had nothing to do with his death! But I'll explain later.)

Now, excuse me a minute while I turn the fan on – I'm still sweating, sir – and let me sit down on the floor, and watch the fan chop up the light of the chandelier.

The rest of today's narrative will deal mainly with the sorrowful tale of how I was corrupted from a sweet, innocent village fool into a citified fellow full of debauchery, depravity, and wickedness.

All these changes happened in me because they happened first in Mr Ashok. He returned from America an innocent man, but life in Delhi corrupted him – and once the master of the Honda City becomes corrupted, how can the driver stay innocent?

Now, I thought I knew Mr Ashok, sir. But that's presumption on the part of any servant.

The moment his brother left, he changed. He began

wearing a black shirt with the top button open, and changed his perfume.

'To the mall, sir?'

'Yes.'

'Which mall, sir? The one where Madam used to go?'

But Mr Ashok would not take the bait. He was punching the buttons of his mobile phone and he just grunted, 'Sahara Mall, Balram.'

'That's the one Madam liked going to, sir.'

'Don't keep talking about Madam in every other sentence.'

I sat outside the mall and wondered what he was doing there. There was a flashing red light on the top floor, and I guessed that it was a disco. Lines of young men and women were standing outside the mall, waiting to go up to that red light. I trembled with fear to see what these city girls were wearing.

Mr Ashok didn't stay long in there, and he came out alone. I breathed out in relief.

'Back to Buckingham, sir?'

'Not yet. Take me to the Sheraton Hotel.'

As I drove into the city, I noticed that something was different about the way Delhi looked that night.

Had I never before seen how many painted women stood at the sides of the roads? Had I never seen how many men had stopped their cars, in the middle of the traffic, to negotiate a price with these women?

I closed my eyes; I shook my head. *What's happening to you tonight?*

At this point, something took place that cleared my confusion – but also proved very embarrassing to me and to Mr Ashok. I had stopped the car at a traffic signal; a girl began crossing the road in a tight T-shirt, her chest bobbing up and down like three kilogrammes of *brinjals* in a bag. I glanced at the rearview mirror – and there was Mr Ashok, his eyes also bobbing up and down.

I thought, *Aha! Caught you, you rascal!*

And his eyes shone, for he had seen *my* eyes, and he was thinking the exact same thing: *Aha! Caught you, you rascal!*

We had caught each other out.

(This little rectangular mirror inside the car, Mr Jiabao – has no one ever noticed before how *embarrassing* it is? How, every now and then, when master and driver find each other's eyes in this mirror, it swings open like a door into a changing room, and the two of them have suddenly caught each other naked?)

I was blushing. Mercifully, the light turned green, and I drove on.

I swore not to look in the rearview mirror again that night. Now I understood why the city looked so different – why my beak was getting stiff as I was driving.

Because *he* was horny. And inside that sealed car, master and driver had somehow become one body that night.

It was with great relief that I drove the Honda into the gate of the Maurya Sheraton Hotel, and brought that excruciating trip to an end.

Now, Delhi is full of grand hotels. In ring roads and sewage pipes you might have an edge in Beijing, but in pomp and splendour, we're second to none in Delhi. We've got the Sheraton, the Imperial, the Taj Palace, Taj

Mansingh, the Oberoi, the Intercontinental, and many more. Now, the five-star hotels of Bangalore I know inside out, having spent thousands of rupees eating kebabs of chicken, mutton, and beef in their restaurants, and picking up sluts of all nationalities in their bars, but the five-stars of Delhi are things of mystery to me. I've been to them all, but I've never stepped past the front door of one. We're not allowed to do that; there's usually a fat guard at the glass door up at the front, a man with a waxed moustache and beard, who wears a ridiculous red circus turban and thinks he's someone important because the American tourists want to have their photo taken with him. If he so much as sees a driver *near* the hotel, he'll glare – he'll shake a finger like a schoolteacher.

That's the driver's fate. Every other servant thinks he can boss over us.

There are strict rules at the five-stars about where the drivers keep their cars while their masters are inside. Sometimes they put you in a parking spot downstairs. Sometimes in the back. Sometimes up at the front, near the trees. And you sit there and wait, for an hour, two hours, three hours, four hours, yawning and doing nothing, until the guard at the door, the fellow with the turban, mumbles into a microphone, saying, 'Driver So-and-So, you may come to the glass door with the car. Your master is waiting for you.'

The drivers were waiting near the parking lot of the hotel, in their usual key-chain-swirling, *paan*-chewing, gossipmongering, ammonia-releasing circle. Crouching and jabbering like monkeys.

The driver with the diseased lips was sitting apart

from them, engrossed in his magazine. On this week's cover, there was a photo of a woman lying on a bed, her clothes undone; her lover stood next to her, raising a knife over her head.

MURDER WEEKLY

RUPEES 4.50

EXCLUSIVE TRUE STORY:

'HE WANTED HIS MASTER'S WIFE'

LOVE – RAPE – REVENGE!

'Been thinking about what I said, Country-Mouse?' he asked me, as he flipped through a story.

'About getting your master something he'd like? Hashish, or girls, or golf balls? Genuine golf balls from the US Consulate?'

'He's not that kind.'

The pink lips twisted into a smile. 'Want to know a secret? My master likes film actresses. He takes them to a hotel in Jangpura, with a big, glowing T sign on it, and hammers them there.'

He named three famous Mumbai actresses his master had 'hammered'.

'And yet he looks like a goody-goody. Only I know – and I tell you, all the masters are the same. One day you'll believe me. Now come read a story with me.'

We read like that, in total silence. After the third murder story, I went to the side, to a clump of trees, to take an ammonia break. He walked along with me.

Our piss hit the bark of the tree just inches apart.

'I've got a question for you.'

'About city girls again?'

'No. About what happens to old drivers.'

'Huh?'

'I mean what will happen to me a few years from now? Do I make enough money to buy a house and then set up a business of my own?'

'Well,' he said, 'a driver is good till he's fifty or fifty-five. Then the eyes go bad and they kick you out, right? That's thirty years from now, Country-Mouse. If you save from today, you'll make enough to buy a small home in some slum. If you've been a bit smarter and made a little extra on the side, then you'll have enough to put your son in a good school. He can learn English, he can go to university. That's the best-case scenario. A house in a slum, a kid in college.'

'*Best*-case?'

'Well, on the other hand, you can get typhoid from bad water. Boss sacks you for no reason. You get into an accident – plenty of worst-case scenarios.'

I was still pissing, but he put a hand on me. 'There's something I've got to ask you, Country-Mouse. Are you all right?'

I looked at him sideways. 'I'm fine. Why do you ask?'

'I'm sorry to tell you this, but some of the drivers are talking about it openly. You sit by yourself in your master's car the whole time, you talk to yourself... You know what you need? A woman. Have you seen the slum behind the malls? They're not bad-looking – nice and plump. Some of us go there once a week. You can come too.'

'DRIVER BALRAM, WHERE ARE YOU?'

It was the call from the microphone at the gate of

the hotel. Mr Turban was at the microphone – speaking in the most pompous, stern voice possible: 'DRIVER BALRAM REPORT AT ONCE TO THE DOOR. NO DELAY. YOUR MASTER WANTS YOU.'

I zipped up and ran, wiping my wet fingers on the back of my trousers.

Mr Ashok was walking out of the hotel with his hands around a girl when I brought the car up to the gate.

She was a slant-eyed one, with yellow skin. A foreigner. A Nepali. Not even of his caste or background. She sniffed about the seats – the seats that I had polished – and jumped on them.

Mr Ashok put his hands on the girl's bare shoulders. I took my eyes away from the mirror.

I have never approved of debauchery inside cars, Mr Jiabao.

But I could smell the mingling of their perfumes – I knew exactly what was going on behind me.

I thought he would ask me to drive him home now, but no – the carnival of fun just went on and on. He wanted to go to PVR Saket.

Now, PVR Saket is the scene of a big cinema, which shows ten or twelve films at the same time, and charges over a hundred and fifty rupees per film – yes, that's right, a hundred and fifty rupees! That's not all: you've also got plenty of places to drink beer, dance, pick up girls, that sort of thing. A small bit of America in India.

Beyond the last shining shop begins the second PVR. Every big market in Delhi is two markets in one – there is always a smaller, grimier mirror image of the real market, tucked somewhere into a by-lane.

This is the market for the servants. I crossed over to this second PVR – a line of stinking restaurants, tea stalls, and giant frying pans where bread was toasted in oil. The men who work in the cinemas, and who sweep them clean, come here to eat. The beggars have their homes here.

I bought a tea and a potato *vada*, and sat under a banyan tree to eat.

'Brother, give me three rupees.' An old woman, looking lean and miserable, with her hand stretched out.

'I'm not one of the rich, mother – go to that side and ask them.'

'Brother—'

'Let me eat, all right? Just leave me alone!'

She went. A knife-grinder came and set up his stall right next to my tree. Holding two knives in his hand, he sat on his machine – it was one of the foot-pedalled whetstones – and began pedalling. Sparks began buzzing a couple of inches away from me.

'Brother, do you have to do your work *here*? Don't you see a human being is trying to eat?'

He stopped pedalling, blinked, then put the blades to the whizzing whetstone again, as if he hadn't heard a word I'd said.

I threw the potato *vada* at his feet:

'How *stupid* can you people get?'

The old beggar woman crossed with me, into the other PVR. She hitched up her sari, took a breath, and then began her routine: 'Sister, just give me three rupees. I haven't eaten since morning…'

A giant pile of old books lay in the centre of the

market, arranged in a large, hollow square, like the *man-dala* made at weddings to hold the sacred fire. A small man sat cross-legged on a stack of magazines in the centre of the square of books, like the priest in charge of this *mandala* of print. The books drew me towards them like a big magnet, but as soon as he saw me, the man sitting on the magazines snapped, 'All the books are in English.'

'So?'

'Do you read English?' he barked.

'Do *you* read English?' I retorted.

There. That did it. Until then his tone of talking to me had been servant-to-servant; now it became man-to-man. He stopped and looked me over from top to bottom.

'No,' he said, breaking into a smile, as if he appreciated my balls.

'So how do you sell the books without knowing English?'

'I know which book is what from the cover,' he said. 'I know this one is Harry Potter.' He showed it to me. 'I know this one is James Hadley Chase.' He picked it up. 'This is Kahlil Gibran – this is Adolf Hitler – Desmond Bagley – *The Joy of Sex*. One time the publishers changed the Hitler cover so it looked like Harry Potter, and life was hell for a week after that.'

'I just want to stand around the books. I had a book once. When I was a boy.'

'Suit yourself.'

So I stood around that big square of books. Standing around books, even books in a foreign language, you feel a kind of electricity buzzing up towards you, Your

Excellency. It just happens, the way you get erect around girls wearing tight jeans.

Except here what happens is that your *brain* starts to hum.

Forty-seven hundred rupees. In that brown envelope under my bed.

Odd sum of money – wasn't it? There was a mystery to be solved here. Let's see. Maybe she started off giving me five thousand, and then, being cheap, like all rich people are – remember how the Mongoose made me get down on my knees for that one-rupee coin? – deducted three hundred.

That's not *how the rich think, you moron. Haven't you learned yet?*

She must have taken out ten thousand at first. Then cut it in half, and kept half for herself. Then taken out another hundred rupees, another hundred, and another hundred. That's how cheap they are.

So that means they really owe you ten thousand. But if she thought she owed you ten thousand, then what she truly owed you was, what – ten times more?

'No, a *hundred* times more.'

The small man, putting down the newspaper he was reading, turned to me from inside his *mandala* of books. 'What did you say?' he shouted.

'Nothing.'

He shouted again. 'Hey, what do you do?'

I grabbed an imaginary wheel and turned it one hundred and eighty degrees.

'Ah, I should have known. Drivers are smart men – they hear a lot of interesting things. Right?'

'Other drivers might. I go deaf inside the car.'

'Sure, sure. Tell me, you must know English – some of what they talk must stick to you.'

'I told you, I don't listen. How can it stick?'

'What does this word in the newspaper mean? Pri-va-see.'

I told him, and he smiled gratefully. 'We had just started the English alphabet when I got taken out of school by my family.'

So he was another of the half-baked. My caste.

'Hey,' he shouted again. 'Want to read some of this?' He held up a magazine with an American woman on the cover – the kind that rich boys like to buy. 'It's good stuff.'

I flicked through the magazine. He was right, it *was* good stuff.

'How much does this magazine sell for?'

'Sixty rupees. Would you believe that? Sixty rupees for a used magazine. And there's a fellow in Khan Market who sells magazines from England that cost five hundred and eight rupees each! Would you believe that?'

I raised my head to the sky and whistled. 'Amazing how much money they have,' I said, aloud, yet as if talking to myself. 'And yet they treat us like animals.'

It was as if I had said something to disturb him, because he lowered and raised his paper a couple of times; then he came to the very edge of the *mandala* and, partially hiding his face with the paper, whispered something.

I cupped a hand around my ear. 'Say that again?'

He looked around and said, a bit louder this time, 'It won't last for ever, though. The current *situation*.'

'Why not?' I moved towards the *mandala*.

'Have you heard about the Naxals?' he whispered over the books. 'They've got guns. They've got a whole army. They're getting stronger by the day.'

'Really?'

'Just read the papers. The Chinese want a civil war in India, see? Chinese bombs are coming to Burma, and into Bangladesh, and then into Calcutta. They go down south into Andhra Pradesh, and up into the Darkness. When the time is right, all of India will…'

He opened his palms.

We talked like this for a while – but then our friendship ended as all servant–servant friendships must: with our masters bellowing for us. A gang of rich kids wanted to be shown a smutty American magazine – and Mr Ashok came walking out of a bar, staggering, stinking of liquor; the Nepali girl was with him.

On the way back, the two of them were talking at the top of their voices; and then the petting and kissing began. My God, and he a man who was still lawfully married to another woman! I was so furious that I drove right through four red lights, and almost smashed into an oxcart that was going down the road with a load of kerosene cans, but they never noticed.

'Good night, Balram,' Mr Ashok shouted as he got out, hand in hand with her.

'Good night, Balram!' she shouted.

They ran into the apartment and took turns jabbing the call button for the lift.

When I got to my room, I searched under the bed. It was still there, the maharaja tunic that he had given me – the turban and dark glasses too.

I drove the car out of the apartment block, dressed like a maharaja, with the dark glasses on. No idea where I was going – I just drove around the malls. Each time I saw a pretty girl I hooted the horn at her and her friends.

I played his music. I ran his A/C at full blast.

I drove back to the building, took the car down into the garage, folded the dark glasses into my pocket, and took off the tunic.

I spat over the seats of the Honda City, and wiped them clean.

*

The next morning, he didn't come down or call me up to his room. I took the lift, and stood near the door. I was feeling guilty about what I'd done the previous night. I wondered if I should make a full confession. I reached for the bell a few times, and then sighed and gave up.

After a while, there were soft noises from inside. I put my ear to the wood and listened.

'But I *have* changed.'

'Don't keep apologizing.'

'I had more fun last evening than in four years of marriage.'

'When you left for New York, I thought I'd never see you again. And now I have. That's the main thing for me.'

I turned away from the door and slapped my forehead. My guilt was growing by the minute. *She was his old lover, you fool – not some pick-up!*

Of course – he would never go for a slut. I had always known that he was a good man: a cut above me.

I pinched my left palm as punishment.

And put my ear to the door again.

The phone began to ring from inside. Silence for a while, and then he said, 'That's Puddles. And that's Cuddles. You remember them, don't you? They always bark for me. Here, take the phone, listen...'

'Bad news?' Her voice, after a few minutes. 'You look upset.'

'I have to go see a cabinet minister. I hate doing that. They're all so *slimy*. The business I'm in... it's a bad one. I wish I were doing something else. Something clean. Like outsourcing. Every day I wish it.'

'Why don't you do something else, then? It was the same when they told you not to marry me. You couldn't say no then either.'

'It's not that simple, Uma. They're my father and brother.'

'I wonder if you *have* changed, Ashok. The first call from Dhanbad, and you're back to your old self.'

'Look, let's not fight again. I'll send you back in the car now.'

'Oh, no. I'm not going back with your driver. I know his kind, the village kind. They think that any unmarried woman they see is a whore. And he probably thinks I'm a Nepali, because of my eyes. You know what that means for him. I'll go back on my own.'

'This fellow is all right. He's part of the family.'

'You shouldn't be so trusting, Ashok. Delhi drivers are all rotten. They sell drugs, and prostitutes, and God knows what else.'

'Not this one. He's stupid as hell, but he is honest. He'll drive you back.'

'No, Ashok. I'll get a taxi. I'll call you in the evening?'

I realized that she was edging towards the door, and I turned and tiptoed away.

There was no word from him until evening, and then he came down for the car. He made me go from one bank to another bank. Sitting in the driver's seat, I watched through the corner of my eye; he was collecting money from the automatic cash machines – four different ones. Then he said, 'Balram, go to the city. You know the big house that's on the Ashoka Road, where we went to with Mukesh Sir once?'

'Yes, sir. I remember. They've got two big Alsatian guard dogs, sir.'

'Exactly. Your memory's good, Balram.'

I saw in the spy mirror that Mr Ashok was pressing the buttons on his mobile phone as I drove. Probably telling the minister's servant that he was coming with the cash. So now I understood at last what work my master was doing as I drove him through Delhi.

'I'll be back in twenty minutes, Balram,' Mr Ashok said when we got to the minister's bungalow. He stepped out with the red bag and slammed the door.

A security guard with a rifle sat in a metal booth over the red wall of the minister's house, watching me carefully. The two Alsatian dogs, roaming the compound, barked now and then.

It was the hour of sunset. The birds of the city began to make a row as they flew home. Now, Delhi, Mr Premier, is a big city, but there are wild places in it – big parks, protected forests, stretches of wasteland – and things can suddenly come out of these wild places. As I was watching the red wall of the minister's house, a peacock flew up over the guard's booth and perched there; for an instant its deep blue neck and its long tail turned golden in the setting sunlight. Then it vanished.

In a little while it was night.

The dogs began barking. The gate opened. Mr Ashok came out of the minister's house with a fat man – the same man who had come out that day from the President's House. I guessed that he was the minister's assistant. They stopped in front of the car and talked.

The fat man shook hands with Mr Ashok, who was clearly eager to leave him – but ah, it isn't so easy to let go of a politician – or even a politician's sidekick. I got out of the car, pretending to check the tyres, and moved into eavesdropping distance.

'Don't worry, Ashok. I'll make sure the minister gives your father a call tomorrow.'

'Thank you. My family appreciates your help.'

'What are you doing after this?'

'Nothing. Just going home to Gurgaon.'

'A young man like you going home this early? Let's have some fun.'

'Don't you have to work on the elections?'

'The elections? All wrapped up. It's a landslide. The minister said so this morning. Elections, my friend, can be managed in India. It's not like in America.'

Brushing aside Mr Ashok's protests, the fat man forced his way into the car. We had just started down the road when he said, 'Ashok, let me have a whisky.'

'Here, in the car? I don't have any.'

The fat man seemed astonished. 'Everyone has whisky in their car in Delhi, Ashok, didn't you know this?'

He told me to go back to the minister's bungalow. He went inside and came back with a pair of glasses and a bottle. He slammed the door, breathed out, and said, 'Now this car is fully equipped.'

Mr Ashok took the bottle and got ready to pour the fat man a glass, when he smacked his lips in annoyance. 'Not you, you fool. The driver. He is the one who pours the drinks.'

I turned around at once and turned myself into a barman.

'This driver is very talented,' the fat man said. 'Sometimes they make a mess of pouring a drink.'

'You'd never guess that his caste was a teetotal one, would you?'

I tightened the cap on the bottle and left it next to the gearbox. I heard the clinking of glasses behind me and two voices saying, 'Cheers!'

'Let's go,' the minister's sidekick said. 'Let's go to the Sheraton, driver. There's a good restaurant down in the basement there, Ashok. Quiet place. We'll have some fun there.'

I turned the ignition key and took the dark egg of the Honda City down the streets of New Delhi.

'A man's car is a man's palace. I can't believe you've never done this.'

'Well, you'd never try it in America – would you?'

'That's the whole advantage of being in Delhi, dear boy!' The fat man slapped Mr Ashok's thigh.

He sipped, and said, 'What's your situation, Ashok?'

'Coal trading, these days. People think it's only technology that's booming. But coal – the media pays no attention to coal, does it? The Chinese are consuming coal like crazy and the price is going up everywhere. Millionaires are being made, left, right, and centre.'

'Sure, sure,' the fat man said. 'The China Effect.' He sniffed his glass. 'But that's not what we in Delhi mean when we say *situation*, dear boy!'

The minister's sidekick smiled. 'Basically, what I'm asking is, who services you – down *there*?' He pointed at a part of Mr Ashok's body that he had no business pointing at.

'I am separated. Going through a divorce.'

'I'm sorry to hear that,' the fat man said. 'Marriage is a good institution. Everything's coming apart in this country. Families, marriages – everything.'

He sipped some more whisky and said, 'Tell me, Ashok, do you think there will be a civil war in this country?'

'Why do you say that?'

'Four days ago, I was in a court in Ghaziabad. The judge gave an order that the lawyers didn't like, and they simply refused to accept his order. They went mad – they dragged the judge down and beat him, in his own court. The matter was not reported in the press. But I saw it with my own eyes. If people start beating the judges – in their own courtrooms – then what is the future for our country?'

Something icy cold touched my neck. The fat man was rubbing me with his glass.

'Another drink, driver.'

'Yes, sir.'

Have you ever seen this trick, Your Excellency? A man steering the car with one hand, and picking up a whisky bottle with the other hand, hauling it over his shoulder, then pouring it into a glass, even as the car is moving, without spilling a drop! The skills required of an Indian driver! Not only does he have to have perfect reflexes, night vision, and infinite patience, he also has to be the consummate barman!

'Would you like some more, sir?'

I glanced at the minister's sidekick, at the fat, corrupt folds of flesh under his chin – then glanced at the road to make sure I wasn't driving into anything.

'Pour one for your master now.'

'No, I don't drink much, really. I'm fine.'

'Don't be silly, Ashok. I insist – fellow, pour one for your master.'

So I had to turn and do the amazing one-hand-on-the-wheel-one-hand-with-the-whisky-bottle trick all over again.

The fat man went quiet after the second drink. He wiped his lips.

'When you were in America you must have had a lot of women? I mean – the *local* women.'

'No.'

'No? What does that mean?'

'I was faithful to Pinky – my wife – the whole time.'

'My. You were faithful. What an idea. Faithfully married. No wonder it ended in divorce. Have you *never* had a white woman?'

'I told you.'

'God. Why is it *always* the wrong kind of Indian who goes abroad? Listen, do you want one now? A European girl?'

'*Now?*'

'Now,' he said. 'A female from Russia. She looks just like that American actress.' He mentioned a name. 'Want to do it?'

'A whore?'

The fat man smiled. 'A friend. A magical friend. Want to do it?'

'No. Thanks. I'm seeing someone. I just met someone I knew a long—'

The fat man took out his mobile phone and punched some numbers. The light of the phone made a blue halo on his face.

'She's there right now. Let's go see her. She's a stunner, I tell you. Just like that American actress. Do you have thirty thousand on you?'

'No. Listen. I'm seeing someone. I'm not—'

'No problem. I'll pay now. You can pay later. Just put it into the next envelope you give the minister.' He put his hand on Mr Ashok's hand and winked, then leaned over and gave instructions to me. I looked at Mr Ashok in the rearview mirror as hard as I could.

A whore? That's for people like me, sir. Are you sure you want this?

I wish I could have told him this openly – but who was I? Just the driver.

I took orders from the fat man. Mr Ashok said nothing – just sat there sucking his whisky like a boy with a soda. Maybe he thought it was a joke, or maybe he was too frightened of the fat man to say no.

But I will defend his honour to my deathbed. *They* corrupted him.

The fat man made me drive to a place in Greater Kailash – another housing colony where people of quality live in Delhi. Touching my neck with his icy glass when I had to make a turn, he guided me to the place. It was as large as a small palace, with big white columns of marble up the front. From the amount of garbage thrown outside the walls of the house, you knew that rich people lived here.

The fat man held open the car door as he spoke into a phone. Five minutes later he slammed the door shut. I began sneezing. A weird perfume had filled the back of the car.

'Stop that sneezing and drive us towards Jangpura, son.'

'Sorry, sir.'

The fat man smiled. He turned to the girl who had got into the car and said, 'Speak to my friend Ashok in Hindi, please.'

I looked into the rearview mirror, and caught my first glimpse of this girl.

It's true, she did look like an actress I had seen somewhere or other. The name of the actress, though, I didn't know. It's only when I came to Bangalore and mastered the use of the Internet – in just two quick sessions, mind you! – that I found her photo and name on Google.

Kim Basinger.

That was the name the fat man had mentioned. And it was true – the girl who got in with the fat man did look exactly like Kim Basinger! She was tall and beautiful, but the most remarkable thing about her was her hair – golden and glossy, just like in the shampoo advertisements!

'How are you, Ashok?' She said it in perfect Hindi. She put her hand out and took Mr Ashok's hand.

The minister's assistant chuckled. 'There. India has progressed, hasn't it? She's speaking in Hindi.'

He slapped her on the thigh. 'Your Hindi has improved, dear.'

Mr Ashok leaned back to speak to the fat man over her shoulder. 'Is she Russian?'

'Ask her, don't ask me, Ashok. Don't be shy. She's a friend.' 'Ukrainian,' she said in her accented Hindi. 'I am a Ukrainian student in India.'

I thought: I would have to remember this place, Ukraine. And one day I would have to go there!

'Ashok,' the fat man said. 'Go on, touch her hair. It's real. Don't be scared – she's a friend.' He chuckled. 'See – didn't hurt, did it, Ashok? Say something in Hindi to Mr Ashok, dear. He's still frightened of you.'

'You're a handsome man,' she said. 'Don't be frightened of me.'

'Driver.' The fat man leaned forward and touched me with his cold glass again. 'Are we near Jangpura?'

'Yes, sir.'

'When you go down the Masjid Road, you'll see a hotel with a big neon T sign on it. Take us there.'

I got them there in ten minutes – you couldn't miss the hotel, the big T sign on it glowed like a lantern in the dark.

Taking the golden-haired woman with him, the fat

man went up to the hotel reception, where the manager greeted him warmly. Mr Ashok walked behind them and kept looking from side to side, like a guilty little boy about to do something very bad.

Half an hour passed. I was outside, my hands on the wheel the whole time. I punched the little ogre. I began to gnaw at the wheel.

I kept hoping he'd come running out, arms flailing, and screaming, *Balram, I was on the verge of making a mistake! Save me – let's drive away at once!*

An hour later Mr Ashok came out of the hotel – alone, and looking ill.

'The meeting's over, Balram,' he said, letting his head fall back on the seat. 'Let's go home.'

I didn't start the car for a second. I kept my finger on the ignition key.

'Balram, let's go home, I said!'

'Yes, sir.'

When we got back to Gurgaon, he staggered out towards the lift. I did not leave the car. I let five minutes pass, and then drove back to Jangpura, straight to the hotel with the T on it.

I parked in a corner and watched the door of the hotel. I wanted her to come out.

A rickshaw-puller drove up next to me, a small, unshaven, stick-thin man, who looked dead tired as he wiped his face and legs clean with a rag, and went to sleep on the ground. On the seat of his rickshaw was a white advertising sticker:

IS EXCESS WEIGHT A PROBLEM FOR YOU?

The mascot of the gym – an American with enormous white muscles – smiled at me from above the slogan. The rickshaw-puller's snoring filled the air.

Someone in the hotel must have seen me. After a while, the door opened: a policeman came out, peered at me, and then began walking down the steps.

I turned the key; I took the car back to Gurgaon.

Now, I've driven around Bangalore at night too, but I never get that feeling here that I did in Delhi – the feeling that if something is burning inside me as I drive, the city will know about it – she will burn with the same thing.

My heart was bitter that night. The city knew this – and under the dim orange glow cast everywhere by the weak streetlamps, she was bitter.

Speak to me of civil war, I told Delhi.

I will, she said.

An overturned flower urn on a traffic island in the middle of a road; next to it three men sit with open mouths. An older man with a beard and white turban is talking to them with a finger upraised. Cars drive by him with their dazzling headlights, and the noise drowns out his words. He looks like a prophet in the middle of the city, unnoticed except by his three apostles. They will become his three generals. That overturned flower urn is a symbol of some kind.

Speak to me of blood on the streets, I told Delhi.

I will, she said.

I saw other men discussing and talking and reading in

the night, alone or in clusters around the streetlamps. By the dim lights of Delhi, I saw hundreds that night, under trees, shrines, intersections, on benches, squinting at newspapers, holy books, journals, Communist Party pamphlets. What were they reading about? What were they talking about?

But what else?

Of the end of the world.

And if there is blood on these streets – I asked the city – do you promise that he'll be the first to go – that man with the fat folds under his neck?

A beggar sitting by the side of the road, a nearly naked man coated with grime, and with wild unkempt hair in long coils like snakes, looked into my eyes:

Promise.

Coloured pieces of glass have been embedded into the boundary wall of Buckingham Towers B Block – to keep robbers out. When headlights hit them, the shards glow, and the wall turns into a Technicolored, glass-spined monster.

The gatekeeper stared at me as I drove in. I saw rupee notes shining in his eyes.

This was the second time he had seen me going out and returning on my own.

In the car park, I got out of the driver's seat and carefully closed the door. I opened the passenger's door, and went inside, and passed my hand along the leather. I passed my hands from one side of the leather seats to the other three times, and then I found what I was looking for.

I held it up to the light.

A strand of golden hair!
I've got it in my desk to this day.

The Sixth Night

The dreams of the rich, and the dreams of the poor – they never overlap, do they?

See, the poor dream all their lives of getting enough to eat and looking like the rich. And what do the rich dream of?

Losing weight and looking like the poor.

Every evening, the compound around Buckingham Towers B Block becomes an exercise ground. Plump, paunchy men and even plumper, paunchier women, with big circles of sweat below their arms, are doing their evening 'walking'.

See, with all these late-night parties, all that drinking and munching, the rich tend to get fat in Delhi. So they walk to lose weight.

Now, where should a human being walk? In the outdoors – by a river, inside a park, around a forest.

However, displaying their usual genius for town planning, the rich of Delhi had built this part of Gurgaon with no parks, lawns, or playgrounds – it was just buildings, shopping malls, hotels, and more buildings. There was a pavement outside, but that was for the poor to live on. So if you wanted to do some 'walking'. it had to be done around the concrete compound of your own building.

Now, while they walked around the apartment block, the fatsoes made their thin servants – most of them drivers – stand at various spots on that circle with bottles of mineral water and fresh towels in their hands. Each time they completed a circuit around the building, they stopped next to their man, grabbed the bottle – gulp – grabbed the towel – wipe, wipe – then it was off on round two.

Vitiligo-Lips was standing in one corner of the compound, with his bottle and his master's sweaty towel. Every few minutes, he turned to me with a twinkle in his eyes – his boss, the steel man, who was bald until two weeks ago, now sported a head of thick black hair – an expensive toupee job he had gone all the way to England for. This toupee was the main subject of discussion in the monkey-circle these days – the other drivers had offered Vitiligo-Lips ten rupees to resort to the old tricks of braking unexpectedly, or taking the car full speed over a pothole, to knock off his master's toupee at least once.

The secrets of their masters were spilled and dissected every evening by the monkey-circle – though if any of them made the divorce a topic of discussion, he knew he would have to deal with me. On Mr Ashok's privacy I allowed no one to infringe.

I was standing just a few feet from Vitiligo-Lips, with my master's bottle of mineral water in my hand and his sweat-stained towel on my shoulder.

Mr Ashok was about to complete his circle – I could

smell his sweat coming towards me. This was round number three for him. He took the bottle, drained it, wiped his face with his towel, and draped it back on my shoulder.

'I'm done, Balram. Bring the towel and bottle up, okay?'

'Yes, sir,' I said, and watched him go into the apartment block. He took a walk once or twice a week, but it clearly wasn't enough to counter his nights of debauchery – I saw a big, wet paunch pressing against his white T-shirt. How repulsive he was, these days.

I signalled to Vitiligo-Lips before going down to the car park.

Ten minutes later, I smelled the steel man's sweat and heard footsteps. Vitiligo-Lips had come down. I called him over to the Honda City – it was the only place in the world I felt fully safe any more.

'What is it, Country-Mouse? Want another magazine?'

'Not that. Something else.'

I got down on my haunches; I squatted by one of the tyres of the City. I scraped the grooves of the tyre with a fingernail. He squatted too.

I showed him the strand of golden hair – I kept it tied around my wrist, like a locket. He brought my wrist to his nose – he rubbed the strand between his fingers, sniffed it, and let my wrist down.

'No problem.' He winked. 'I told you your master would get lonely.'

'Don't talk about him!' I seized his neck. He shook me off.

227

'Are you crazy? You tried to choke me!'

I scraped the grooves of the tyre again. 'How much will it cost?'

'High-class or low-class? Virgin or non-virgin? All depends.'

'I don't care. She just has to have golden hair – like in the shampoo advertisements.'

'Cheapest is ten, twelve thousand.'

'That's too much. He won't pay more than four thousand seven hundred.'

'Six thousand five hundred, Country-Mouse. That's the minimum. White skin has to be respected.'

'All right.'

'When does he want it, Country-Mouse?'

'I'll tell you. It'll be soon. And another thing – I want to know another thing.'

I put my face on the tyre and breathed in the smell of the rubber. For strength.

'How many ways are there for a driver to cheat his master?'

*

Mr Jiabao, I am aware that it is a common feature of those Cellophane-wrapped business books to feature small 'sidebars'. At this stage of the story, to relieve you of tedium, I would like to insert my own 'sidebar' into the narrative of the modern entrepreneur's growth and development.

*

How does the enterprising driver earn a little extra cash?

1. When his master is not around, he can siphon petrol from the car, with a funnel. Then sell the petrol.
2. When his master orders him to make a repair to the car, he can go to a corrupt mechanic; the mechanic will inflate the price of the repair, and the driver will receive a cut. This is a list of a few entrepreneurial mechanics who help entrepreneurial drivers:

   - Lucky Mechanics, in Lado Serai, near the Qutub
   - R.V. Repairs, in Greater Kailash Part Two
   - Nilofar Mechanics, in DLF Phase One, in Gurgaon.

3. He should study his master's habits, and then ask himself: 'Is my master careless? If so, what are the ways in which I can benefit from his carelessness?' For instance, if his master leaves empty English liquor bottles lying around in the car, he can sell the whisky bottles to the bootleggers. Johnnie Walker Black brings the best resale value.

4. As he gains in experience and confidence and is ready to try something riskier, he can turn his master's car into a freelance taxi. The stretch of the road from Gurgaon to Delhi is excellent for this; lots of Romeos come to see

their girlfriends who work in the call centres. Once the entrepreneurial driver is sure that his master is not going to notice the absence of the car – and that none of his master's friends are likely to be on the road at this time – he can spend his free time cruising around, picking up and dropping off paying customers.

*

At night I lay in my mosquito net, the lightbulb on in my room, and watched the dark roaches crawling on top of the net, their antennae quivering and trembling, like bits of my own nerves: and I lay in bed, too agitated even to reach out and crush them. A cockroach flew down and landed right above my head.

You should have asked them for money when they made you sign that thing. Enough money to sleep with twenty white-skinned girls. It flew away. Another landed on the same spot.

Twenty?

A hundred. Two hundred. Three hundred, a thousand, ten thousand golden-haired whores. And even that would still not have been enough. That would not start to be enough.

Over the next two weeks, I did things I am still ashamed to admit. I cheated my employer. I siphoned his petrol; I took his car to a corrupt mechanic who billed him for work that was not necessary; and three times, while driving back to Buckingham B, I picked up a pay-ing customer.

The strangest thing was that each time I looked at the

cash I had made by cheating him, instead of guilt, what did I feel?

Rage.

The more I stole from him, the more I realized how much he had stolen from me.

To go back to the analogy I used when describing Indian politics to you earlier, I was growing a belly at last.

Then one Sunday afternoon, when Mr Ashok had said he wouldn't need me again that day, I gulped two big glasses of whisky for courage, then went to the servants' dormi-tory. Vitiligo-Lips was sitting beneath the poster of a film actress – each time his master 'hammered' an actress, he put her poster up on the wall – playing cards with the other drivers.

'Well, you can say what you want, but I know that these jokers aren't going to win re-election.'

He looked up and saw me.

'Well, look who's here. It's the yoga guru, paying us a rare visit. Welcome, honoured sir.'

They showed me their teeth. I showed them my teeth.

'We were discussing the elections, Country-Mouse. You know, it's not like the Darkness here. The elections aren't rigged. Are you going to vote this time?'

I summoned him with a finger.

He shook his head. 'Later, Country-Mouse, I'm having too much fun discussing the elections.'

I waved the brown envelope in the air. He put his cards down at once.

I insisted that we walk down to the car park; he counted the money there, in the shadow of the Honda City.

'Good, Country-Mouse. It's all here. And where is your master? Will you drive him there?'

'I am my own master.'

He didn't get it for a minute. Then his jaw dropped – he rushed forward – he hugged me. 'Country-Mouse!' He hugged me again. 'My man!'

He was from the Darkness too – and you feel proud when you see one of your own kind showing some ambition in life.

He drove me in the Qualis – his master's Qualis – to the hotel, explaining on the way that he ran an informal 'taxi' service when the boss wasn't around.

This hotel was in South Extension, Part Two – one of the best shopping areas in Delhi. Vitiligo-Lips locked his Qualis, smiled reassuringly, and walked with me up to the reception desk. A man in a white shirt and black bow tie was running his finger down the entries in a long ledger; leaving his finger on the book, he looked at me as Vitiligo-Lips explained things into his ear.

The manager shook his head. 'A golden-haired woman – for him?'

He put his hands on the counter and leaned over so he could see me from the toes up.

'For *him*?'

Vitiligo-Lips smiled. 'Look here, the rich of Delhi have had all the golden-haired women they want; who knows what they'll want next? Green-haired women from the moon. Now it's going to be the working class that lines up for the white women. This fellow is the future of your business, I tell you – treat him well.'

The manager seemed uncertain for a moment; then

he slammed the ledger shut and showed me an open palm. 'Give me five hundred rupees extra.' He grinned. 'Working-class surcharge.'

'I don't have it!'

'Give me five hundred or forget it.'

I took out the last three hundred rupees I had. He took the cash, straightened his tie, and then went up the stairs. Vitiligo-Lips patted me on the shoulder and said, 'Good luck, Country-Mouse – do it for all of us!'

I ran up the stairs.

Room 114A. The manager was standing at the door, with his ear to it. He whispered, 'Anastasia?'

He knocked, then put his ear to the door again and said, 'Anastasia, are you in?'

He pushed the door open. A chandelier, a window, a green bed – and a girl with golden hair sitting on the bed.

I sighed, because this one looked nothing like Kim Basinger. Not half as pretty. That was when it hit me – in a way it never had before – how the rich *always* get the best things in life, and all that we get is their leftovers.

The manager brought both his palms up to my face; he opened and closed them, and then did it again.

Twenty minutes.

Then he made a knocking motion with his fist – followed by a kicking motion with his shiny black boot.

'Get it?'

That's what would happen to me after twenty minutes. 'Yes.'

He slammed the door. The woman with the golden hair still wasn't looking at me.

I had only summoned up the courage to sit down by her side when there was banging on the door outside.

'When you hear that – it's over! Get it?' The manager's voice.

'All right!'

I moved closer to the woman on the bed. She neither resisted nor encouraged. I touched a curl of her hair and pulled it gently to get her to turn her face towards me. She looked tired, and worn out, and there were bruises around her eyes, as if someone had scratched her.

She gave me a big smile – I knew it well: it was the smile a servant gives a master.

'What's your name?' she asked in Hindi.

This one too! They must have a Hindi language school for girls in this country, Ukraine, I swear!

'Munna.'

She smiled. 'That's not a real name. It just means "boy".'

'That's right. But it's my name,' I said. 'My family gave me no other name.'

She began laughing – a high-pitched, silvery laugh that made her whole golden head of hair bob up and down. My heart beat like a horse's. Her perfume went straight to my brain.

'You know, when I was young, I was given a name in my language that just meant "girl". My family did the same thing to me!'

'Wow,' I said, curling my legs up on the bed.

We talked. She told me she hated the mosquitoes in this hotel and the manager, and I nodded. We talked for a while like this, and then she said, 'You're not a bad-looking fellow – and you're quite sweet', and then ran her finger through my hair.

At this point, I jumped out of the bed. I said, 'Why are you here, sister? If you want to leave this hotel, why don't you? Don't worry about the manager. I'm here to protect you! I am your own brother, Balram Halwai!'

Sure, I said that – in the Hindi film they'll make of my life.

'Seven thousand sweet rupees for twenty minutes! Time to get started!'

That was what I actually said.

I climbed on top of her – and held her arms behind her head with one hand. Time to dip my beak in her. I let the other hand run through her golden curls.

And then I shrieked. I could not have shrieked louder if you had shown me a lizard.

'What happened, Munna?' she asked.

I jumped off the bed, and *slapped* her.

My, these foreigners can yell when they want to.

Immediately – as if the manager had been there all the time, his ear to the door, grinning – the door burst open, and he came in.

'This,' I shouted at him, pulling the girl by her hair, 'is not real gold.'

The roots were black! It was all a dye job!

He shrugged. 'What do you expect, for seven thousand? The real thing costs forty, fifty.'

I leapt at him, caught his chin in my hand, and rammed it against the door. 'I want my money back!'

The woman let out a scream from behind me. I turned

around – that was the mistake I made. I should've finished off that manager right there and then.

Ten minutes later, with a scratched and bruised face, I came tumbling out the front door. It slammed behind me.

Vitiligo-Lips hadn't waited. I had to take a bus back home; I was rubbing my head the whole time. Seven thousand rupees – I wanted to cry! *Do you know how many water buffaloes you could have bought for that much money?* – I could feel Granny's fingers wringing my ears.

Back in Buckingham Towers at last – after a one-hour traffic jam on the road – I washed the wound on my head in the common sink, and then spat a dozen times. To hell with everything – I scratched my groin. I needed that. I slouched towards my room, kicked opened the door, and froze.

Someone was inside the mosquito net. I saw a silhouette in the lotus position.

'Don't worry, Balram. I know what you were doing.'

A man's voice. Well, at least it wasn't Granny – that was my first thought.

Mr Ashok lifted up a corner of the net and looked at me, a sly grin on his face.

'I know exactly what you were doing.'

'Sir?'

'I was calling your name and you weren't responding. So I came down to see. But I know exactly what you were doing… that other driver, the man with pink lips, he told me.'

My heart pounded. I looked down at the ground.

'He said you were at the temple, offering prayers for my health.'

'Yes, sir,' I said, with sweat pouring down my face in relief. 'That's right, sir.'

'Come inside the net,' he said softly. I went in and sat next to him inside the mosquito net. He was looking at the roaches walking above us.

'You live in such a hole, Balram. I never knew. I'm sorry.'

'It's all right, sir. I'm used to it.'

'I'll give you some money, Balram. You go into some better housing tomorrow, okay?'

He caught my hand and turned it over. 'Balram, what are all these red marks on your palm? Have you been pinching yourself?'

'No, sir... it's a skin disease. I've got it here too, behind my ear – see – all those pink spots?'

He came close, filling my nostrils with his perfume. Bending my ear with a finger, gently, he looked.

'My. I never noticed. I sit behind you every day and I never—'

'A lot of people have this disease, sir. A lot of poor people.'

'Really. I haven't noticed. Can you get it treated?'

'No, sir. The diseases of the poor can never get treated. My father had TB and it killed him.'

'It's the twenty-first century, Balram. Anything can be treated. You go to the hospital and get it treated. Send me the bill, I'll pay it.'

'Thank you, sir,' I said. 'Sir... do you want me to take you somewhere in the City?'

He opened his lips and then closed them without making any noise. He did this a couple of times, and then he said, 'My way of living is all wrong, Balram. I know it, but I don't have the courage to change it. I just don't have... the *balls*.'

'Don't think so much about it, sir. And, sir, let's go upstairs, I beg you. This is not a place for a man of quality like yourself.'

'I let people exploit me, Balram. I've never done what I've wanted, my whole life. I...'

His head sagged; his whole body looked tired and worn.

'You should eat something, sir,' I said. 'You look tired.'

He smiled – a big, trusting baby's smile.

'You're always thinking of me, Balram. Yes, I want to eat. But I don't want to go to another hotel, Balram. I'm sick of hotels. Take me to the kind of place you go to eat, Balram.'

'Sir?'

'I'm sick of the food I eat, Balram. I'm sick of the life I lead. We rich people, we've lost our way, Balram. I want to be a simple man like you, Balram.'

'Yes, sir.'

We walked outside, and I led him across the road and into a tea shop.

'Order for us, Balram. Order the commoners' food.'

I ordered okra, cauliflower, radish, spinach, and *dhal*. Enough to feed a whole family, or one rich man.

He ate and burped and ate some more.

'This food is fantastic. And just twenty-five rupees! You people eat so well!'

When he was done, I ordered him a *lassi*, and when he took the first sip, he smiled. 'I like eating your kind of food!'

I smiled and thought, *I like eating your kind of food too*.

*

'The divorce papers will come through soon. That's what the lawyer said.'

'All right.'

'Should we start looking already?'

'For another lawyer?'

'No. For another girl.'

'It's too early, Mukesh. It's been just three months since she left.'

I had driven Mr Ashok to the train station. The Mongoose had come to town again, from Dhanbad. Now I was driving both of them back to the apartment.

'All right. Take your time. But you must remarry. If you stay a divorced man, people won't respect you. They won't respect us. It's the way our society works. Listen to me. Last time you didn't listen, when you married a girl from outside our caste, our religion – you even refused to take dowry from her parents. This time, *we'll* pick the girl.'

I heard nothing; I could tell that Mr Ashok was clenching his teeth.

'I can see you're getting worked up,' the Mongoose said. 'We'll talk about it later. For now, take this.' He handed his brother a red bag that he had brought with him from Dhanbad.

Mr Ashok clicked open the bag and peered inside – and at once the Mongoose slammed the bag shut.

'Are you crazy? Don't open that here in the car. It's for Mukeshan. The fat man. The assistant. You know him, don't you?'

'Yes, I know him.' Mr Ashok shrugged. 'Didn't we already pay those bastards off?'

'The minister wants more. It's election time. Every time there's elections, we hand out cash. Usually to both sides, but this time the government is going to win for sure. The opposition is in a total mess. So we just have to pay off the government, which is good for us. I'll come with you the first time, but it's a lot of money, and you may have to go a second and third time too. And then there are a couple of bureaucrats we have to grease. Get it?'

'It seems like this is all I get to do in Delhi. Take money out of banks and bribe people. Is this what I came back to India for?'

'Don't be sarcastic. And remember, ask for the bag back each time. It's a good bag, Italian-made. No need to give them any additional gifts. Understand? Oh, hell. Not another *fucking* traffic jam.'

'Balram, play Sting again. It's the best music for a traffic jam.'

'This driver knows who Sting is?'

'Sure, he knows it's my favourite CD. Show us the Sting CD, Balram. See – see – he knows Sting!'

I put the CD into the player.

Ten minutes passed, and the cars had not moved an inch. I replaced Sting with Enya; I replaced Enya with Eminem. Vendors came to the car with baskets of oranges, or strawberries in plastic cases, or newspapers, or novels in English. The beggars were on the attack too. One beggar was carrying another on his shoulders and going from car to car; the fellow on his shoulders had no legs below his knees. They went together from car to car, the fellow without the legs moaning and groaning and the other fellow tapping or scratching on the windows of the car.

Without thinking much about it, I cracked open the egg.

Rolling down the glass, I held out a rupee – the fellow with the deformed legs took it and saluted me; I rolled the window up and resealed the egg.

The talking in the backseat stopped at once.

'Who the hell told you to do that?'

'Sorry, sir,' I said.

'Why the hell did you give that beggar a rupee? What cheek! Turn the music off.'

They really gave it to me that evening. Though their talk was normally in a mix of Hindi and English, the two brothers began speaking in chaste Hindi – entirely for my benefit.

'Don't we give money each time we go to the temple?' the elder thug said. 'We donate *every* year to the cancer institute. I buy that card that the schoolchildren come around selling.'

'The other day I was speaking to our accountant and he was saying, "Sir, you have no money in your bank. It's all gone." Do you know how high the taxes are in this country?' the younger thug said. 'If we gave any money, what would we have to eat?'

That was when it struck me that there really was no difference between the two of them. They were both their father's seed.

For the rest of the drive home, the Mongoose pointedly kept his eyes on the rearview mirror. He looked as if he had smelled something funny.

When we reached Buckingham B, he said, 'Come upstairs, Balram.'

'Yes, sir.'

We stood side by side in the lift. When he opened the door of the apartment, he pointed to the floor. 'Make yourself comfortable.'

I squatted below the photo of Cuddles and Puddles and put my hands between my knees. He sat down on a chair, and rested his face in his palm, and just stared at me.

His brow was furrowed. I could see a thought forming in his mind.

He got up from his chair, walked over to where I was crouched, and got down on one knee. He sniffed the air.

'Your breath smells of aniseed.'

'Yes, sir.'

'People chew that to hide the liquor on their breath. Have you been drinking?'

'No, sir. My caste, we're teetotallers.'

He kept sniffing, coming closer all the time.

I took in a big breath; held it in the pit of my belly; then I forced it out, in a belch, right to his face.

'That's disgusting, Balram,' he said with a look of horror. He stood up and took two steps back.

'Sorry, sir.'

'Get out!'

I came out sweating.

The next day, I drove him and Mr Ashok to some minister's or bureaucrat's house in New Delhi; they went out with the red bag. Afterwards, I took them to a hotel, where they had lunch – I gave the hotel staff instructions: no potatoes in the food – then drove the Mongoose to the railway station.

I put up with his usual threats and warnings – no A/C, no music, no wasting fuel, blah blah blah. I stood on the platform and watched as he ate his snack. When the train left, I danced around the platform and clapped my hands. Two homeless urchins were watching me, and they laughed – they clapped their hands too. One of them began singing a song from the latest Hindi film, and we danced together on the platform.

Next morning, I was in the apartment, and Mr Ashok was fiddling with the red bag and getting ready to leave, when the phone began to ring.

I said, 'I'll take the bag down, sir. I'll wait in the car.'

He hesitated, then held the bag out in my direction. 'I'll join you in a minute.'

I closed the door of the apartment. I walked to the lift, pressed the button, and waited. It was a heavy bag, and I had to shift it about in my palm.

The lift had reached the fourth floor.

I turned and looked at the view from the balcony of the thirteenth floor – the lights were shining from Gurgaon's malls, even in broad daylight. A new mall had opened in the past week. Another one was under construction. The city was growing.

The lift was coming up fast. It was about to reach the eleventh floor.

I turned and ran.

Kicking the door of the fire escape open, hurrying down two flights of dark stairs, I clicked the red bag open.

All at once, the entire stairwell filled up with dazzling light – the kind that only money can give out.

Twenty-five minutes later, when Mr Ashok came down, punching the buttons on his mobile phone, he found the red bag waiting for him on his seat. I held up a shining silver disc as he closed the door.

'Shall I play Sting for you, sir?'

As we drove, I tried hard not to look at the red bag – it was torture for me, just like when Pinky Madam used to sit in short skirts.

At a red light, I looked at the rearview mirror. I saw my thick moustache and my jaw. I touched the mirror. The angle of the image changed. Now I saw long beautiful eyebrows curving on either side of powerful, furrowed brow muscles; black eyes were shining below those tensed muscles. The eyes of a cat watching its prey.

Go on, just look at the red bag, Balram – that's not stealing, is it?

I shook my head.

And even if you were to steal it, Balram, it wouldn't be stealing.

How so? I looked at the creature in the mirror.

See – Mr Ashok is giving money to all these politicians in Delhi so that they will excuse him from the tax he has to pay. And who owns that tax, in the end? Who but the ordinary people of this country – you!

'What is it, Balram? Did you say something?'

I tapped the mirror. My moustache rose into view again, and the eyes disappeared, and it was only my own face staring at me now.

'This fellow in front of me is driving rashly, sir. I was just grumbling.'

'Keep your cool, Balram. You're a good driver, don't let the bad ones get to you.'

The city knew my secret. One morning, the President's House was covered in smog and blotted out from the road; it seemed as though there were no government in Delhi that day. And the dense pollution that was hiding the prime minister and all his ministers and bureaucrats said to me:

They won't see a thing you do. I'll make sure of that.

I drove past the red wall of Parliament House. A guard with a gun was watching me from a lookout post on the red wall – he put his gun down the moment he saw me.

Why would I stop you? I'd do the same, if I could.

At night a woman walked with a Cellophane bag; my headlights shone into the bag and turned the Cellophane transparent. I saw four large dark fruits inside the bag – and each dark fruit said, *You've already done it. In your heart you've already taken it.* Then the headlights passed; the Cellophane turned opaque; the four dark fruits vanished.

Even the road – the smooth, polished road of Delhi that is the finest in all of India – knew my secret.

One day at a traffic signal, the driver of the car next to me lowered the window and spat out: he had been chewing *paan*, and a vivid red puddle of expectorate splashed on the hot midday road and festered there like a living thing, spreading and sizzling. A second later, he spat again – and now there was a second puddle on the road. I stared at the two puddles of red, spreading spit – and then:

The left-hand puddle of spit seemed to say:	**But the right-hand puddle of spit seemed to say:**
Your father wanted you to to be an honest man.	Your father wanted you to be a *man*.
Mr Ashok does not hit you or spit on you, like people did to your father.	Mr Ashok made you take the blame when his wife killed that child on the road.
Mr Ashok pays you well, 4,000 rupees a month. He has been raising your salary without your even asking.	This is a pittance. You live in a city. What do you save? Nothing.
Remember what the Buffalo did to his servant's family. Mr Ashok will ask his father to do the same to your family once you run away.	The very fact that Mr Ashok threatens your family makes your blood boil!

I turned my face away from the red puddles. I looked at the red bag sitting in the centre of my rearview mirror, like the exposed heart of the Honda City.

That day I dropped Mr Ashok off at the Imperial

Hotel, and he said, 'I'll be back in twenty minutes, Balram.'

Instead of parking the car, I drove to the train station, which is in Pahar Ganj, not far from the hotel.

People were lying on the floor of the station. Dogs were sniffing at the garbage. The air was mouldy. *So this is what it will be like*, I thought.

The destinations of all the trains were up on a blackboard.

Benaras

Jammu

Amritsar

Mumbai

Ranchi

What would be *my* destination, if I were to come here with a red bag in my hand?

As if in answer, shining wheels and bright lights began flashing in the darkness.

Now, if you visit any train station in India, you will see, as you stand waiting for your train, a row of bizarre-looking machines with red lightbulbs, kaleidoscopic wheels, and whirling yellow circles. These are your-fortune-and-weight-for-one-rupee machines that stand on every rail platform in the country.

They work like this. You put your bags down to the side. You stand on them. Then you insert a one-rupee coin into the slot.

The machine comes to life; levers start to move inside, things go clankety-clank, and the lights flash like crazy. Then there is a loud noise, and a small stiff chit of cardboard coloured either green or yellow will pop out of the machine. The lights and noise calm down. On this chit will be written your fortune, and your weight in kilograms.

Two kinds of people use these machines: the children of the rich, or the fully grown adults of the poorer class, who remain all their lives children.

I stood gazing at the machines, like a man without a mind. Six glowing machines were shining at me: light-bulbs of green and yellow and kaleidoscopes of gold and black that were turning around and around.

I got up on one of the machines. I sacrificed a rupee – it gobbled the coin, made noise, gave off more lights, and released a chit.

LUNNA SCALES CO.
NEW DELHI 110 055
YOUR WEIGHT

59

'Respect for the law is the
first command of the gods.'

I let the fortune-telling chit fall on the floor and I laughed.

Even here, in the weight machine of a train station, they try to hoodwink us. Here, on the threshold of a man's freedom, just before he boards a train to a new life, these flashing fortune machines are the final alarm bell of the Rooster Coop.

The sirens of the coop were ringing – its wheels turning – its red lights flashing! A rooster was escaping from the coop! A hand was thrust out – I was picked up by the neck and shoved back into the coop.

I picked the chit up and re-read it.

My heart began to sweat. I sat down on the floor.

Think, Balram. Think of what the Buffalo did to his servant's family.

Above me I heard wings thrashing. Pigeons were sitting on the roof beams all around the station; two of them had flown from a beam and began wheeling directly over my head, as if in slow motion – pulled into their breasts, I saw two sets of red claws.

Not far from me I saw a woman lying on the floor, with nice full breasts inside a tight blouse. She was snoring. I could see a one-rupee note stuffed into her cleavage, its lettering and colour visible through the weave of her bright green blouse. She had no luggage. That was all she had in the world. One rupee. And yet look at her – snoring blissfully, without a care in the world.

Why couldn't things be so simple for me?

A low growling noise made me turn. A black dog was turning in circles behind me. A pink patch of skin – an open wound – glistened on its left butt; and the dog had twisted on itself in an attempt to gnaw at the wound. The wound was just out of reach of its teeth, but the dog was going crazy from pain – trying to attack the wound with its slavering mouth, it kept moving in mad, precise, pointless circles.

I looked at the sleeping woman – at her heaving breasts. Behind me the growling went on and on.

That Sunday, I asked Mr Ashok's permission, saying I wanted to go to a temple, and went into the city. I took a bus down to Qutub, and from there a jeep-taxi down to G.B. Road.

This, Mr Premier, is the famous 'red-light district' (as they say in English) of Delhi.

An hour here would clear all the evil thoughts out of my head. When you retain semen in your lower body, it leads to evil movements in the fluids of your upper body. In the Darkness we know this to be a fact.

It was just five o'clock and still light, but the women were waiting for me, as they wait for all men, at all times of the day.

Now, I've been to these streets before – as I've confessed to you – but this time was different. I heard them above me – the women – jeering and taunting from the grilled windows of the brothels – but this time I couldn't bear to look up at them.

A *paan*-maker sat on a wooden stall outside the gaudy blue door of a brothel, using a knife to spread spices on moist leaves that he had picked out of a bowl of water, which is the first step in the preparation of *paan*; in the small square space below his stall sat another man, boiling milk in a vessel over the hissing blue flame of a gas stove.

'What's the matter with you? Look at the women.'

The pimp, a small man with a big nose covered in red warts, had caught me by the wrist.

'You look like you can afford a foreign girl. Take a Nepali girl. Aren't they beauties? Look up at them, son!'

He took my chin – maybe he thought I was a shy virgin, out on my first expedition here – and forced me to look up.

The Nepalis up there, behind the barred window, were really good-looking: very light-skinned and with those Chinese eyes that just drive us Indian men mad. I shook the pimp's hand off my face.

'Take any one! Take all! Aren't you man enough, son?'

Normally this would have been enough for me to burst into the brothel, hollering for blood.

But sometimes what is most animal in a man may be the best thing in him. From my waist down, nothing stirred. *They're like parrots in a cage. It'll be one animal fucking another animal.*

'Chew *paan* – it will help if you're having trouble getting it up!' the seller of *paan* shouted from his stand. He held up a fresh, wet *paan* leaf, and shook it so the droplets splashed on my face.

'Drink hot milk – it helps too!' shouted the small, shrunken man below him who was boiling the milk.

I watched the milk. It seethed, and spilled down the sides of the stainless steel vessel; the small, shrunken man smiled – he provoked the boiling milk with a spoon – it became frothier and frothier, hissing with outrage.

I charged into the *paan*-seller, pushing him off his perch, scattering his leaves, and spilling his water. I kicked the midget in his face. Screams broke out from above. The pimps rushed at me; shoving and kicking for dear life, I ran out of that street.

Now, G.B. Road is in Old Delhi, about which I should say something. Remember, Mr Premier, that Delhi is the capital of not one but *two* countries – two Indias. The Light and the Darkness both flow in to Delhi. Gurgaon, where Mr Ashok lived, is the bright, modern end of the city, and this place, Old Delhi, is the other end. Full of things that the modern world forgot all about – rickshaws, old stone buildings, and Muslims. On a Sunday, though, there is something more: if you keep pushing through the crowd that is always there, go past the men cleaning the other men's ears by poking rusty metal rods into them, past the men selling small fish trapped in green bottles full of brine, past the cheap shoe market and the cheap shirt market, you will come to the great secondhand book market of Darya Ganj.

You may have heard of this market, sir, since it is one of the wonders of the world. Tens of thousands of dirty, rotting, blackened books on every subject – Technology, Medicine, Sexual Pleasure, Philosophy, Education, and Foreign Countries – heaped upon the pavement from Delhi Gate onwards all the way until you get to the market in front of the Red Fort. Some books are so old they crumble when you touch them; some have silverfish feasting on them – some look like they were retrieved from a flood, or from a fire. Most shops on the pavement are shuttered down; but the restaurants are still open, and the smell of fried food mingles with the smell of rotting paper. Rusting exhaust fans turn slowly in the ventilators of the restaurants like the wings of giant moths.

I went amid the books and sucked in the air: it was like oxygen after the stench of the brothel.

There was a thick crowd of book buyers fighting over the books with the sellers, and I pretended to be one of the buyers. I leapt into the books, picking them up, reading them like this, flip, flip, flip, until a bookseller shouted, 'You going to buy it or read it for free?'

'It's no good,' I would say, and put the book down and go to the next bookseller, and pick up something he had, and flip flip flip. Never paying anyone a single rupee, flipping through books for free, I kept looting bookseller after bookseller all evening long!

Some books were in Urdu, the language of the Muslims – which is all just scratches and dots, as if some crow dipped its feet in black ink and pressed them to the page. I was going through one such book when a bookseller said, 'Can you read Urdu?'

He was an old Muslim, with a pitch-black face that was bedewed with sweat, like a begonia leaf after the rains, and a long white beard.

I said: 'Can *you* read Urdu?'

He opened the book, cleared his throat, and read, '"*You were looking for the key for years.*" Understood that?' He looked at me, wide furrows on his black forehead.

'Yes, Muslim uncle.'

'Shut up, you liar. And listen.'

He cleared his throat again.

'"*You were looking for the key for years/But the door was always open!*"'

He closed the book. 'That's called poetry. Now get lost.'

'Please, Muslim uncle,' I begged. 'I'm just a rickshaw-puller's son from the Darkness. Tell me all about poetry. Who wrote that poem?'

He shook his head, but I kept flattering him, telling him how fine his beard was, how fair his skin was (ha!), how it was obvious from his nose and forehead that he wasn't some pigherd who had converted but a true-blue Muslim who had flown here on a magic carpet all the way from Mecca, and he grunted with satisfaction. He read me another poem, and another one – and he explained the true history of poetry, which is a kind of secret, a magic known only to wise men. Mr Premier, I won't be saying anything new if I say that the history of the world is the history of a ten-thousand-year war of brains between the rich and the poor. Each side is eternally trying to hoodwink the other side: and it has been this way since the start of time. The poor win a few battles (the peeing in the potted plants, the kicking of the pet dogs, etc.) but of course the rich have won the war for ten thousand years. That's why, one day, some wise men, out of compassion for the poor, left them signs and symbols in poems, which appear to be about roses and pretty girls and things like that, but when understood correctly spill out secrets that allow the poorest man on earth to conclude the ten-thousand-year-old brain-war on terms favourable to himself. Now, the four greatest of these wise poets were Rumi, Iqbal, Mirza Ghalib, and another fellow whose name I was told but have forgotten.

(Who *was* that fourth poet? It drives me crazy that I can't recall his name. If you know it, send me an email.)

'Muslim uncle, I have another question for you.'

'What do I look like? Your schoolteacher? Don't keep asking me questions.'

'The last one, I promise. Tell me, Muslim uncle, can a man make himself vanish with poetry?'

'What do you mean – like vanish through black

magic?' He looked at me. 'Yes, that can be done. There are books for that. You want to buy one?'

'No, not vanish like that. I meant can he... can he...'

The bookseller had narrowed his eyes. The sweat beads had grown larger on his huge black forehead.

I smiled at him. 'Forget I asked that, Muslim uncle.'

And then I warned myself never to talk to this old man again. He knew too much already.

My eyes were burning from squinting at books. I should have been heading back towards Delhi Gate to catch a bus. There was a foul taste of book in my mouth – as if I had inhaled so much particulated old paper from the air. Strange thoughts brew in your heart when you spend too much time with old books.

But instead of going back to the bus, I wandered farther into Old Delhi. I had no idea where I was going. Everything grew quiet the moment I left the main road. I saw some men sitting on a charpoy smoking, others lying on the ground and sleeping; eagles flew above the houses. Then the wind blew an enormous gust of buffalo into my face.

Everyone knows there is a butchers' quarter some-where in Old Delhi, but not many have seen it. It is one of the wonders of the old city – a row of open sheds, and big buffaloes standing in each shed with their butts towards you, and their tails swatting flies away like windshield wipers, and their feet deep in immense pyr-amids of shit. I stood there, inhaling the smell of their bodies – it had been so long since I had smelled buffalo! The horrible city air was driven out of my lungs.

A rattling noise of wooden wheels. I saw a buffalo

coming down the road, pulling a large cart behind it. There was no human sitting on this cart with a whip; the buffalo just knew on its own where to go. And it was coming down the road. I stood to the side, and as it passed me, I saw that this cart was full of the faces of dead buffaloes; faces, I say – but I should say skulls, stripped even of the skin, except for the little black bit of skin at the tip of the nose from which the nostril hairs still stuck out, like last defiant bits of the personality of the dead buffalo. The rest of the faces were gone. Even the eyes had been gouged out.

And the living buffalo walked on, without a master, drawing its load of death to the place where it knew it had to go.

I walked along with that poor animal for a while, staring at the dead, stripped faces of the buffaloes. And then the strangest thing happened, Your Excellency – I swear the buffalo that was pulling the cart turned its face to me, and said, in a voice not unlike my father's:

'Your brother Kishan was beaten to death. Happy?'

It was like experiencing a nightmare in the minutes before you wake up; you know it's a dream, but you can't wake up just yet.

'Your aunt Luttu was raped and then beaten to death. Happy? Your grandmother Kusum was kicked to death. Happy?'

The buffalo glared at me.

'Shame!' it said, and then it took a big step forward and the cart passed by, full of dead skinned faces, which seemed to me at that moment the faces of my own family.

*

The next morning, Mr Ashok came down to the car, smiling, and with the red bag in his hand. He slammed the door.

I looked at the ogre and swallowed hard.

'Sir...'

'What is it, Balram?'

'Sir, there's something I've been meaning to tell you for a while.' And I took my fingers off the ignition key. I swear, I was ready to make a full confession right there... had he said the right word... had he touched my shoulder the right way.

But he wasn't looking at me. He was busy with the mobile phone and its buttons.

Punch, punch, punch.

To have a madman with thoughts of blood and theft in his head, sitting just ten inches in front of you, and not to know it. Not to have a hint, even. What *blindness* you people are capable of. Here you are, sitting in glass buildings and talking on the phone night after night to Americans who are thousands of miles away, but you don't have the faintest idea what's happening to the man who's driving your car!

What is it, Balram?

Just this, sir – that I want to smash your skull open!

He leaned forward – he brought his lips right to my ear – I was ready to melt.

'I understand, Balram.'

I closed my eyes. I could barely speak.

'You do, sir?'

'You want to get married.'

'…'

'Balram. You'll need some money, won't you?'

'Sir, no. There's no need of that.'

'Wait, Balram. Let me take out my wallet. You're a good member of the family. You never ask for more money – I know that other drivers are constantly asking for overtime and insurance: but you never say a word. You're old-fashioned. I like that. We'll take care of all the wedding expenses, Balram. Here, Balram – here's… here's…'

I saw him take out a thousand-rupee note, put it back, then take out a five-hundred, then put it back, and take out a hundred.

Which he handed to me.

'I assume you'll be going to Laxmangarh for the wedding, Balram?'

'…'

'Maybe I'll come along,' he said. 'I really like that place. I want to go up to that fort this time. How long ago was it that we were there, Balram? Six months ago?'

'Longer than that, sir.' I counted the months off on my fingers. 'Eight months ago.'

He counted the months too. 'Why, you're right.'

I folded the hundred-rupee note and put it in my chest pocket.

'Thank you for this, sir,' I said, and turned the ignition key.

Early next morning I walked out of Buckingham B onto the main road. Though it was a brand-new building, there was already a leak in the drainage pipe, and a large patch of sewage darkened the earth outside the compound wall; three stray dogs were sleeping on the wet patch. A good way to cool off – summer had started, and even the nights were unpleasant now.

The three mutts seemed so comfortable. I got down on my haunches and watched them.

I put my finger on the dark sewage puddle. So cool, so tempting.

One of the stray dogs woke up; it yawned and showed me all its canines. It sprang to its feet. The other mutts got up too. A growling began, and a scratching of the wet mud, and a showing of teeth – they wanted me off their kingdom.

I surrendered the sewage to the dogs and headed for the malls. None of them had opened yet. I sat down on the pavement.

No idea where to go next.

That's when I saw the small dark marks in the pavement.

Paw prints.

An animal had walked on the concrete before it had set.

I got up and walked after the animal. The space between the prints grew wider – the animal had begun to sprint.

I walked faster.

The paw prints of the accelerating animal went all the way around the malls, and then behind the malls, and at last, where the pavement ended and raw earth began, they vanished.

Here I had to stop, because five feet ahead of me a row

of men squatted on the ground in a nearly perfect straight line. They were defecating.

I was at the slum.

Vitiligo-Lips had told me about this place – all these construction workers who were building the malls and giant apartment buildings lived here. They were from a village in the Darkness; they did not like outsiders coming in, except for those who had business after dark. The men were defecating in the open like a defensive wall in front of the slum: making a line that no respectable human should cross. The wind wafted the stench of fresh shit towards me.

I found a gap in the line of the defecators. They squatted there like stone statues.

These people were building homes for the rich, but they lived in tents covered with blue tarpaulin sheets, and partitioned into lanes by lines of sewage. It was even worse than Laxmangarh. I picked my way around the broken glass, wire, and shattered tube lights. The stench of faeces was replaced by the stronger stench of industrial sewage. The slum ended in an open sewer – a small river of black water went sluggishly past me, bubbles sparkling in it and little circles spreading on its surface. Two children were splashing about in the black water.

A hundred-rupee note came flying down into the river. The children watched with open mouths, and then ran to catch the note before it floated away. One child caught it, and then the other began hitting him, and they began to tumble about in the black water as they fought.

I went back to the line of crappers. One of them had

finished up and left, but his position had been filled.

I squatted down with them and grinned.

A few immediately turned their eyes away: they were still human beings. Some stared at me blankly as if shame no longer mattered to them. And then I saw one fellow, a thin black fellow, was grinning back at me, as if he were proud of what he was doing.

Still crouching, I moved myself over to where he was squatting and faced him. I smiled as wide as I could. So did he.

He began to laugh – and I began to laugh – and then all the crappers laughed together.

'We'll take care of your wedding expenses,' I shouted.

'We'll take care of your wedding expenses!' he shouted back.

'We'll even fuck your wife for you, Balram!'

'We'll even fuck your wife for you, Balram!'

He began laughing – laughing so violently that he fell down face-first into the ground, still laughing, exposing his stained arse to the stained sky of Delhi.

As I walked back, the malls had begun to open. I washed my face in the common toilet and wiped my hands clean of the slum. I walked into the car park, found an iron wrench, aimed a couple of practice blows, and then took it to my room.

A boy was waiting for me near my bed, holding a letter between his teeth as he adjusted the buttons on his pants. He turned around when he heard me; the letter flew out of his mouth and to the ground. The wrench fell out of my hand at the same time.

'They sent me here. I took the bus and train and asked

people and came here.' He blinked. 'They said you have to take care of me and make me a driver too.'

'Who the hell are you?'

'Dharam,' he said. 'I'm Luttu Auntie's fourth son. You saw me when you came to Laxmangarh last time. I was wearing a red shirt. You kissed me here.' He pointed to the top of his head.

Picking up the letter, he held it out to me.

Dear grandson,

It has been a long time since you came to visit us – and an even longer time, a total of eleven months and two days, since you last sent us any money. The city has corrupted your soul and made you selfish, vain-glorious, and evil. I knew from the start that this would happen, because you were a spiteful, insolent boy. Every chance you got you just stared at yourself in a mirror with open lips, and I had to wring your ears to make you do any work. You are just like your mother. It is her nature and not your father's sweet nature that you have. So far we have borne our sufferings patiently, but we will not do so. You must send us money again. If you don't, we'll tell your master. Also we have decided to arrange for your wedding on our own, and if you do not come here, we will send the girl to you by bus. I say these things not to threaten you but out of love. After all, am I not your own grandmother? And how I used to stuff your mouth with sweets! Also, it is your duty to look after Dharam, and take care of him as if he were your own son. Now take care of your health, and

remember that I am preparing lovely chicken dishes
for you, which I will send to you by mail – along with
the letter that I will write to your master.

Your loving Granny,
Kusum

I folded the letter, put it in my pocket, and then slapped the boy so hard that he staggered back, hit the side of the bed, and fell into it, pulling down the mosquito net as he fell.

'Get up,' I said. 'I'm going to hit you again.'

I picked up the wrench and held it over him – then threw it to the floor.

The boy's face had turned blue, and his lip was split and bleeding, and he still hadn't said a word.

I sat in the mosquito net, sipping from a half bottle of whisky. I watched the boy.

I had come to the edge of the precipice. I had been ready to slay my master – this boy's arrival had saved me from murder (and a lifetime in prison).

That evening, I told Mr Ashok that my family had sent me a helper, someone to keep the car tidy, and instead of getting angry that he would now have to feed another mouth – which is what most of the masters would have done – he said, 'He's a cute boy. He looks like you. What happened to his face?'

I turned to Dharam. 'Tell him.'

He blinked a couple of times. He was thinking it over. 'I fell off the bus.'

Smart boy.

'Take care in the future,' Mr Ashok said. 'This is great, Balram – you'll have company from now on.'

Dharam was a quiet little fellow. He didn't ask for anything from me, he slept on the floor where I told him to, he minded his own business. Feeling guilty for what I'd done, I took him to the tea shop.

'Who teaches at the school these days, Dharam? Is it still Mr Krishna?'

'Yes, Uncle.'

'Is he still stealing the money for the uniforms and the food?'

'Yes, Uncle.'

'Good man.'

'I went for five years and then Kusum Granny said that was enough.'

'Let's see what you learned in five years. Do you know the eight-times table?'

'Yes, Uncle.'

'Let's hear it.'

'Eight ones are eight.'

'That's easy – what's next?'

'Eight twos are sixteen.'

'Wait.' I counted out on my fingers to make sure he had got it right. 'All right. Go on.'

'Order me a tea too, won't you?' Vitiligo-Lips sat down next to me. He smiled at Dharam.

'Order it yourself,' I said.

He pouted. 'Is that any way for you to be talking to me, working-class hero?'

Dharam was watching us keenly, so I said, 'This boy is from my village. From my family. I'm talking to him now.'

'Eight threes are twenty-four.'

'I don't care who he is,' Vitiligo-Lips said. 'Order me a tea, working-class hero.'

He flexed his palm near my face – five fingers. That meant, *I want five hundred rupees*.

'I've got nothing.'

'Eight fours are thirty-two.'

He drew a line across his neck and smiled. *Your master will know everything*.

'What's your name, boy?'

'Dharam.'

'What a nice name. Do you know what it means?'

'Yes, sir.'

'Does your uncle know what it means?'

'Shut up,' I said.

It was the time of the day when the tea shop got cleaned. One of the human spiders dropped a wet rag on the floor and started to crawl with it, pushing a growing wavelet of stinking ink-black water ahead of him. Even the mice scampered out of the shop. The customers sitting at the tables were not spared – the black puddle splashed them as it passed. Bits of *beedis*, shiny plastic wrappers, punched bus tickets, snippets of onion, sprigs of fresh coriander floated on the black water; the reflection of a naked electric bulb shone out of the scum like a yellow gemstone.

As the black water went past, a voice inside me said, '*But your heart has become even blacker than that, Munna.*'

That night Dharam woke up when he heard the shrieking. He came to the mosquito net.

'Uncle, what's going on?'

'Turn on the light, you fool! Turn on the light!'

He did so, and saw me paralysed inside the net: I could not even point at the thing. A thick-bodied grey gecko had come down from the wall and was on my bed.

Dharam began to grin.

'I'm not joking, you moron – get it out of my bed!'

He stuck his hand into the net, grabbed the lizard, and smashed it under his foot.

'Throw it somewhere far, far away – outside the room, outside the apartment building.'

I saw the bewildered look in his eyes: *Afraid of a lizard – a grown man like my uncle!*

Good, I thought, just as he was turning off the lights. *He'll never suspect that I'm planning anything.*

An instant later, my grin faded.

What *was* I planning?

I began to sweat. I stared at the anonymous palm prints that had been pressed into the white plaster of the wall.

A cane began tapping on concrete – the nightwatchman of Buckingham B was doing his rounds with his long cane. When the tapping of the cane died out there was no noise inside the room, except for the buzzing of the cockroaches as they chewed on the walls or flew about. It was another hot, humid night. Even the cockroaches must have been sweating – I could barely breathe.

Just when I thought I'd never go to sleep, I began reciting a couplet, over and over again.

I was looking for the key for years
But the door was always open.

And then I was asleep.

*

I should have noticed the stencilled signs on the walls in which a pair of hands smashed through shackles – I should have stopped and listened to the young men in red headbands shouting from the trucks – but I had been so wrapped up in my own troubles that I had paid no attention at all to something very important that was happening to my country.

Two days later, I was taking Mr Ashok down to Lodi Gardens along with Ms Uma; he was spending more and more time with her these days. The romance was blossoming. My nose was getting used to her perfume – I no longer sneezed when she moved.

'So you *still* haven't done it, Ashok? Is it going to be like last time all over again?'

'It's not so simple, Uma. Mukesh and I have had a fight over you already. I will put my foot down. But give me some time, I need to get over the divorce – Balram, why have you turned the music up so loud?'

'I like it loud. It's romantic. Maybe he's done it deliberately.'

'Look, it'll happen. Trust me. It's just... Balram, why the hell haven't you turned the music down? Sometimes these people from the Darkness are so stupid.'

'I told you that already, Ashok.'

Her voice dropped.

I caught the words 'replacement', 'driver', and 'local' in English.

Have you thought about getting a replacement driver – a local driver?

He mumbled his reply.

I could not hear a word. But I did not have to.

I looked at the rearview mirror: I wanted to confront him, eye to eye, man to man. But he wouldn't look at me in the mirror. Didn't dare face me.

I tell you, you could have heard the grinding of my teeth just then. I thought I was making plans for him? *He'd* been making plans for me! The rich are always one step ahead of us – aren't they?

Well, not this time. For every step he'd take, I'd take *two*.

Outside on the road, a streetside vendor was sitting next to a pyramid of motorbike helmets that were wrapped in plastic and looked like a pile of severed heads.

Just when we were about to reach the gardens, we saw that the road was blocked on all sides: a line of trucks had gathered in front of us, full of men who were shouting:

'Hail the Great Socialist! Hail the voice of the poor of India!'

'What the hell is going on?'

'Haven't you seen the news today, Ashok? They are announcing the results.'

'Fuck,' he said. 'Balram, turn Enya off, and turn on the radio.'

The voice of the Great Socialist came on. He was being interviewed by a radio reporter.

'The election shows that the poor will not be ignored. The Darkness will not be silent. There is no water in our taps, and what do you people in Delhi give us? You give us mobile phones. Can a man drink a phone when he is thirsty? Women walk for miles every morning to find a bucket of clean—'

'Do you want to become prime minister of India?'

'Don't ask me such questions. I have no ambitions for myself. I am simply the voice of the poor and the disenfranchised.'

'But surely, sir—'

'Let me say one last word, if I may. All I have ever wanted was an India where any boy in any village could dream of becoming the prime minister. Now, as I was saying, women walk for...'

According to the radio, the ruling party had been hammered at the polls. A new set of parties had come to power. The Great Socialist's party was one of them. He had taken the votes of a big part of the Darkness. As we drove back to Gurgaon, we saw hordes of his supporters pouring in from the Darkness. They drove where they wanted, did what they wanted, whistled at any woman they felt like whistling at. Delhi had been invaded.

Mr Ashok did not call me the rest of the day; in the evening he came down and said he wanted to go to the Imperial Hotel. He was on the mobile phone the whole time, punching buttons and making calls and screaming:

'We're *totally* fucked, Uma. This is why I hate this business I'm in. We're at the mercy of these...'

'Don't yell at me, Mukesh. *You* were the one who said the elections were a foregone conclusion. Yes, *you*! And now we'll *never* get out of our income-tax mess.'

'All right, I'm *doing* it, Father! I'm going to meet him right now at the Imperial!'

He was still on the phone when I dropped him off at the Imperial Hotel. Forty-two minutes passed, and then he came out with two men. Leaning down to the window, he said, 'Do whatever they want, Balram. I'm taking a taxi back from here. When they're done bring the car back to Buckingham.'

'Yes, sir.'

The two men slapped him on the back; he bowed, and opened the doors for them himself. If he was kissing arse like this, they had to be politicians.

The two men got in. My heart began to pound. The man on the right was my childhood hero – Vijay, the pigherd's son turned bus conductor turned politician from Laxmangarh. He had changed uniforms again: now he was wearing the polished suit and tie of a modern Indian businessman.

He ordered me to drive towards Ashoka Road; he turned to his companion and said, 'The sister-fucker finally gave me his car.'

The other man grunted. He lowered the window and spat. 'He knows he has to show us some respect now, doesn't he?'

Vijay chortled. He raised his voice. 'Do you have anything to drink in the car, son?'

I turned around: fat nuggets of gold were studded into his rotting black molars.

'Yes, sir.'

'Let's see it.'

I opened the glove compartment and handed him the bottle.

'It's good stuff. Johnnie Walker Black. Son, do you have glasses too?'

'Yes, sir.'

'Ice?'

'No, sir.'

'It's all right. Let's drink it neat. Son, pour us a drink.'

I did so, while keeping the Honda City going with my left hand. They took the glasses and drank the whisky like it was lemon juice.

'If he doesn't have it ready, let me know. I'll send some boys over to have a word with him.'

'No, don't worry. His father always paid up in the end. This kid has been to America and has his head full of shit. But he'll pay up too, in the end.'

'How much?'

'Seven. I was going to settle for five, but the sister-fucker himself offered six – he's a bit soft in the head – and then I said seven, and he said okay. I told him if he didn't pay, we'd screw him and his father and his brother and the whole coal-pilfering and tax-evading racket they have. So he began to sweat, and I know he'll pay up.'

'Are you sure? I'd love to send some boys over. I just love to see a rich man roughed up. It's better than an erection.'

'There will be others. This one isn't worth the trouble. He said he'll bring it on Monday. We're going to do it at the Sheraton. There's a nice restaurant down in the base-ment. Quiet place.'

'Good. He can buy us dinner as well.'

'Goes without saying. They have lovely kebabs there.'

One of the two men gargled the scotch in his mouth, gulped it in, burped, and sucked his teeth.

'You know what the best part of this election is?'

'What?'

'The way we've spread down south. We've got a foothold in Bangalore too. And you know that's where the future is.'

'The south? Bullshit.'

'Why not? One in every three new office buildings in India is being built in Bangalore. It *is* the future.'

'*Fuck* all that. I don't believe a word. The south is full of Tamils. You know who the Tamils are? Negroes. We're the sons of the Aryans who came to India. We made them our slaves. And now they give us lectures. *Negroes*.'

'Son' – Vijay leaned forward with his glass – 'another drink for me.'

I poured them out the rest of the bottle that night.

At around three in the morning, I drove the City back to the apartment block in Gurgaon. My heart was beating so fast, I didn't want to leave the car at once. I wiped it down and washed it three times over. The bottle was lying on the floor of the car. Johnnie Walker Black – even an empty one is worth money on the black market. I picked it up and went towards the servants' dormitory.

For a Johnnie Walker Black, Vitiligo-Lips wouldn't mind being woken up.

I walked rotating the bottle with my wrist, feeling its weight. Even empty, it wasn't so light.

I noticed that my feet were slowing down, and the bottle was rotating faster and faster.

I was looking for the key for years...

The smashing of the bottle echoed through the hollow of the car park – the sound must have reached the lobby and ricocheted through all the floors of the building, even to the thirteenth floor.

I waited for a few minutes, expecting someone to come running down.

No one. I was safe.

I held what was left of the bottle up to the light. Long and cruel and clawlike jags.

Perfect.

With my foot I gathered the broken pieces of the bottle, which lay all around me, into a pile. I wiped the blood off my hand, found a broom, and swept the area clean. Then I got down on my knees and looked around for any pieces I had failed to pick up; the car park echoed with the line of a poem that was being recited over and over:

But the door was always open.

Dharam was sleeping on the floor; cockroaches were crawling about his head. I shook him awake and said, 'Lie inside the mosquito net.' He got in sleepily; I lay on the floor, braving the cockroaches. There was still some blood on my palm: three small red drops had formed on my flesh, like a row of ladybirds on a leaf. Sucking my palm like a boy, I went to sleep.

Mr Ashok did not want me to drive him anywhere on Sunday morning. I washed the dishes in the kitchen, wiped the fridge, and said, 'I'd like to take the morning off, sir.'

'Why?' he asked, lowering the newspaper. 'You've

never asked for a whole morning off before. Where are you off to?'

And you have never before asked me where I was going when I left the house. What has Ms Uma done to you?

'I want to spend some time with the boy, sir. At the zoo. I thought he would like to see all those animals.'

He smiled. 'You're a good family man, Balram. Go, have fun with the boy.' He went back to reading his newspaper – but I caught a gleam of cunning in his eye as he went over the English print of the newspaper.

As we walked out of Buckingham Towers B Block, I told Dharam to wait for me, then went back and watched the entrance to the building. Half an hour passed, and then Mr Ashok was down at the lobby. A small dark man – of the servant class – had come to see him. Mr Ashok and he talked for a while, and then the small man bowed and left. They looked like two men who had just concluded a deal.

I went back to where Dharam was waiting. 'Let's go!'

He and I took the bus to the Old Fort, which is where the National Zoo is. I kept my hand on Dharam's head the whole time – he must have thought it was out of affection, but it was only to stop my hand from trembling – it had been shaking all morning like a lizard's tail that has fallen off.

The first strike would be mine. Everything was in place now, nothing could go wrong – but like I told you, I am not a brave man.

The bus was crowded, and the two of us had to stand for the entire journey. We both sweated like pigs. I had forgotten what a bus trip in summer was like. When we stopped at a red light, a Mercedes-Benz pulled up along-side the bus. Behind his upraised window, cool in his egg, the chauffeur grinned at us, exposing red teeth.

There was a long line at the ticket counter of the zoo. There were lots of families wanting to go into the zoo, and that I could understand. What puzzled me, though, was the sight of so many young men and women going into the zoo, hand in hand: giggling, pinching each other, and making eyes, as if the zoo were a romantic place. That made no sense to me.

Now, Mr Premier, every day thousands of foreigners fly into my country for enlightenment. They go to the Himalayas, or to Benaras, or to Bodh Gaya. They get into weird poses of yoga, smoke hashish, shag a *sadhu* or two, and think they're getting enlightened.

Ha!

If it is enlightenment you have come to India for, you people, forget the Ganga – forget the ashrams – go straight to the National Zoo in the heart of New Delhi.

Dharam and I saw the golden-beaked storks sitting on palm trees in the middle of an artificial lake. They swooped down over the green water of the lake, and showed us traces of pink on their wings. In the background, you could see the broken walls of the Old Fort.

Iqbal, that great poet, was so right. The moment you recognize what is beautiful in this world, you stop being a slave. To hell with the Naxals and their guns shipped from China. If you taught every poor boy how to paint, that would be the end of the rich in India.

I made sure Dharam appreciated the gorgeous rise and fall of the fort's outline – the way its loopholes filled up with blue sky – the way the old stones glittered in the light.

We walked for half an hour, from cage to cage. The lion and the lioness were apart from each other and not talking, like a true city couple. The hippo was lying in a giant pond full of mud; Dharam wanted to do what others were doing – throw a stone at the hippo to stir it up – but I told him that would be a cruel thing. Hippos lie in mud and do nothing – that's their nature.

Let animals live like animals; let humans live like humans. That's my whole philosophy in a sentence.

I told Dharam it was time to leave, but he made faces and pleaded. 'Five minutes, Uncle.'

'All right, five minutes.'

We came to an enclosure with tall bamboo bars, and there – seen in the interstices of the bars, as it paced back and forth in a straight line – was a tiger.

Not *any* kind of tiger.

The creature that gets born only once every generation in the jungle.

I watched him walk behind the bamboo bars. Black stripes and sunlit white fur flashed through the slits in the dark bamboo; it was like watching the slowed-down reels of an old black-and-white film. He was walking in the same line, again and again – from one end of the bamboo bars to the other, then turning around and re-peating it over, at exactly the same pace, like a thing under a spell.

He was hypnotizing himself by walking like this – that was the only way he could tolerate this cage.

Then the thing behind the bamboo bars stopped

moving. It turned its face to my face. The tiger's eyes met my eyes, like my master's eyes have met mine so often in the mirror of the car.

All at once, the tiger vanished.

A tingling went from the base of my spine into my groin. My knees began to shake; I felt light. Someone near me shrieked. 'His eyes are rolling! He's going to faint!' I tried to shout back at her, 'It's *not* true: I'm *not* fainting!' I tried to show them all I was fine, but my feet were slipping. The ground beneath me was shaking. Something was digging its way towards me: and then claws tore out of mud and dug into my flesh and pulled me down into the dark earth.

My last thought, before everything went dark, was that *now* I understood those pinches and raptures – *now* I understood why lovers come to the zoo.

That evening, Dharam and I sat on the floor in my room, and I spread a blue letter before him. I put a pen in his hands.

'I'm going to see how good a letter-writer you are, Dharam. I want you to write to Granny and tell her what happened today at the zoo.'

He wrote it down in his slow, beautiful hand. He told her about the hippos, and the chimpanzees, and the swamp deer.

'Tell her about the tiger.'

He hesitated, then wrote: *We saw a white tiger in a cage.*

'Tell her *everything*.'

He looked at me, and wrote: *Uncle Balram fainted in front of the white tiger in the cage.*

'Better still – I'll dictate; write it down.'

He wrote it all down for ten minutes, writing so fast that his pen got black and oozy with overflowing ink – he stopped to wipe the nib against his hair, and went back to the writing. In the end he read out what he had written:

I called out to the people around me, and we carried Uncle to a banyan tree. Someone poured water on his face. The good people slapped Uncle hard and made him wake up. They turned to me and said, 'Your uncle is raving – he's saying goodbye to his grandmother. He must think he's going to die.' Uncle's eyes were open now. 'Are you all right, Uncle?' I asked. He took my hand and he said, 'I'm sorry, I'm sorry, I'm sorry.' I asked, 'Sorry for what?' And he said, 'I can't live the rest of my life in a cage, Granny. I'm so sorry.' We took the bus back to Gurgaon and had lunch at the tea shop. It was very hot, and we sweated a lot. And that was all that happened today.

'Write whatever you want after that to her, and post it tomorrow, as soon as I leave in the car – but not before. Understand?'

*

It was raining all morning, a light, persistent kind of rain. I heard the rain, though I could not see it. I went to the Honda City, placed the incense stick inside, wiped the seats, wiped the stickers, and punched the ogre in the mouth. I threw a bundle near the driver's seat. I shut all the doors and locked them.

Then, taking two steps back from the Honda City, I bowed low to it with folded palms.

I went to see what Dharam was doing. He was looking lonely, so I made a paper boat for him, and we sailed it in the gutter outside the apartment block.

After lunch, I called Dharam into my room.

I put my hands on his shoulders; slowly I turned him around so he faced away from me. I dropped a rupee coin on the ground.

'Bend down and pick that up.'

He did so, and I watched. Dharam combed his hair just like Mr Ashok did – with a parting down the middle; when you stood up over him, there was a clear white line down his scalp, leading up to the spot on the crown where the strands of a man's hairline radiate from.

'Stand up straight.'

I turned him around a full circle. I dropped the rupee again.

'Pick it up one more time.'

I watched the spot.

Telling him to sit in a corner of the room and keep watch over me, I went inside my mosquito net, folded my legs, closed my eyes, touched my palms to my knees, and breathed in.

I don't know how long I sat like the Buddha, but it lasted until one of the servants shouted out that I was wanted at the front door. I opened my eyes – Dharam was sitting in a corner of the room, watching me.

'Come here,' I said – I gave him a hug, and put ten rupees into his pocket. He'd need that.

'Balram, you're late! The bell is ringing like crazy!'

I walked to the car, inserted the key, and turned the engine on. Mr Ashok was standing at the entrance with an umbrella and a mobile phone. He was talking on the phone as he got into the car and slammed the door.

'I still can't believe it. The people of this country had a chance to put an efficient ruling party back in power, and instead they have voted in the most outrageous bunch of thugs. We don't deserve—' He put the phone aside for a moment and said, 'First to the city, Balram – I'll tell you where' – and then resumed the phone talk.

The roads were greasy with mud and water. I drove slowly.

'...parliamentary democracy, Father. We will never catch up with China for this single reason.'

First stop was in the city – at one of the usual banks. He took the red bag and went in, and I saw him inside the glass booth, pressing the buttons of the cash machine. When he came back, I could feel that the weight of the bag on the backseat had increased. We went from bank to bank, and the weight of the red bag grew. I felt its pressure increase on my lower back – as if I were taking Mr Ashok and his bag not in a car, but the way my father would take a customer and his bag – in a rickshaw.

Seven hundred thousand rupees.

It was enough for a house. A motorbike. And a small shop. A new life.

My seven hundred thousand rupees.

'Now to the Sheraton, Balram.'

'Yes, sir.'

I turned the key – started the car, changed gear. We moved.

'Play some Sting, Balram. Not too loud.'

'Yes, sir.'

I put the CD on. The voice of Sting came on. The car picked up speed. In a little while, we passed the famous bronze statue of Gandhi leading his followers from darkness to the light.

Now the road emptied. The rain was coming down lightly. If we kept going this way, we would come to the hotel – the grandest of all in the capital of my country, the place where visiting heads of state, like yourself, always stay. But Delhi is a city where civilization can appear and disappear within five minutes. On either side of us right now there was just wilderness and rubbish.

In the rearview mirror I saw him paying attention to nothing but his mobile phone. A blue glow from the phone lit up his face. Without looking up, he asked me, 'What's wrong, Balram? Why has the car stopped?'

I touched the magnetic stickers of the goddess Kali for luck, then opened the glove compartment. There it was – the broken bottle, with its claws of glass.

'There's something off with the wheel, sir. Just give me a couple of minutes.'

Before I could even touch it, I swear, the door of the car opened. I was out in the drizzle.

There was soggy black mud everywhere. Picking my way over mud and rainwater, I squatted near the left rear wheel, which was hidden from the road by the body of the car. There was a large clump of bushes to one side – and a stretch of wasteland beyond.

You've never seen the road this empty. You'd swear it's been arranged just for you.

The only light inside the car was the blue glow from his mobile phone. I rapped against his glass with a finger. He turned to me without lowering the window.

I mouthed out the words, 'There's a problem, sir.'

He did not lower the window; he did not step out. He was playing with his mobile phone: punching the buttons and grinning. He must be sending a message to Ms Uma.

Pressed to the wet glass, my lips made a grin.

He released the phone. I made a fist and thumped on his glass. He lowered the window with a look of displeasure. Sting's soft voice came through the window.

'What is it, Balram?'

'Sir, will you step out, there is a problem.'

'What problem?'

His body just wouldn't budge! It knew – the body knew – though the mind was too stupid to figure it out.

'The wheel, sir. I'll need your help. It's stuck in the mud.'

Just then headlights flashed on me: a car was coming down the road. My heart skipped a beat. But it just drove right past us, splashing muddy water at my feet.

He put a hand on the door and was about to step out, but some instinct of self-preservation still held him back.

'It's raining, Balram. Do you think we should call for help?'

He wriggled and moved away from the door.

'Oh, no, sir. Trust me. Come out.'

He was still wriggling – his body was moving as far from me as it could. *I'm losing him*, I thought, and this forced me to do something I knew I would hate myself for, even years later. I *really* didn't want to do this – I *really* didn't want him to think, even in the two or three minutes he had left to live, that I was *that* kind of driver – the one that resorts to blackmailing his master – but he had left me no option:

'It's been giving problems ever since that night we went to the hotel in Jangpura.'

He looked up from the mobile phone at once.

'The one with the big T sign on it. You remember it, don't you, sir? Ever since that night, sir, nothing has been the same with this car.'

His lips parted, then closed. He's thinking: *Blackmail?* Or an innocent reference to the past? Don't give him time to settle.

'Come out of the car, sir. Trust me.'

Putting the mobile on the seat, he obeyed me. The blue light of the mobile phone filled the inside of the dark car for a second – then went out.

He opened the door farthest from me and got out near the road. I got down on my knees and hid behind the car.

'Come over this side, sir. The bad tyre is on this side.'

He came, picking his way through the mud.

'It's *this* one, sir – and be careful, there's a broken bottle lying on the ground.' There was so much garbage by the roadside that it lay there looking perfectly natural.

'Here, let me throw it away. *This* is the tyre, sir. Please take a look.'

He got down on his knees. I rose up over him, holding the bottle held behind my back with a bent arm.

Down below me, his head was just a black ball – and in the blackness, I saw a thin white line of scalp between the neatly parted hair, leading like a painted line on a highway to the spot on the crown of his skull – the spot from which a man's hair radiates out.

The black ball moved; grimacing to protect his eyes against the drizzle, he looked up at me.

'It seems fine.'

I stood still, like a schoolboy caught out by his teacher. I thought: *That landlord's brain of his has figured it out. He's going to stand up and hit me in the face.*

But what is the use of winning a battle when you don't even *know* that there is a war going on?

'Well, you know more about this car than I do, Balram. Let me take another look.'

And he peered again at the tyre. The black highway appeared before me once more, with the white paint marks leading to the crown spot.

'There *is* a problem, sir. You should have got a replacement a long time ago.'

'All right, Balram.' He touched the tyre. 'But I really think we—'

I rammed the bottle down. The glass ate his bone. I rammed it three times into the crown of his skull, smashing through to his brains. It's a good, strong bottle, Johnnie Walker Black – well worth its resale value.

The stunned body fell into the mud. A hissing sound came out of its lips, like wind escaping from a tyre.

I fell to the ground – my hand was trembling, the bottle slipped out, and I had to pick it up with my left hand. The thing with the hissing lips got up onto its hands and knees; it began crawling around in a circle, as if looking for someone who was meant to protect it.

Why didn't I gag him and leave him in the bushes,

stunned and unconscious, where he wouldn't be able to do a thing for hours, while I escaped? Good question – and I've thought about it many a night, as I sit at my desk, looking at the chandelier.

The first possible reply is that he could always recover, break out of his gag, and call the police. So I had to kill him.

The second possible reply is that his family was going to do such terrible things to my family: I was just getting my revenge in advance.

I like the second reply better.

Putting my foot on the back of the crawling thing, I flattened it to the ground. Down on my knees I went, to be at the right height for what would come next. I turned the body around, so it would face me. I stamped my knee on its chest. I undid the collar button and rubbed my hand over its clavicles to mark out the spot.

When I was a boy in Laxmangarh, and I used to play with my father's body, the junction of the neck and the chest, the place where all the tendons and veins stick out in high relief, was my favourite spot. When I touched this spot, the pit of my father's neck, I controlled him – I could make him stop breathing with the pressure of a finger.

The Stork's son opened his eyes – just as I pierced his neck – and his lifeblood spurted into my eyes.

I was blind. I was a free man.

When I got the blood out of my eyes, it was all over for Mr Ashok. The blood was draining from the neck quite fast – I believe that is the way the Muslims kill their chickens.

But then tuberculosis is a worse way to go than this, I assure you.

After dragging the body into the bushes, I plunged my hands and face into the rainwater and muck. I picked up the bundle near my feet – the white cotton T-shirt, the one with lots of white space and just one word in English – and changed into it. Reaching for the gilded box of tissues, I wiped my face and hands clean. I pulled out all the stickers of the goddess, and threw them on Mr Ashok's body – just in case they'd help his soul go to heaven.

And then, getting into the car, turning the ignition key, putting my foot on the accelerator, I took the Honda City, finest of cars, most faithful of accomplices, on one final trip. Since there was no one else in the car, my left hand reached out to turn Sting off – then stopped and relaxed.

From now on I could play the music as long as I wanted.

In the railway station, thirty-three minutes later, the coloured wheels in the fortune machines were coruscat-ing. I stood in front of them, staring at the glowing and the whirling, and wondering, *Should I go back to get Dharam?*

If I left him there now, the police would certainly arrest him as an accomplice. They would throw him into jail with a bunch of wild men – and you know what happens to little boys when they get put into dens like that, sir.

On the other hand, if I went back now all the way to Gurgaon, someone might discover the body... and then all this (I tightened my grip on the bag) would have been a waste.

I squatted on the floor of the station, pressed down by indecision. There was a squealing noise to my left. A plastic bucket was tumbling about, as if it were alive: then a grinning black face popped out of the bucket. A little creature, a baby boy. A homeless man and woman, covered in filth, sat on either side of the bucket, gazing blankly into the distance. Between his fatigued parents, this little thing was having the time of his life, playing with the water and splashing it on passers-by. 'Don't do it, little boy,' I said. He splashed more water, squealing with pleasure each time he hit me. I raised my hand. He ducked into his bucket and kept thrashing from the inside.

I reached into my pockets, searched for a rupee coin, checked to make sure it wasn't a two-rupee coin, and rolled it towards the bucket.

Then I sighed, and got up, and cursed myself, and walked out of the station.

Your lucky day, Dharam.

The Seventh Night

Can you hear that, Mr Jiabao? I'll turn it up for you.

The health minister today announced a plan to elimi-nate malaria in Bangalore by the end of the year. He has instructed all city officials to work without holiday until malaria is a thing of the past. Forty-five million rupees will be allocated to malaria eradication.

In other news, the chief minister of the state today announced a plan to eliminate malnutrition in Bangalore in six months. He declared that there would be not one hungry child in the city by the end of the year. All officials are to work single-mindedly towards this goal, he declared. Five hundred million rupees will be allocated for malnutrition eradication.

In other news, the finance minister declared that this year's budget will include special incentives to turn our villages into high-technology paradises...

This is the kind of news they feed us on All India Radio, night after night: and tomorrow at dawn it'll be in the papers too. People just swallow this crap. Night after night, morning after morning. Amazing, isn't it?

But enough of the radio. It's turned off. Now let me look up to my chandelier for inspiration.

Wen!

Old friend!

Tonight we bring this glorious tale to a conclusion. As I was doing my yoga this morning – that's right, I wake up at eleven in the morning every day and go straight into an hour of yoga – I began reflecting on the progress of my story, and realized that I'm almost done. All that remains to be told is how I changed from a hunted criminal into a solid pillar of Bangalorean society.

Incidentally, sir, while we're on the topic of yoga – may I just say that an hour of deep breathing, yoga, and meditation in the morning constitutes the perfect start to the entrepreneur's day. How I would handle the stresses of this fucking business without yoga, I have no idea. Make yoga a must in all Chinese schools – that's my suggestion.

But back to the story, now.

First, I want to explain one thing about a fugitive's life. Being a man on the run isn't all about fear – a fugitive is entitled to his share of fun too.

That evening as I was sweeping up the pieces of the Johnnie Walker bottle in the car park, I worked out a plan for how I would get to Bangalore. It wouldn't be on a direct train – no. Someone might see me, and then the police would know where I had gone. Instead, I would transfer myself from train to train, zigzagging my way down to Bangalore.

Although my schedule was shot to pieces when I went to get Dharam – he was sleeping in the net, and I woke him up and said we were going on a holiday to the South, and dragged him out – and it was hard to keep my red bag in one hand and Dharam in the other hand (for the train station is a dangerous place for a little boy, you know – lots of shady characters around), still I began to move in this zigzag way south from Delhi.

On the third day of travelling like this, red bag in hand, I was at Hyderabad, waiting in line at the station tea shop to buy a cup of tea before my train left. (Dharam was guarding the seat in the compartment.) There was a gecko just above the tea shop, and I was looking at it with concern, hoping it would move before it was my turn to get tea.

The gecko turned to the left – it ran over a large piece of paper posted on the wall – it stood still for a moment, like that, then darted to the side.

That large piece of paper on the wall was a police poster – my police poster. It had already arrived here. I looked at it with a smile of pride.

A smile that lasted just a second. For some bizarre reason – you'll see how sloppily things get done in India – my poster had been stapled to another poster, of two guys from Kashmir – two terrorists wanted for bombing something or other.

You'd almost think, looking at the posters, that I was a terrorist too. How annoying.

I realized that I was being watched. A fellow with his hands behind his back was looking at the poster, and at me, most intently. I began to tremble. I edged away from the poster, but I was too late. The moment he saw me leaving, he ran up to me, caught my wrist, and stared at my face.

Then he said, 'What's it say? That poster you're reading?'

'Read it for yourself.'

'Can't.'

Now I understood why he had come running. It was the desperation of an illiterate man to get the attention of the literate man. From his accent I knew he was from the Darkness too.

'It's the wanted-men list for this week,' I said. 'Those two are terrorists. From Kashmir.'

'What did they do?'

'They blew up a school. They killed eight children.'

'And this fellow? The one with the moustache?' He tapped my photo with a knuckle of his right hand.

'He's the guy who caught them.'

'How did he do that?'

To create the illusion I was reading the printing on the wall, I squinted at the two posters, and moved my lips.

'This fellow was a driver. Says here he was in his car, and these two terrorist guys came up to him.'

'Then?'

'Says he pretended he didn't know they were terrorists, and took them for a ride around Delhi in his car. Then he stopped the car in a dark spot, and smashed a bottle and cut their necks with it.' I slashed two necks with my thumb.

'What kind of bottle?'

'An English liquor bottle. They tend to be pretty solid.'

'I know,' he said. 'I used to go to the English liquor shop for my master every Friday. He liked Smir-fone.'

'Smir-noff,' I said, but he wasn't listening. He was peering again at the photo in the poster.

Suddenly he put his hand on my shoulder.

'You know who this fellow in the poster looks like?'

'Who?' I asked.

He grinned.

'Me.'

I looked at his face, and at the photo.

'It's true,' I said, slapping him on the back.

I *told* you: it could be the face of half the men in India.

And then, because I felt sorry for that poor illiterate, thinking he had just endured what my father must have endured at so many railway stations – being mocked and hoodwinked by strangers – I bought him a cup of tea, before going back to the train.

*

Sir:

I am not a politician or a parliamentarian. Not one of those extraordinary men who can kill and move on, as if nothing had happened. It took me four weeks in Bangalore to calm my nerves.

For those four weeks I did the same thing again and again. I left the hotel – a small, seedy place near the train station that I had taken after leaving a deposit of five hundred rupees – every morning at eight and walked around with a bag full of cash in my hands for four hours (I dared not leave it in the hotel room) before returning for lunch.

Dharam and I ate together. What he did to keep himself amused in the mornings I don't know, but he was in good spirits. This was the first holiday he had had in his whole life. His smiles cheered me up.

Lunch was four rupees a plate. The food is good value

in the south. It is strange food, though, vegetables cut up and served in watery curries. Then I went up to my room and slept. At four o'clock I came down and ordered a pack of Parle Milk biscuits and a tea, because I did not know yet how to drink the coffee.

I was eager to try coffee. You see, poor people in the north of this country drink tea, and poor people in the south drink coffee. Who decided that things should be like this, I don't know, but it's like this. So this was the first time I was smelling coffee on a daily basis. I was dying to try it out. But before you could drink it, you had to know *how* to drink it. There was an etiquette, a routine, associated with it that fascinated me. It was served in a cup set into a tumbler, and then it had to be poured in certain quantities and sipped at a certain speed from the tumbler. How the pouring was to be done, how the sipping was to be done, I did not know. For a while I only watched.

It took me a week to realize that everyone was doing it differently. One man poured all the coffee into his tumbler at once; another never used the tumbler at all.

They're all strangers here, I said to myself. *They're all drinking coffee for the first time.*

That was another of the attractions of Bangalore. The city was full of outsiders. No one would notice one more.

I spent four weeks in that hotel near the railway station, doing nothing. I admit there were doubts in my mind. Should I have gone to Mumbai instead? But the police would have thought of that at once – everyone goes to Mumbai in the films after they kill someone, don't they?

Calcutta! I should have gone *there*.

One morning Dharam said, 'Uncle, you look so depressed. Let's go for a walk.' We walked through a park where drunken men lay on benches amid wild overgrown weeds. We came out onto a broad road; on the other side of the road stood a huge stone building with a golden lion on top of it.

'What is this building, Uncle?'

'I don't know, Dharam. It must be where the ministers live in Bangalore.'

On the gable of the building I saw a slogan:

GOVERNMENT WORK IS GOD'S WORK

'You're smiling, Uncle.'

'You're right, Dharam. I *am* smiling. I think we'll have a good time in Bangalore,' I said and I winked at him.

I moved out of the hotel and took a flat on rent. Now I had to make a living in Bangalore – I had to find out how I could fit into this city.

I tried to hear Bangalore's voice, just as I had heard Delhi's.

I went down M.G. Road and sat down at the Café Coffee Day, the one with the outdoor tables. I had a pen and a piece of paper with me, and I wrote down everything I overheard.

I completed that computer program in two and a half minutes.

An American today offered me four hundred thousand dollars for my start-up and I told him, 'That's not enough!'

Is Hewlett-Packard a better company than IBM?

Everything in the city, it seemed, came down to one thing.

Outsourcing. Which meant doing things in India for Americans over the phone. Everything flowed from it – real estate, wealth, power, sex. So I would have to join this outsourcing thing, one way or the other.

The next day I took an autorickshaw up to Electronics City. I found a banyan tree by the side of a road, and I sat down under it. I sat and watched the buildings until it was evening and I saw all the SUVs racing in; and then I watched until two in the morning, when the SUVs began racing out of the buildings.

And I thought, *That's it. That's how I fit in.*

Let me explain, Your Excellency. See, men and women in Bangalore live like the animals in a forest do. Sleep in the day and then work all night, until two, three, four, five o'clock, depending, because their masters are on the other side of the world, in America. Big question: how will the boys and girls – girls especially – get from home to the workplace in the late evening and then get back home at three in the morning? There is no night bus system in Bangalore, no train system like in Mumbai. The girls would not be safe on buses or trains anyway. The men of this city, frankly speaking, are animals.

That's where entrepreneurs come in.

The next thing I did was to go to a Toyota Qualis dealer in the city and say, in my sweetest voice, 'I want to drive your cars.' The dealer looked at me, puzzled.

I couldn't believe I had said that. Once a servant, always a servant: the instinct is always there, inside you, somewhere near the base of your spine. (If you ever came to my office, Mr Premier, I would probably try to press you feet at once!)

I pinched my left palm. I smiled as I held it pinched and said – in a deep, gruff voice, 'I want to *rent* your cars.'

*

The last stage in my amazing success story, sir, was to go from being a social entrepreneur to a business entrepreneur. This part wasn't easy at all.

I called them all up, one after the other, the officers of all the outsourcing companies in Bangalore. Did they need a taxi service to pick up their employees in the evening? Did they need a taxi service to drop off their employees late at night?

And you know what they all said, of course.

One woman was kind enough to explain:

'You're too late. Every business in Bangalore already has a taxi service to pick up and drop off their employees at night. I'm sorry to tell you this.'

It was just like starting out in Dhanbad – I got depressed. I lay in bed a whole day.

What would Mr Ashok do? I wondered.

Then it hit me. I wasn't alone – I had someone on my side! I had thousands on my side!

You'll see my friends when you visit Bangalore – fat, paunchy men swinging their canes, on Brigade Road, poking and harassing vendors and shaking them down for money.

I'm talking of the police, of course.

The next day I paid a local to be a translator – you

know, I'm sure, that the people of the north and the south in my country speak different languages – and went to the nearest police station. In my hand I had the red bag. I acted like an important man, and made sure the policemen saw the red bag by swinging it a lot, and gave them a business card I had just had printed. Then I insisted on seeing the big man there, the inspector. At last they let me into his office – the red bag had done the trick.

The big man sat at a huge desk, with shiny badges on his khaki uniform and the red marks of religion on his forehead. Behind him were three portraits of gods. But not the one I was looking for.

Oh, thank God. There was one of Gandhi too. It was in the corner.

With a big smile – and a *namaste* – I handed him the red bag. He opened it cautiously.

I said, via the translator, 'Sir, I want to make a small offering of my gratitude to you.'

It's amazing. The moment you show cash, *everyone* knows your language.

'Gratitude for what?' the inspector asked in Hindi, peering into the bag with one eye closed.

'For all the good you are going to do me, sir.'

He counted the money – ten thousand rupees – heard what I wanted, and asked for double. I gave him a bit more, and he was happy. I tell you, Mr Premier, my poster was right there, the one that I had seen earlier, the whole time I was negotiating with him. The WANTED poster, with the dirty little photo of me.

Two days later, I called up the nice woman at the

Internet company who had turned me down, and heard a shocking tale. Her taxi service had been disrupted. A police raid had discovered that most of the drivers did not have licences.

'I'm so sorry, madam,' I said. 'I offer you my sympathies. In addition, I offer you my company. White Tiger Drivers.'

'Do all your drivers have licences?'

'Of course, madam. You can call the police and check.'

She did just that, and called me back. I think the police must have put in a good word for me. And that was how I got my own – as they say in English – 'start-up.'

I was one of the drivers in the early days, but then I gave up. I don't really think I ever enjoyed driving, you know? Talking is much more fun. Now the start-up has grown into a big business. We've got sixteen drivers who work in shifts with twenty-six vehicles. Yes, it's true: a few hundred thousand rupees of someone else's money, and a lot of hard work, can make magic happen in this country. Put together my real estate and my bank holdings, and I am worth fifteen times the sum I borrowed from Mr Ashok. See for yourself at my website. See my motto: 'We Drive Technology Forward.' In *English!* See the photos of my fleet: twenty-six shining new Toyota Qualises, all fully air-conditioned for the summer months, all contracted out to famous technology companies. If you like my SUVs, if you want your call-centre boys and girls driven home in style, just click where it says:

CONTACT ASHOK SHARMA NOW!

Yes, Ashok! That's what I call myself these days. Ashok Sharma, North Indian entrepreneur, settled in Bangalore.

If you were sitting here with me, under this big chandelier, I would show you all the secrets of my business. You could stare at the screen of my silver Macintosh laptop and see photos of my SUVs, my drivers, my garages, my mechanics, and my paid-off policemen.

All of them belong to me – Munna, whose destiny was to be a sweet-maker!

You'll see photos of my boys too. All sixteen of them. Once I was a driver to a master, but now I am a master of drivers. I don't treat them like servants – I don't slap, or bully, or mock anyone. I don't insult any of them by calling them my 'family', either. They're my employees, I'm their boss, that's all. I make them sign a contract and I sign it too, and both of us must honour that contract. That's all. If they notice the way I talk, the way I dress, the way I keep things clean, they'll go up in life. If they don't, they'll be drivers all their lives. I leave the choice up to them. When the work is done I kick them out of the office: no chitchat, no cups of coffee. A White Tiger keeps no friends. It's too dangerous.

Now, despite my amazing success story, I don't want to lose contact with the places where I got my real education in life.

The road and the pavement.

I walk about Bangalore in the evenings, or in the early mornings, just to listen to the road.

One evening when I was near the train station, I saw a dozen or so manual labourers gathered together in front of a wall and talking in low tones. They were speaking in a strange language; they were the locals of the place. I didn't have to understand their words to know what they were saying. In a city where so many had streamed in from outside, they were the ones left behind.

They were reading something on that wall. I wanted to see what it was, but they stopped their talking and crowded in front of the wall. I had to threaten to call the police before they parted and let me see what they had been reading.

It was a stencilled image of a pair of hands smashing its manacles:

THE GREAT SOCIALIST IS COMING TO BANGALORE

In a couple of weeks he arrived. He had a big rally here and gave a terrific speech, all about fire and blood and purging this country of the rich because there was going to be no fresh water for the poor in ten years because the world was getting hotter. I stood at the back and listened. At the end people clapped like crazy. There is a lot of anger in this town, that's for sure.

Keep yours ears open in Bangalore – in any city or town in India – and you will hear stirrings, rumours, threats of insurrection. Men sit under lampposts at night and read. Men huddle together and discuss and point fingers to the heavens. One night, will they all join together – will they destroy the Rooster Coop?

Ha!

Maybe once in a hundred years there is a revolution that frees the poor. I read this in one of those old text-book pages people in tea stalls use to wrap greasy samosas with. See, only four men in history have led successful revolutions to free the slaves and kill their masters, this page said:

Alexander the Great.
Abraham Lincoln of America.
Mao of your country.

And a fourth man. It may have been Hitler, I can't remember. But I don't think a fifth name is getting added to the list anytime soon.

An Indian revolution?

No, sir. It won't happen. People in this country are still waiting for the war of their freedom to come from somewhere else – from the jungles, from the mountains, from China, from Pakistan. That will never happen. Every man must make his own Benaras.

The book of your revolution sits in the pit of your belly, young Indian. Crap it out, and read.

Instead of which, they're all sitting in front of colour TVs and watching cricket and shampoo advertisements.

On the topic of shampoo advertisements, Mr Premier, I must say that golden-coloured hair sickens me now. I don't think it's healthy for a woman to have that colour of hair. I don't trust the TV or the big outdoor posters of white women that you see all over Bangalore. I go from my own experience now, from the time I spend in five-star hotels. (That's right, Mr Jiabao: I don't go to 'red light districts' any more. It's not right to buy and sell women who live in birdcages and get treated like animals. I only buy girls I find in five-star hotels.)

Based on my experience, Indian girls are the best.

(Well, *second*-best. I tell you, Mr Jiabao, it's one of the most thrilling sights you can have as a man in Bangalore, to see the eyes of a pair of Nepali girls flashing out at you from the dark hood of an autorickshaw.)

In fact, the sight of these golden-haired foreigners – and you'll discover that Bangalore is full of them these days – has only convinced me that the white people are on the way out. All of them look so emaciated – so puny. You'll never see one of them with a decent belly. For this I blame the president of America; he has made buggery perfectly legal in his country, and men are marrying other men instead of women. This was on the radio. This is leading to the decline of the white man. Then white people use mobile phones too much, and that is destroying their brains. It's a known fact. Mobile phones cause cancer in the brain and shrink your masculinity; the Japanese invented them to diminish the white man's brain and balls at the same time. I overheard this at the bus stand one night. Until then I had been very proud of my Nokia, showing it to all the call-centre girls I was hoping to dip my beak into, but I threw it away at once. Every call that you make to me, you have to make it on a landline. It hurts my business, but my brain is too important, sir: it's all that a thinking man has in this world.

White men will be finished within my lifetime. There are blacks and reds too, but I have no idea what they're up to – the radio never talks about them. My humble prediction: in twenty years' time, it will be just us yellow men and brown men at the top of the pyramid, and we'll rule the whole world.

And God save everyone else.

Now I should explain about that long interruption in my narrative two nights ago.

It will also allow me to illustrate the differences between Bangalore and Laxmangarh. Understand, Mr Jiabao, it is not as if you come to Bangalore and find that everyone is moral and upright here. This city has its share of thugs and politicians. It's just that here, if a man wants to be good, he *can* be good. In Laxmangarh, he doesn't even have this choice. That is the difference between this India and that India: the *choice*.

See, that night, I was sitting here, telling you my life's story, when my landline began to ring. Still chatting to you, I picked up the receiver and heard Mohammad Asif's voice.

'Sir, there's been some trouble.'

That's when I stopped talking to you.

'What kind of trouble?' I asked. I knew Mohammad Asif had been on duty that night, so I braced myself for the worst.

There was a silence, and then he said, 'I was taking the girls home when we hit a boy on a bicycle. He's dead, sir.'

'Call the police at once,' I said.

'But sir – I am at fault. I hit him, sir.'

'That's exactly why you will call the police.'

The police were there when I got to the scene with an empty van. The Qualis was parked by the side of the road; the girls were all still inside.

There was a body, a boy, lying on the ground, bloodied.

The bike was on the ground, smashed and twisted.

Mohammad Asif was standing off to the side, shaking his head. Someone was yelling at him – yelling with the passion that you only see on the face of the relative of a dead man.

The policeman on the scene had stalled everyone. He nodded when he saw me. We knew each other well by now.

'That's the dead boy's brother, sir,' he whispered to me. 'He's in a total rage. I haven't been able to get him out of here.'

I shook Mohammad Asif out of his trance. 'Take my car and get these women home, first of all.'

'Let my boy go,' I told the policeman loudly. 'He's got to get the people in there home. Whatever you want to deal with, you deal with me.'

'How can you let him go?' the brother of the dead boy yelled at the policeman.

'Look here, son,' I said, 'I am the owner of this vehicle. Your fight is with me, not with this driver. He was following my orders, to drive as fast as he could. The blood is on my hands, not his. These girls need to go home. Come with me to the police station – I offer myself as your ransom. Let them go.'

The policeman played along with me. 'It's a good idea, son. We need to register the case at the station.'

While I kept the brother engaged by pleading to his reason and human decency, Mohammad Asif and all the girls got into my van and slipped away. That was the first objective – to get the girls home. I have signed a contract with their company, and I honour all that I sign.

I went to the police station with the dead boy's brother. The policemen on night duty brought me coffee. They did not bring the boy coffee. He glared at me as I took the cup; he looked ready to tear me to pieces. I sipped.

'The assistant commissioner will be here in five minutes,' one of the policemen said.

'Is he the one who's going to register the case?' the brother asked. 'Because no one has done it so far.'

I sipped some more.

The assistant commissioner who sat in the station was a man whom I had lubricated often. He had fixed a rival for me once. He was the worst kind of man, who had nothing in his mind but taking money from everyone who came to his office. Scum.

But he was *my* scum.

My heart lifted at the sight of him. He had come all the way to the station at night to help me out. There is honesty among thieves, as they say. He understood the situation immediately. Ignoring me, he went up to the brother and said, 'What is it you want?'

'I want to file an F.I.R.,' the brother said. 'I want this crime recorded.'

'What crime?'

'The death of my brother. By this man's' – pointing a finger at me – 'vehicle.'

The assistant commissioner looked at his watch. 'My God, it's late. It's almost five o'clock. Why don't you go home now? We'll forget you were here. We'll *let* you go home.'

'What about this man? Will you lock him up first?'

The assistant commissioner put his fingers together.

He sighed. 'See, at the time of the accident, your brother's bicycle had no working lights. That is illegal, you know. There are other things that will come out. I promise you, things will come out.'

The boy stared. He shook his head, as if he hadn't heard correctly. 'My brother is dead. This man is a killer. I don't understand what's going on here.'

'Look here – go home. Have a bath. Pray to God. Sleep. Come back in the morning. We'll file the F.I.R. then, all right?'

The brother understood at last why I had brought him to the station – he understood at last that the trap had shut on him. Maybe he had only seen policemen in Hindi movies until now.

Poor boy.

'This is an outrage! I'll call the papers! I'll call the lawyers! I'll call the police!'

The assistant commissioner, who was not a man given to humour, allowed himself a little smile. 'Sure. Call the police.'

The brother stormed out, shouting more threats.

'The number plates will be changed tomorrow,' the assistant commissioner said. 'We'll say it was a hit-and-run. Another car will be substituted. We keep battered cars for this purpose here. You're very lucky that your Qualis hit a man on a bicycle.'

I nodded.

A man on a bicycle getting killed – the police don't even have to register the case. A man on a motorbike getting killed – they would *have* to register that. A man in a *car* getting killed – they would have thrown me in jail.

'What if he goes to the papers?'

The assistant commissioner slapped his belly. 'I've got every pressman in this town in here.'

I did not hand him an envelope at once. There is a time and a place for these things. Now was the time to smile, and say thanks, and sip the hot coffee he had offered me; now was the time to chat with him about his sons – they're both studying in America, he wants them to come back and start an Internet company in Bangalore – and nod and smile and show him my clean, shining, fluoridated teeth. We sipped cup after cup of steaming coffee under a calendar that had the face of the goddess Lakshmi on it – she was showering gold coins from a pot into the river of prosperity. Above her was a framed portrait of the god of gods, a grinning Mahatma Gandhi.

A week from now I'll go to see him again with an envelope, and then he won't be so nice. He'll count the money in front of me and say, *This is all? Do you know how much it costs to keep two sons studying in a foreign college? You should see the American Express bills they send me every month!* And he'll ask for another envelope. Then another, then another, and so on. There is no end to things in India, Mr Jiabao, as Mr Ashok so correctly used to say. You'll have to keep paying and paying the fuckers. But I complain about the police the way the rich complain; not the way the poor complain.

The difference is everything.

The next day, sir, I called Mohammad Asif to the office. He was burning with shame over what he had done – I didn't need to reproach him.

And it was not his fault. Not mine either. Our outsourcing companies are so cheap that they force their taxi operators to promise them an impossible number of runs every night. To meet such schedules, we have to drive recklessly; we have to keep hitting and hurting people on the roads. It's a problem every taxi operator in this city faces. Don't blame *me*.

'Don't worry about it, Asif,' I said. The boy looked so devastated.

I've come to respect Muslims, sir. They're not the brightest lot, except for those four poet fellows, but they make good drivers, and they're honest people, by and large, although a few of them seem to get this urge to blow trains up every year. I wasn't going to fire Asif over this.

But I did ask him to find out the address of the boy, the one we had killed.

He stared at me.

'Why go, sir? We don't have to fear anything from the parents. Please don't do this.'

I made him find the address and I made him give it to me.

I took cash out of my locker in crisp new one-hundred-rupee notes; I put them in a brown envelope. I got into a car and drove myself to the place.

The mother was the one who opened the door. She asked me what I wanted, and I said, 'I am the owner of the taxi company.'

I didn't have to tell her which one.

She brought me a cup of coffee in a cup set in a metal tumbler. They have exquisite manners, these South Indians.

I poured the coffee into the tumbler, and sipped the correct way.

There was a photo of a young man, with a large jasmine garland around it, up on the wall.

I said nothing until I finished the coffee. Then I put the brown envelope on the table.

An old man had come into the room now, and he stood staring at me.

'First of all, I want to express my deep sorrow at the death of your son. Having lost relatives myself – so many of them – I know the pain that you have suffered. He should not have died.'

'Second, the fault is mine. Not the driver's. The police have let me off. That is the way of this jungle we live in. But I accept my responsibility. I ask for your forgiveness.'

I pointed to the brown envelope lying on the table.

'There are twenty-five thousand rupees in here. I don't give it to you because I have to, but because I want to. Do you understand?'

The old woman would not take the money.

But the old man, the father, was eyeing the envelope. 'At least you were man enough to come,' he said.

'I want to help your other son,' I said. 'He is a brave boy. He stood up to the police the other night. He can come and be a driver with me if you want. I will take care of him if you want.'

The woman clenched her face and shook her head. Tears poured out of her eyes. It was understandable. She might have had the hopes for that boy that my mother had for me. But the father was amenable; men are more reasonable in such matters.

I thanked him for the coffee, bowed respectfully before the bereaved mother, and left.

Mohammad Asif was waiting for me at the office when I got back. He shook his head and said, 'Why? Why did you waste so much money?'

That's when I thought, *Maybe I've made a mistake.* Maybe Asif will tell the other drivers I was frightened of the old woman, and they will think they can cheat me. It makes me nervous. I don't like showing weakness in front of my employees. I know what that leads to.

But I had to do something different; don't you see? I can't live the way the Wild Boar and the Buffalo and the Raven lived, and probably *still* live, back in Laxmangarh.

I am in the Light now.

*

Now, what happens in your typical *Murder Weekly* story – or Hindi film, for that matter? A poor man kills a rich man. Good. Then he takes the money. Good. But then he gets dreams in which the dead man pursues him with bloody fingers, saying, *Mur-der-er, mur-der-er.*

Doesn't happen like that in real life. Trust me. It's one of the reasons I've stopped going to Hindi films.

There was just that one night when Granny came chasing me on a water buffalo, but it never happened again.

The real nightmare you get is the *other* kind. You toss about in the bed dreaming that you haven't done it – that you lost your nerve and let Mr Ashok get away – that you're still in Delhi, still the servant of another man, and then you wake up.

The sweating stops. The heartbeat slows.

You did it! You killed him!

About three months after I came to Bangalore, I went to a temple and performed last rites there for all of them: Kusum, Kishan, and all my aunts, cousins, nephews, and nieces. I even said a prayer for the water buffalo. Who knows who has lived and who has not? And then I said to Kishan, and to Kusum, and to all of them: 'Now leave me in peace.'

And they have, sir, by and large.

One day I read a story in a newspaper: 'Family of 17 Murdered in North Indian Village.' My heart began to thump – seventeen? That can't be right – that's not mine. It was just one of those two-inch horror stories that appear every morning in the papers – they didn't give a name to the village. They just said it was somewhere in the Darkness – near Gaya. I read it again and again – seventeen! There aren't seventeen at home... I breathed out... But what if someone's had children...?

I crumpled that paper and threw it away. I stopped reading the newspaper for a few months after that. Just to be safe.

Look, here's what would have happened to them. Either the Stork had them killed, or had some of them killed, and the others beaten. Now, even if by some miracle he – or the police – didn't do that, the neighbours would have shunned them. See, a bad boy in one family casts the village's reputation into the dust. So the villagers would have forced them out – and they'd have to go to Delhi, or Calcutta, or Mumbai, to live under some concrete bridge, begging for their food, and without a hope for the future. That's not much better than being dead.

What's that you say, Mr Jiabao? Do I hear you call me a cold-blooded monster?

There is a story I think I heard at a train station, sir, or maybe I read it on the torn page that had been used to wrap an ear of roasted corn I bought at the market – I can't remember. It was a story of the Buddha. One day a cunning Brahmin, trying to trick the Buddha, asked him, 'Master, do you consider yourself a man or a god?'

The Buddha smiled and said, 'Neither. I am just one who has woken up while the rest of you are still sleeping.'

I'll give you the same answer to your question, Mr Jiabao. You ask, 'Are you a man or a demon?'

Neither, I say. I have woken up, and the rest of you are still sleeping, and that is the only difference between us.

I shouldn't think of them at all. My family.

Dharam certainly doesn't.

He's figured out what's happened by now. I told him at first we were going on a holiday, and I think he bought it for a month or two. He doesn't say a word, but sometimes I see him watching me out of the corner of his eye.

He knows.

At night we eat together, sitting across the table, watching each other and not saying much. After he's done eating, I give him a glass of milk. Two nights ago, after he finished his milk, I asked him, 'Don't you ever think of your mother?'

Not a word.

'Your father?'

He smiled at me and then he said, 'Give me another glass of milk, won't you, Uncle?'

I got up. He added, 'And a bowl of ice cream too.'

'Ice cream is for Sundays, Dharam,' I said.

'No. It's for today.'

And he smiled at me.

Oh, he's got it all figured out, I tell you. Little black-mailing thug. He's going to keep quiet as long as I keep feeding him. If I go to jail, he loses his ice cream and glasses of milk, doesn't he? That must be his thinking. The new generation, I tell you, is growing up with no morals at all.

He goes to a good school here in Bangalore – an English school. Now he pronounces English like a rich man's son. He can say 'pizza' the way Mr Ashok said it. (And doesn't he love eating pizza – that nasty stuff?) I watch with pride as he does his long division on clean white paper at the dinner table. All these things I never learned.

One day, I know, Dharam, this boy who is drinking my milk and eating my ice cream in big bowls, will ask me, *Couldn't you have spared my mother? Couldn't you have written to her telling her to escape in time?*

And then I'll have to come up with an answer – or kill him, I suppose. But that question is still a few years away. Till then we'll have dinner together, every evening, Dharam, last of my family, and me.

That leaves only one person to talk about.

My ex.

I thought there was no need to offer a prayer to the gods for him, because his family would be offering very expensive prayers all along the Ganga for his soul. What can a poor man's prayers mean to the 36,000,004 gods in comparison with those of the rich?

But I do think about him a lot – and, believe it or not, I do miss him. He didn't deserve his fate.

I should have cut the Mongoose's neck.

*

Now, Your Excellency, a great leap forward in Sino-Indian relations has been taken in the past seven nights. *Hindi-Chini Bhai Bhai*, as they say. I have told you all you need to know about entrepreneurship – how it is fostered, how it overcomes hardships, how it remains steadfast to its true goals, and how it is rewarded with the gold medal of success.

Sir: although my story is done, and my secrets are now your secrets, if you allow me, I would leave you with one final word.

(That's an old trick I learned from the Great Socialist – just when his audience is yawning, he says 'one final word' – and then he goes on for two more hours. Ha!)

When I drive down Hosur Main Road, when I turn into Electronics City Phase 1 and see the companies go past, I can't tell you how exciting it is to me. General Electric, Dell, Siemens – they're all here in Bangalore. And so many more are on their way. There is construction everywhere. Piles of mud everywhere. Piles of stones. Piles of bricks. The entire city is masked in smoke, smog, powder, cement dust. It is under a veil. When the veil is lifted, what will Bangalore be like?

Maybe it will be a disaster: slums, sewage, shopping malls, traffic jams, policemen. But you never know. It may turn out to be a decent city, where humans can live like humans and animals can live like animals. A new

Bangalore for a new India. And then I can say that, in my own way, I helped to make New Bangalore.

Why not? Am I not a part of all that is changing this country? Haven't I succeeded in the struggle that every poor man here should be making – the struggle not to take the lashes your father took, not to end up in a mound of indistinguishable bodies that will rot in the black mud of Mother Ganga? True, there was the matter of murder – which is a wrong thing to do, no question about it. It has darkened my soul. All the skin-whitening creams sold in the markets of India won't clean my hands again.

But isn't it likely that everyone who counts in this world, including our prime minister (including *you*, Mr Jiabao), has killed someone or other on their way to the top? Kill enough people and they will put up bronze statues to you near Parliament House in Delhi – but that is glory, and not what I am after. All I wanted was the chance to be a man – and for that, one murder was enough.

What comes next for me? I *know* that's what you're wondering.

Let me put it this way. This afternoon, driving down M.G. Road, which is our posh shopping road with lots of American shops and technology companies, I saw the Yahoo! people putting up a new sign outside their office:

HOW BIG CAN YOU THINK?

I took my hands off the wheel and held them wider than an elephant's cock.

'*That* big, sister-fucker!'

I love my start-up – this chandelier, and this silver lap-top, and these twenty-six Toyota Qualises – but honestly, I'll get bored of it sooner or later. I'm a *first-gear* man, Mr Premier. In the end, I'll have to sell this start-up to some other moron – *entrepreneur*, I mean – and head into a new line. I'm thinking of real estate next. You see, I'm always a man who sees 'tomorrow' when others see 'today'. The whole world will come to Bangalore tomor-row. Just drive to the airport and count the half-built glass-and-steel boxes as you pass them. Look at the names of the American companies that are building them. And when all these Americans come here, where do you think they're all going to sleep? On the road?

Ha!

Anywhere there's an empty apartment, I take a look at it, I wonder, *How much can I get from an American for this in 2010?* If the place has a future as the home of an American, I put a down payment on it at once. The fut-ure of real estate is Bangalore, Mr Jiabao. You can join in the killing if you want – I'll help you out!

After three or four years in real estate, I think I might sell everything, take the money, and start a school – an English-language school – for poor children in Banga-lore. A school where you won't be allowed to corrupt anyone's head with prayers and stories about God or Gandhi – nothing but the facts of life for these kids. A school full of White Tigers, unleashed on Bangalore! We'd have this city at our knees, I tell you. I could become the Boss of Bangalore. I'd fix that assistant com-missioner of police at once. I'd put him on a bicycle and have Asif knock him over with the Qualis.

All this dreaming I'm doing – it may well turn out to be nothing.

See, sometimes I think I will never get caught. I think the Rooster Coop needs people like me to break out of it. It needs masters like Mr Ashok – who, for all his numerous virtues, was not much of a master – to be weeded out, and exceptional servants like me to replace them. At such times, I gloat that Mr Ashok's family can put up a reward of a million dollars on my head, and it will not matter. I have switched sides: I am now one of those who cannot be caught in India. At such moments, I look up at this chandelier, and I just want to throw my hands up and holler, so loudly that my voice would carry over the phones in the call-centre rooms all the way to the people in America:

I've made it! I've broken out of the coop!

But at other times someone in the street calls out, 'Balram', and I turn my head and think, *I've given myself away.*

Getting caught – it's always a possibility. There's no end to things in India, as Mr Ashok used to say. You can give the police all the brown envelopes and red bags you want, and they might still screw you. A man in a uniform may one day point a finger at me and say, *Time's up, Munna.*

Yet even if all my chandeliers come crashing down to the floor – even if they throw me in jail and have all the other prisoners dip their beaks into me – even if they make me walk the wooden stairs to the hangman's noose – I'll never say I made a mistake that night in Delhi when I slit my master's throat.

I'll say it was all worthwhile to know, just for a day, just for an hour, just for a *minute*, what it means not to be a servant.

I think I am ready to have children, Mr Premier.

Ha!

Yours for ever,
Ashok Sharma
The White Tiger
Of Bangalore
boss@whitetiger-technologydrivers.com